Craig Zerf
Plob

Small Dog Publishing Limited

Who is Craig Zerf?

Craig wrote his first novel at the age of four and, by age seven, he was one of the most prolific writers in the Northern hemisphere. Unfortunately none of these tomes were published. This rejection forced him into seeking a career in the Dark Arts of business management. His unhealthy obsession with medieval bladed weapons and riveted metal clothing caused his initial fast rise in the corporate world to be curtailed when it was recommended by senior management that he seek professional help.

He told them to sod off and wrote Plob instead.

He has now published a trio of award-winning fantasy/humour books in the Plob series and also writes best-selling thriller novels as C. Marten-Zerf.

As Craig Zerf
Plob
Plob goes south
Plob srikes back

As C. Marten-Zerf
The Broken Men
Choice of Weapon

To my wife, Polly and my son, Axel.
For without her there would be no today and without him, no tomorrow.

The only way to get somewhere is by leaving someplace else.

- Terence Reis (Musician & poet)

Prologue

The sandy-haired toddler stomped solidly across the slate floor and sat in front of the fire that stuttered away in the large hearth. The damp logs hissed and popped, giving off more smoke than warmth as the toddler blew on them in an attempt to encourage flame. He coughed and then giggled as the wood smoke wafted out and enveloped him in a sharp smelling cloak of blue-white mist.

Still laughing he fumbled in the front pocket of his simple smock and took out a small wooden soldier, perhaps four inches high. He set it down in front of him and mumbled the magic words that his beloved granddad had taught him. As he finished the simple incantation, the soldier started slashing at the remaining wisps of smoke that hung in the air around the little boy who clapped his hands together in delight.

A handsome blonde woman, her pale face pinched with anxiety, turned from the window and snapped at him, 'Move away from the fire - all that smoke isn't good for you.'

The toddler moved back from the hearth and the women started to chew once again at her fingernails as she returned to her vigil. She wondered how the battle was going and prayed fervently that her husband and her father, the boy's dad and granddad, were still alive.

In the background the toddler laughed and clapped his hands again as the wooden soldier moved magically across the floor.

The thunderbolt rent the air, crackling and sizzling as it struck the foremost row of goblins. A flight of arrows followed, whistling through the sky and falling onto the evil host like a rain of steel. The captain of the guard called out for the magician, the little boy's grandfather, to hit the enemy with another bolt - but he was nowhere to be seen. He had disappeared. In their time of greatest need and peril he had forsaken them - so the captain called him coward and cursed his name. Then he sounded his horn and the men of Maudlin gave a loud shout and ran at the enemy, the tips of their upheld swords and spears glowing like fired torches in the fast setting sun. They knew that, without the help of their magician, it was to be the last charge. They knew that the enemy was too numerous to defeat - they knew all of these things but, because they were men, and this is what men do - they charged anyway.

And then, without warning, the hobgoblins turned as one and melted from the field of battle.

The enemy never came to Maudlin again.

And, back at the house with the fire and the slate floor, the blonde woman tried unsuccessfully to console the toddler as he cried and cried and cried. ‘My g’andad gone - my g’andad gone - my g’andad gone.’

Chapter 1

Plob.

Reetworthy Plob.

Reetworthy Plob the third.

Not much of a name. Especially for a knight at arms. A keeper of the sword of the nation and a general all round protagonist of the hugely heroic variety. This was fortunate indeed as Plob - Reetworthy Plob - Reetworthy Plob the third - was none of the aforementioned. In fact Plob was a lofty, sturdily built, earnest, marginally attractive, sandy-haired pubescent teenager with all of the corresponding adolescent faults and foibles thereof.

Also he was a magician's assistant.

Nay. Let us elaborate. He was, in all verity, *the* magician's assistant. The magician being, of course, Smegly the Magnificent. Master magician and first advisor to King Mange the Particularly Inept, son of King Plaug the Completely Inept who in turn was sired by King Spot the Utterly Useless. So, as far as kings go, things were definitely on the up.

And who knew? If the present king could ever find a significant other, the offspring might even mature to be dubbed Mangol the Not Completely Foolish.

All said and done, this was not particularly likely as the king was a solid holder of the second ugliest man in the kingdom title. The ugliest, of course, being Mister Struben the night soil collector, who lived over on the other side of the river, in the small run-down house with the wobbly chimney. Next to the widow Tomb's cottage (Ah, now you've got it), and he was the official mascot of the PBP (Police Brutality Party), the motto thereof being 'Beat them, Bash them, Till they look like Struben.' As well as this, the king had severely ruinous breath, a staggeringly serious lisp and a large root-vegetable-like growth protruding from the centre of his forehead that he insists everyone refers to as his twin brother, Mucous.

Plob. Reetworthy Plob. Reetworthy Plob the Third.

It wasn't that it was an awful name. It merely wasn't right for a magician. Plob the Magnificent. It didn't work. Even Plob the Awfully Good seemed wrong.

Blurg. Now there was a name. If only he'd been called Blurg.

Blurg the Brilliant. Blurg the Superb. The name sent shivers down Plob's spine and puckered up his adolescent skin into hundreds of little goose bumps momentarily swinging the scales from marginally attractive to marginally unattractive. He grinned to himself. Well there's no harm in imagining, he thought.

The thing is Plob hadn't actually been destined to be a magician; in fact it would be safe to say that the last thing that his parents wanted Plob to be was a magician. Not because they had any sort of irrational dislike of magicians as such, it was simply because Plob's grandfather, Slodong the third, had been a magician. A good magician. One of the best and, as such, his unexpected, and mainly unsubstantiated, fall into immorality and cowardice had been all the more shocking.

It had allegedly happened many years ago during the last, and final, winter war against the Far Eastern Hobgoblins who came swarming over the mountains almost every winter to attack the city of Maudlin without warning. The king's guards had rallied the townsfolk and, with the help of Slodong and his thunderbolt and fireball earth-magiks, valiantly repelled the first wave of Goblin forces and then…disaster. Without either notification or forewarning the magician cravenly disappeared to leave the outnumbered townsfolk to a death worse, possibly, even than fate. Not as in gone-out-for-lunch or having-a-quick-lie-down disappear but a proper puff-of-smoke-and-now-for-my-next-magical-trick disappearance. The only thing that saved the town from definite and total destruction was the fortunately immediate, simultaneous and completely incomprehensible change of heart by the leader and General in chief of the Hobgoblin hordes who, without much further ado, ceased his attack and ordered the withdrawal of his minions from the area of Maudlin never to be seen again. And so Maudlin was mysteriously and inexplicably saved, although through no help from the allegedly timorous and fearful magician, Slodong the third, whose name was, from that day forth, vilified and despised as the moniker of a coward.

Plob, however, who still remembered his grandfather with a childlike hero worship and a great fondness was convinced that he had sacrificed himself, via some arcane device, in order to save the Maudlinians by somehow causing the Hobgoblin leader's change of heart. When still but a toddler he had determined to become a magician himself in order to discover what his grandfather had done and how he had done it. Thus he would cleanse his name and honour forever after, and have it remembered in the roles of heroes as Plob thought right.

Anyway, it did no good to complain as people quipped, 'if the name was good enough for your father and your father's father before him then it's good enough for you.' Which is true, or would be, if it was. But it isn't. So it's not. The fact is that his father was not Reetworthy Plob the second and his father before him was not Reetworthy Plob the first. So - Reetworthy Plob the third was actually Reetworthy Plob the third the first. Which was all very confusing until one realized that Reetworthy Plob the third's father was Plobeeble Scone the third and his mother was Margelin Rutty the third and thereby one could deduce that Plob's family name was the third, as in Mr and Mrs the third and their son Plob.

Anyway, it was such a long explanation that when faced with the 'it was good enough for your father etc.' quip he simply smiled in his marginally attractive pleasant enough pubescent way and nodded. Long explanations aside though, Plob was not the sort of boy who would disagree as he wouldn't have wanted to be, well, disagreeable. In short Plob was a nice boy. It wasn't his fault he was a teenager, and anyway, he was sure to grow out of it. Cured from puberty by an onrush of age as it were.

And it was better than living in the village of B'uknighum across the valley where, due to a misunderstood royal decree by King Spot the Utterly Useless, everyone had to be named Xbltqwb Buttney.

This had, in turn, made it impossible to trace ones family lineage and had resulted in such serious interbreeding that now all of the residents of B'ukninghum looked and acted the same. They were buck toothed and chinless, big on ending all sentences with the words 'rather' or 'what' and, on the whole, totally harmless. Everyone tended to ignore them and left them alone to their 'rah rahs,' 'beastlys' and 'the peasants need a damn good thrashings'.

Still, though, sometimes he thought that it simply wasn't fair.

It simply wasn't fair, thought Bill. That's all. It wasn't bloody fair.He swore softly under his breath. Bill had never wanted to be a plumber, it had just sort of happened. He'd got home from his local London comprehensive one afternoon, after failing his final school exams, and his father had thrown the *Islington Times* down in front of him. Heavily circled in blood-red ink were two positions vacant ads. Pet shop assistant and trainee plumber. 'Choose,' his father had bellowed.

His father shouted at everyone; he'd been deaf as a post ever since he'd stopped being able to hear and, as a result, conducted all his conversations at the same volume as a teenager wearing a iPod.

Bill stared at the two circles, his mind racing. 'W-W-Well,' he stuttered. Bill stuttered a lot. Coincidently his stutter had started around the same time as his father's shouting. They made a right pair, his mum had said, his father screaming 'speak up' whilst Billy stammered away like a motorboat 'B-B-B-B-B-B.'

One morning his mum had got up early, gone downstairs to the kitchen and gassed herself. She left a note to his father. 'M-m-make your own t-t-tea, you stupid deaf b-b-bastard.' That was the first inkling that Bill had that his parents were less than happy together.

'I-I-I love animals. I think that I'll g-g-g-go for the p-p-pet shop ass-ass-ass-assistant.'

'Don't be daft,' his father bellowed, punching Bill in the mouth, 'I circled that one as a joke.'

So Bill became a plumber. Christ, a plumber. A bleeding, buggery, bollocksy, bastard, bum-hole plumber. And not a very good one at that. It's a pity I hate it so much, he thought. 'Cause I've got a good name for a plumber. Bill. It went well with plumber it did. Bill the plumber

Bill the plumber.

'Bil de Plummer - Harrumph,' quoth Smegly. (Master magicians harrumph a lot. They maintain that it impresses the hell out of the general populace).

'When in doubt, Plob you can always fall back on a good Harrumph,' quoth Master Smegly when giving lessons. Master magicians also tend to 'quoth' a lot. Lesser mortals have to make do with 'saying.' It's merely one of those higher mortal lesser mortal words like smote and rend. Lesser mortals hit and tear, higher mortals (such as master magicians) smite with great force and rend asunder.

Any road, Master Smegly was harrumphing, which generally meant that he was in doubt. He turned and strode across the room to the bookcase (Strode is another one. Lessers walk, greaters stride. Actually it's amazing that they achieve anything, what with all that striding, smiting and rending that has to be done).

'Now, let me see, harrumph, epiphany, epoch, evangelist, evil. Yes, that's it, evil.'

He drew the huge tome from the bookcase and laid it down on his workbench with a vast calumph and, consequently, raising a cloud of magically charged dust motes that danced prettily in the sunlight before briefly achieving a semblance of higher consciousness, starting a fledgling civilization, discovering free love and, finally, collapsing in a small sated heap of moist muddy muck . The entire process took place in micro-seconds and passed by un-applauded and unnoticed by all excepting for a somnolent blue-bottle who had seen it all before more times than he could care to remember. In fact, by now, he was so thoroughly depressed by the whole repetitive process of birth, death and rebirth and death once more he had decided to bat himself repeatedly against the closed window pane in an creepy-crawly attempt to cleanse his mind of the whole distressing pageant. On the blue-bottle's third attempt Master Smegly leant over and, with a large nicotine-stained thumb, irritably smeared the fly's essence out onto the glass. Which just goes to show - or does it?

Smegly turned to the distressed young women who had arrived at the door a mere few moments ago with her heart and hands aflutter and the rumour of dire warnings on her youthful red lips. 'This guide, my dear,' he said. 'Has in it a description of every known source of evil - past, present and future. As we can see monsters, politicians, poltergeists, goblins, ghosts and ghouls. Harrumph. Now let us look under B… harrumph, harrumph.'

The wise Master Smegly was obviously hugely perturbed, thought Plob, judging from the quantity of harrumphs coming from his study. He sidled up to the door in order to listen more closely to the happenings.

'No nothing under B. Let's try D…'

Master Smegly flipped over a number of pages and ran his finger down a column.

'No. Nothing here either. Are you sure that you got the names right?'

'Absolutely, master magician. My visions are always crystal clear and I have never been wrong. It came to me only moments before my morning repast. I was thrown into an involuntary trance; the world around grew chill and dark. My sight grew dim and a voice called to me from a great distance. "Ultimate evil is set to enfold your world" it quoth. And yea, I heard screams of agony and saw the flames of hell and I begged, "Forsooth, tell me, I beg of you, does this evil have a name? If you could tell me I would be verily chuffed," and the flames expanded and the screams became an excruciating cacophony of agony and the voice thundered out over all, "Evil has been given a name, and that name is Bil de Plummer." And that was all, Master Smegly. I told my mother and she bade me rush straight over and inform the magician, and this I have done.'

Plob was gobsmacked. Bil. What evil twisted entity would go under such a name?

Bil. The very thought of it caused Plob's usually unflappable mind to flutter on the edges of panic. But no, he must contain this irrational fear. He was, after all, Plob - The master magician's assistant - chosen from over two hundred aspiring applicants coached in from across the country for 'the choosing' that took place only once every ten years.

He heard the clattering of a chair being pushed back as the young miss stood up, followed closely by a rapid-fire string of harrumphs and Plob knew that the interview was over. He quickly scurried off down the corridor, picked up his feather duster and started pretend dusting frantically.

He glanced up momentarily to see the girl clip-clop past, dressed in leather riding boots and tight jodhpurs, swishing her crop from side to side. (Of course she was wearing other items of clothing as well, it's simply that Plob was a teenage boy so he didn't notice them).

Master Smegly came chugging up behind her. 'Come along, Plob. Enough pretend dusting for one day. You heard the conversation and must know that serious things are afoot. I want you to go down to the dungeons and fire up the ovens; we have magiks to perform and auguries to inspect.'

Chapter 2

Inspector Terry Block ran his hand over his No. 2 haircut, savouring the feel of the tennis-ball-like fuzz as it rasped against his palm. His hand shook slightly, despite his uncaring expression and he tried desperately to think of something full of hard East-End wit and good rhyming cockney slang to say about the gruesome scene laid out before him. Unfortunately, as always his solid middle class upbringing belied his Bow-Bells name and Jack-the-lad hairstyle and the best that he could come out with was a muttered profanity.

Block's partner, Hugo Prendergast, rose up from the genuflectory position he had assumed next to the battered, dyed blonde, female corpse and straightened the already rectilinear creases on his dark grey Saville Row trousers. 'At least he left us a body this time,' he drawled in his two-hundred-thousand-pound silk and steel Etonian accent. 'Should make identification a little easier than most of the others. Thank God for His small mercies.'

Block stared at Prendergast with undisguised loathing. 'Bloody posh glory boy,' he mumbled under his breath.

'What's that, old chap?'

Block shook his head. 'Nothing. Come on, let's go back to the station. Drink some coffee and eat doughnuts and pretend that we're American cops with guns and big air-conditioned offices.'

Prendergast raised a quizzical eyebrow and followed his partner down the steps to the white, unmarked Ford Sierra. He would never understand Block, he mused as he climbed into the passenger seat of the K-reg sixteen hundred. It wasn't because Block was middle-class, that in itself wasn't the problem, for, although Prendergast didn't actually have any middle-class friends, he had met a good few of them and, all things considered, they seemed to be a fairly acceptable crowd. Well-educated, clean and hard-working. The problem lay in the fact that Terry Block was the only middle-class chap that he'd ever met that had such staunch working-class aspirations.

The car eventually started on the third try and Block squealed out into the traffic, head down, hands clenched tightly on the slick black plastic steering wheel as a blast of roasting air was funnelled onto him via the broken heating system. And, swearing steadily and rhythmically under his breath like a fallen devotee of Krishna, he immediately started sweating.

Plob woke up sweating, the name of the evil one ringing in his ears. It was bad. Very bad. Worse than even Master Smegly could have anticipated. They had spent the rest of the day after the young miss had left weaving magiks, searching, divining and auguring. Plob sweating and puffing like a blown horse as he shovelled tons of coal into the ovens, moved a score of cast iron cauldrons and hammered a hundred miscast spells back into shape.

It all pointed to the same dastardly conclusion. There was no hint of 'Bil de Plummer.' He was 'the unknown evil.' An evil so dark and dank, so vile and loathsome that even the spirit guides forsook all knowledge of him.

Well either that or that young girl was a crazy, inbred dimwit who'd got it all horribly wrong. But, somehow, Plob didn't think so - and neither did Master Smegly. In fact Smegly's lack of knowledge about 'the evil one' had thrown him into such a fit of harrumphing that that he had eventually hyperventilated and Plob had to rush around trying to find a canvas bag for him to breathe into.

Plob yawned, stretched, fell out of bed, staggered stiffly over to splash himself awake at the washbasin and got dressed. Master Smegly wanted an early start to the day.

Smegly had decided that the king had to be told and that was likely to take up the bulk of the day due to the fact that all would have to be repeated, retold and re-explained in approximately two thousand, two hundred and seventy-four different ways. It wasn't that the king was that bad, he was, actually, slightly worse.

Bill stepped back to survey his work. Mesomorph, ectomorph, endomorph. Blonde, black, brunette. Nice - he thought. Very lifelike - he thought. If it wasn't for that stupid imitation blonde with her badly dyed hair I would have a full set - he thought. And he cackled. As the truly insane are wont to do. Cackle, cackle, cackle, cough, cough, cough. Thirsty work this insane cackling - he thought. No worries though, soon I will be king - he thought. King Bill.

King Mange turned from the window to stare blankly at Master Smegly. And slowly, ever so slowly, Plob could see a flicker of understanding beginning to ignite in the king's vacant eyes. It was about time, he thought, it had already chimed three times past the noon bell and even Master Smegly's vast pool of patience was beginning to dissipate.

But alas, no, it was not to be. The flicker wavered, spluttered and died. Ye Gods, today was worse than most. It seemed as if the king wasn't even trying to understand. As if he was, well, completely, as opposed to partially, inept. Still - it was close now, thought Plob, as Master Smegly began to explain the entire scenario again, this time trying to present it in yet another, perhaps simpler way.

As Smegly's voice droned on, the King's mouth would droop slowly open and then, periodically, and without warning, clap shut with such violence that it caused the king's alleged twin brother to wobble up and down like a large radish on a stick having been struck by a soup ladle. And, as Master Smegly mentioned 'Bil de Plummer' for the umpteenth time, it finally struck home. Flicker, flicker…

'Bad,' said the king.

Smegly immediately stopped talking, knowing that now was a crucial time. To push too hard, to throw more kindling on that tiny spark of understanding could extinguish it completely.

Both Master Smegly and Plob waited with bated breath. (Whatever that means. Really, what is bated breath? How does one bate one's breath? Can one do it on command? You know - 'bate your breath, young man, I'll be with you in a moment.' I don't think so. And, if it is possible, is it a higher or a lesser word? It just seems that your common and garden variety teenager wouldn't go around bating his breath if he could just hold it, or exhale it or draw his last of it. Anyway - it's debateable…Hmmm – Harrumph).

The king's meagre mind cupped the idea to its chest and carefully protected it from the myriad of other constant daily thoughts and bodily functions. And, lo, it burst into flame. A smoky, undernourished, damp firewood, I wouldn't even bother cooking on that sort of flame - but flame nonetheless.

'Very bad,' said the king.

Smegly nodded slowly in gentle affirmation.

'Very, very bad,' repeated the king.

'Yes,' agreed Smegly.

'Yeth!' shouted the King, hugely encouraged by Master Smegly's agreement with his obviously brilliant deduction. And, not one to let go of a good thing, the King squared his shoulders, gave Mucous a quick tug, and gave tongue.

'Very, very bad.'

Sooth, thought Plob, as he politely struggled to maintain his 'master-magician's-assistant-in-the-presence-of-royalty' expression. If this was only partially inept then the grandfather, King Spot the Utterly Useless, must barely have had enough intelligence to dribble. Still, the king was the king and if it was 'partially inept' he wanted, it was 'partially inept' he got. However, it was a little like describing a syphilitic pit bull with rabies as 'a little unsafe to become romantically involved with.'

Plob stared in fascination as the King, after another particularly protracted string of 'verys,' went bright purple in the face due to lack of oxygen, rolled his eyes back in their sockets, and then went into complete panic as he realized that he had forgotten how to breathe. His head swivelled frantically around as he searched for some form of inspiration, his mouth opening and closing like a landed Carp.

Smegly muttered an incantation under his breath, spun around twice in a clockwise direction and released the spell in the king's general direction. The change was instantaneous; the king's lungs began to pump away merrily as he tottered back to his padded throne, sat down and promptly fell into a deep sleep.

Master Smegly turned sadly to Plob and gestured to the door.

'Come, my boy. We have done all that we can. Let us away.'

Plob followed his master out of the castle and into the town.

Chapter 3

The wrench was all right. Yeah. He liked the wrench. It was bright red with a knobble and squiggly bits, and, if you held it exactly right, in the dark, when you looked in the mirror it looked as though you might be holding a sceptre.

King Bill.

King Bill the Incredible.

King Bill the Conqueror.

King Bill the Socially Acceptable.

As opposed to Bill - the guy who fixes other people's crappers.

Bill turned to survey his intimates - all perfect in his eyes, because the pieces that he didn't like had already been cut out and discarded. Embalmed, and vacuum-packed for freshness, his subjects lay stacked in the corner of his crowded room - waiting patiently for his coronation. He held his sceptre up for all to see and grandly saluted his fine, fine people. His beloved vassals. One more blonde one and he would have the full set. And then there would be no stopping him. Then he would be well and truly in.

Plob liked the inn. He didn't get to go there very often. Well, one couldn't afford to on an assistant's wage as it was hard to save when your pay consisted of free lessons. However, when feeling generous, or hugely distracted, Master Smegly would treat Plob to a meal out.

'The complete and utter bastard and Wegren Bumbles inn and eatery'.

It used to be called 'Blurble and Wegrens inn and eatery' but one day Mrs Wegren Bumble had got back early from the market and had found Mr Blurble Bumble asleep. In itself this was not a huge problem.

The fact that he was naked and on top of Mrs Engred Moist, the allegedly insatiable town nymphomaniac, however, definitely caused some problems.

So Wegren kicked Blurble out and re-named the inn.

Master Smegly ordered the plough-man's platter and Plob, after ascertaining, and verifying, that the 'toad in the hole' was guaranteed to contain absolutely no trace whatsoever of any bullfrog, croaker, paddock, pollywog or, in fact, aquatic reptilian species hereto known to man, ordered a double portion.

Although Plob had always hoped that, when he turned thirteen, he would follow in his grandfather's footsteps as a magician, he had spent the majority of his pre-teen years working, in a farmer's dry goods store owned by his father and knew a great many ploughmen. To this day, he had never actually met one who ever had more than a crust of bread and a rind of mouldy old cheese for lunch. This had no apparent semblance to the veritable 'horn-of-plenty' that arrived at their table under the moniker of 'ploughman's-platter.' Three different types of cheese, a mountain of pickles, a selection of breads and, of course, the ubiquitous trio of tired old skin of lettuce, slice of dried out tomato and ragged ring of onion that no one ever ate. (It has been rumoured that every eating establishment has one set of these weary, aged vegetable accoutrement that is carefully handed on from generation to generation, magically preserved and never eaten. Mind you, it has also being rumoured that this rumour is complete rubbish).

And what about 'Shepherd's Pie'? As far as Plob knew, your average shepherd was seldom known to bake whilst herding (or herd whilst baking, for that matter). Plob thought of old Corbin the sheepherder. He was sure that Corbin had never baked a pie. Actually Corbin had probably never even eaten a pie (shepherds or other). All Corbin really ever did was herd sheep, spit a lot and, whenever possible, dry and smoke any and all wild herbs that he could find growing up in the mountains. As a result Corbin was - well - strange. A strange kind of strange, you know, the kind spelt with three or four extra A's - 'Straaaaaange.' (OK, five extra A's).

And he never, ever, baked pie.

Plob's toad-less 'toad in the hole' arrived, greasy sausages shiningly resplendent in their nest of heavy overcooked stodge.

He tucked in.

Smegly hailed a hansom cab as they strolled down the cobbled high street back towards the master's abode in Artefact Street that lay just outside the city's inner walls and was home to most of the skilled artisans in the sprawling town of Maudlin. Ah. This is the life, thought Plob. If only I had the lucre. Eating at inns. Riding in cabs. Dead brill.

The cab pulled over to the side of the street and Plob and Smegly climbed up. Master Smegly informed the cabbie of their destination and the horse set off at a trot. Smegly leant back in his seat and stared at the clouds whilst knuckling his left temple.

'Well, my boy.' He said, sighing. 'I fear the worst. We shall receive no help from the king regarding this evil entropy named Bil. Something has to be done about it and it appears that we're to be on our own with the doing.'

Plob started upright, his brain racing. Well - perhaps not racing, as such, but definitely running along at a quicker pace than usual. Scurrying perhaps.

'Why?' He asked.

'What?' Replied Smegly.

'No.' Plob shook his head. 'I said - Why?'

'Why what?'

'No. Just why.'

Master Smegly stared intently at Plob. A short pause ensued, followed immediately by another that combined with the first and turned it into a medium pause. Plob drew a breath.

'I'm sorry. What I mean is - why do we have to face this alone? Can't we get help? Sort of like a quest. We travel around and collect a noble band of like-minded people to help us in our cause. Like in all the old books - you know - "Glimburble goes on a quest" or "The noble quest of Splurgitude the vain." It's got all the classic ingredients.' Plob continued. 'We've already got the master magician and his assistant. Now all we need is a beautiful maid, a brave and stupendous knight and a great thief. The thief's very important - you have to have a thief, there's always a thief.'

'And a cab driver,' came a voice from up front. 'There's always a cabbie.'

'No there's not,' retorted Plob.

'Is so,' insisted the cabbie.

'Not.'

'Is.'

'Not.'

'Is.'

'Not, not, not, not notnotnot,' shouted Plob, knowing full well that he was sounding juvenile but not being able to stop himself.

'Well – there was in all the stories that I've read,' mumbled the cabbie sulkily as they drew up outside Master Smegly's residence. Smegly paid him off and fished around in the depths of his voluminous robe for the front door key.

'There is so too,' they heard the cabbie shout laughingly as he turned the corner.

'Not,' shouted Plob as he grinned at the cabby's disappearing back.

'You know something, Plob?' said Smegly as they opened the door. 'You're right.'

Plob beamed at the knowledge that his suggestion was being taken seriously.

'Yes. I've never heard of a cabbie being involved in a quest,' said Smegly nodding.

It was always the same. People only ever call a plumber when something went wrong. Burst pipe call the plumber. Blocked drain - call the plumber. Leaking cistern, broken geyser, dripping tap - plumber, plumber, plumber. Nobody ever practised 'preventative plumbing.'

Nobody ever phoned him up and said, 'Hi - there's nothing wrong with my pipes, I'd just like you to pop around and check them out. See if they need any maintenance.' No - instead they waited until the sewers backed up and the crud was running out the door and then they phoned. And, when you'd sorted their problems out and presented them with a bill, they'd always say the same thing. 'This is an outrage. Doctors charge less than this for making a house call.'

And you'd say - 'Well next time phone the doctor and see if he'll wallow around in your shit-infested overflow for an hour for thirty squids, you stupid bastard.'

Except you didn't. What you actually said was 'W-W-W-W-W' and they slammed the door in your face leaving you holding a faeces stained personal check that would probably bounce at any rate.

Because you were Bill the plumber - and you stuttered. And then you'd go back home and stand in the darkened room, in front of the mirror.

With the wrench.

In front of your subjects.

And imagine.

Chapter 4

Horgelbund the pheasant killer. Soldier of fortune. Knight extraordinaire. And a legend…in his own mind.

Actually Horgy was the highly qualified accountant, just orphaned, ex-son of Sir Hord the Incredibly Wealthy, who had recently passed away leaving his one and only living relative, Horgelbund, a portfolio of shares and property that was beyond even the king's tax collectors wildest dreams of avarice.

So, with his despot of a father finally gone, Horgy could do what he always wanted. And, what he always wanted, was to be a knight.

Easier said than done, thought Horgy. He was sure that becoming a knight was the one thing that would be difficult to purchase. One couldn't become a knight by simply shovelling lavatories full of gold in the general direction of the king.

No. There were rules, etiquette, and honour. That sort of thing. So Horgy set about it in the only way that his accounting type brain knew how.

Firstly he obtained a secret copy of the Knights' Charter by bribing one of the middle to minor officials in charge of the hall of secret charters and such at the King's court. Armed, at first, with only this rule-by-rule charter on how knights were chosen by the inner council, he sallied forth.

Rule number one - All knights must be in possession of a serviceable suit of armour complete with all weaponry referred to in regulations 2.2, 6.1 and 14.7 of the 'Rutting' convention. (Shouldn't be a problem).

Rule number two - All knights must be in possession of a steed, mighty of stature and great of heart with a suitably noble name. (Not too much of a problem).

Rule number three - All knights shall show complete proficiency and conversancy with aforementioned armour, weapons and noble steed. (All right, we'll get back to that one).

Rule number four - All knights shall be pure of soul, strong of body, courageous of bent and so noble of character as to be pretty well terminally boring. (Yeah, yeah. No problem. Horgy already had the boring bit down pat).

Rule number five - All knights will prove said courageousness and purity of soul by entering the pit of champions naked and unarmed in order to fight a pride of starving lions to the death.

P.S. This is a brand new rule that has just been added by the royal decree of King Mange the Partially Inept as he feels that there are far too many potentially noble knight types around. He has also decreed that they are outmoded, boring and they make his teeth itch. (Hang on. Half a mo. To the death. That will not do. No. Not at all. Death was nasty. And horrible. It made Horgy come over all icky like. But wait. What was this?) Horgy leaned closer. Hastily scrawled at the bottom of the scroll, in the king's own spidery, inept (sorry - partially inept) hand was an addendum.

Fore inasmuch as aspiring knights may find rule number five pointless, repugnant and generally icky making (Horgy's thoughts exactly) His Royal Highness, King Mange the Partially Inept, the first of that name, may seem fit to pass royal dispensation if, and only if, said aspirant knight sees fit to shovel lavatories full of gold in the general direction of said royal personage (and his twin brother Mucous).

Horgy blinked, re-read the addendum, blinked once again, called for his shovel and fearlessly set out to become a knight.

'By the powerth vethted in me I pronounthe thee – Thir Horgelbund the pheathant killer.'

And, finally, it was so. It had been an arduous battle. Go to the vaults, withdraw gold, shovel in general direction of king. Sell portfolio of shares, collect money, shovel in general direction of king. Dispose of real estate holdings, convert to sovereign, shovel in general direction of king. Shovel, shovel, shovel.

In all truth Horgy (sorry - Sir Horgy) felt less noble knight and more menial labourer of the shovelling variety.

And his praise name, 'Pheasant Killer,' well, it was the best that he could do. It may have been Sir Horgelbund the Brave, if he had proved himself in battle, or Sir Horgelbund the Strong, if he had been possessed of great strength. Even the Chaste, or the Pure, if any of those were vaguely true. But when asked by the committee to present them with a list of stupendous things that he had done in his life (in chronological order restricting it to less than fifty stupendous events and or achievements) he had struggled a little. I mean, stupendous is so subjective, isn't it? Anyway, it ended up being a very short list. A list of three, as it were.

The committee had informed him that 'Sir Horgelbund the Potty Trained' was inappropriate and 'Sir Horgelbund the Knight Able to Pee His Name in The Snow after Drinking Four Pints Of Mead' whilst being impressive, was too long and cumbersome to be considered as a praise name. It was fortunate for Horgy that, just that morning, whilst riding to present his list to the committee, he had trotted over and crushed to death a pheasant attempting to run across the path. As this impressive feat (dare we say stupendous?) had happened in front of witnesses, he hurriedly tacked it onto his list of two, thereby bringing the massive total of stupendous feats up to three.

'Arithe Thir Horgelbund, Pheasant Killer and Knight.'

This part was tricky. Unfortunately Horgy, whilst ordering his suit of armour, had become embarrassed by his titchy measurements (paltry pecs, bitty biceps and teeny triceps) and, in a fit of bravado, had thrown in a good few inches all round.

As a result, not only was it almost too heavy for him to move, he also rattled around inside like a preying mantis in a teapot, thereby ensuring that controlled motor movement was a nigh on impossibility.

Horgy gritted his teeth and stood up. The first six or seven inches were easy going, only because he was still moving inside the suit as opposed to actually moving with it. As his shoulders came up solid against his steel epaulettes his vertical travel came to an abrupt halt. But, not to be shamed in his moment of glory (and very, very costly glory at that) Horgy puckered up, assumed a small-faced expression and took the strain.

Huuuunggruuhhhmmooooograhooww!

There was an embarrassed titter amongst the gathered gentry as, faced with the view of Horgy's steel-rimmed bright red face, lips peeled back and newly-knighted nostrils flared, they all reached the conclusion that Sir Horgelbund was taking a noble and stupendous dump in his shining new metal suit. (Perhaps 'Sir Horgelbund the Potty Trained' would not have been so inappropriate after all). Horgy redoubled his efforts and it was only through a feat of tremendous self-discipline that he managed to prove them wrong.

Inch by straining inch, left side up a little, right side up a little, left side, right side, left, right, Sir Horgy came to his feet. The cheers from the crowd were deafening as, proudly, Sir Horgelbund the Pheasant Killer, sweating like a brood mare in the mating season, lurched zombie-like down the red carpet and in the vague direction of the royal long drops.

It had become an obsession.

Bill sat hunched over his wrench. Lovingly polishing it and imbuing it with his vast store of bitterness and malice.

Imbue, Imbue, Imbue.

As it happened, Master Smegly had taken Plob's suggestion seriously. Indeed he viewed it as more than passingly good. The only problem being that it was decidedly impractical. So, Master Smegly did what all wise old men do when faced with a possibly good, definitely impractical, suggestion from a teenager. Put him in charge of it. This he had already done.

Plob stood back and looked on his work of art that he had nailed to the front door with much satisfaction.

Queft members wanted
Courageous Knight
Nobly thief
Beeyoutiful maid
APPLY WITHINN

Well - that should do it.

Dreenee sighed as she picked up the tray of ales that Mrs Bumble had just drawn. It was late. Her back ached, her feet ached and her eyes smarted from the smog-like quantities of tobacco smoke that seemed to hang constantly in the air of the taproom in 'The complete and utter…'

She was a right stonker, our Dreenee. Possessed of thick blonde tresses and eyes like limpid pools. (Limpid pools of what, I hear you ask. To be honest I'm not sure. Let's settle for limpid pools of some deep, dark blue sort of stuff and leave it at that). She had a large generous mouth that offset her large generous bosom to perfection. And, as she sashayed through the crowded tap room with her tray of ales, she received many an approving comment and friendly sally. None of the comments were ribald. There was no touching. Dreenee was a girl well-liked, well-respected and well-feared.

When she had first started working at the 'Complete and utter…' only two days ago, on her first night, whilst taking her first order, a captain of the king's elite guards had attempted to administer a playful pat on the behind (Dreenee's, not his own). This overture was politely declined.

However, spurred on by his companions, the captain leant over to pat again. As he patted, Dreenee turned to serve his ale, thereby receiving a less than playful grope on her 'not-behind.' This caused a loud burst of laughter from said captain elite and much ribald commentary from aforementioned comrades. It also caused Dreenee to break his collarbone in two places, dislocate his knee and splinter both of his front teeth whilst throwing him out into the street.

She did not drop the tray that she was holding.

She did not spill any of the ale.

Not a drop.

Unbeknown to Dreenee, however, the scented candle of fate was about to burn her imminently patable (or not, as the case might be) posterior. For Dreenee had assaulted none other than the king's second cousin, thrice removed on his mother's side (and once removed by Dreenee) and one hundred and forty third in line to the throne. Which basically meant that almost every known member of the extended royal family (including the budgie and both of the corgis) had to snuff it before he had an even vague chance of getting a stab at running the kingdom.

So - as Dreenee sashayed and jollied around the boards of 'the complete and utter…' with all those interesting parts of her anatomy moving under her dress in that way that girls like Dreenee had without trying - the king's guard was drawn up under royal orders to sally forth and arrest, with extreme prejudice, the person who had dared to cause damage to the captain of royal blood.

One almost felt sorry for them - almost.

Chapter 5

'I'm bored,' snivelled little Kleebles. He always snivelled. He was one of those children that make child battering seem like a sensible option.

His mother turned from her butter churning. 'You must learn to amuse yourself, my dear little Snoggins. I have much work to do.'

'But, Mumykins. I don't know what to do. I don't know what to do I don't know what to do. Idontknowwhatadooooo.'

'Well, dear, why don't you go and groom the horses?'

'No.'

'Muck out the stables?'

'No.'

'Wash the wagon?'

'No.'

'Clean the old…'

'It's fine, I'll find something to do.'

Kleebles dragged himself off to his bedroom, sighing and shrugging and generally being totally hard done by. He poked listlessly around in his room, bored little child's shoulders hunched over in an adult posture of failed world-weariness. Looking for something to play with, but finding nothing that came instantly to grasp.

And then - he saw it. It had never been a favourite of his and, strictly speaking, you needed some friends to play it, but, then again, strictly speaking, he had no friends.

He opened the box and pulled out his Ouija board.

The ten-man detachment of the king's guard dismounted and tethered their horses to the hitching rail outside 'The complete and utter…'

'Right, you 'orrible lot,' bellowed Mr Tipstaff, the age-hardened sergeant-at-arms. 'We are out 'ere this fine day to place under arrest one by standard small-to-medium-size attractive blonde lassie whom has been deemed, by his highness, the Partially Inept, to be a menace to society. So let's be quick about it, and I do not want to catch anyone trying to sneak a sly drink once we're inside. Form up.'

The detachment formed up behind the grizzled old sergeant amidst much comment of the 'Ooh, small-to-medium attractive blonde. I want to be the one who ties her up' variety through to the 'she may be carrying a concealed weapon. I get to search her - really thoroughly'.

The curtains were drawn. The lights were low and Bill posed in front of the mirror, in his newest blue boiler suit with an old bedspread tied across his shoulders like a cloak. Face contorted into a spitting image version of Prince Charles. He stood tall in front of his vacuum-wrapped collection of subjects, held the wrench aloft and adopted what he thought of as a most regal stance.

'Yes,' he shouted at the mirror as he stared at his supposedly royal reflection. 'Finally I am the king. No more plumbing for this fellow. Oh no, no, no. I am king and now I'll show them. King Bill. King Bill the Merciless.'

Yes. It had happened. Bill and sanity had taken separate buses to opposite ends of the country. Bill had gone bye-bye.

Kleebles leaned forward, placed his forefinger on the upturned glass and intoned sonorously. 'Oh, Great Evil one. Send your spirit to enter this glass for I am bored and can think not what else to do. Oh, cancerous and deplorable one, make something happen to relieve this boredom that I feel. Oh, vastly vile and lecherous one, come to my aid, I implore thee.'

And, in that place that is both infinitely far away and uncomfortably close, Evil awoke from his slumber, sat up, and took note.

Terry took an absent minded swig of his seven-hour-old, clammy, skin-covered, over-sweetened half cupful of house brand tea and shuddered. He'd been sitting at his desk since early that morning, poring over the cairns of photos, witness statements, sightings and crank calls. The evidence that constituted the framework of the two confirmed murders and the five missing persons cases that he suspected were the work of one man.

Three missing men, one blond of hair and blue of eye, one black-haired and one haired in a reddish brown mop. The two girls, young, attractive, one raven-haired, the other brunette. The murder victims - yesterday's, a petite, dyed-blonde model and last week's, a slightly built man with lengthy flaxen locks. There was a pattern. A definite pattern. But somehow it still eluded him, gliding tantalisingly through the shoals of his thought just beyond his grasp. Think. Before the next victim…please.

The sergeant's ten-man detachment lay in tatters around him. He couldn't believe it. Firstly, the intelligence report was completely wrong. The girl wasn't small-to-medium. She was a slip of a girl. Almost child height.

Secondly, she wasn't an attractive blonde. She was an outrageously, stunningly, incapacitating sensual golden-haired Aphrodite of such radiant loveliness and beauty that even Mr Tipstaff, a hoary veteran of many an exotic campaign, was struck still by her blatant eroticism.

And, thirdly, it was impossible to arrest someone who could break a man's arm in four places without nary a wobble of her serving tray. The only reason that he himself had escaped with merely two badly bruised and bleeding kneecaps (a complete set, as it were) was his hereto undiscovered penchant for pleading and whining that he had put to full use.

Any road - he was a tough old warrior, and he had work to do. He dragged himself painfully towards the door and out onto the pavement, withdrew his gold-plated alarm whistle from his breast pocket, and blew three piercing blasts, two long and two short (sorry, make that four piercing blasts). Thereby summoning all the king's horses and all the king's men (well, all those within whistle shot).

Evil laughed. It sounded like a thousand nails being driven into the palms of a thousand martyrs. It was, in short, not a good sound. But Evil didn't care. At least it sounded better than those snorting laughs that some people have. You know - Ha ha ha snort. Like a sow on laughing gas.

Evil laughed because he was about to have some serious fun. He rose up, threw his arms wide and released his malevolent thought into the ether.

And what Evil thinks comes to pass.

A billion suns winked out of existence. Ice Ages came and went in the blink of an eye. Pestilence, famine and increased taxation swept through the multiverse. The horsemen of the apocalypse called all of their mates over for a party and went on a drunken rampage.

And - somewhere far away, in a small bedsit in Islington, a young plumber standing next to a pile of dead, vacuum-packed subjects, holding a wrench whilst dressed in a new blue boiler suit with a bedspread as a cloak, was taken from his world and transported, via Evil's satanic highway, to another world and another darkened room containing an Oiuja board and a small terrified boy-child called Kleebles.

Ye Gods, they're everywhere, thought Dreenee as she ran down the street. Soldiers on foot, soldiers on horseback, soldiers in wagons. Who would have thought that three (sorry four) blasts on a whistle could bring the city out in such a military rash.

On reflection she should have simply run away and left the ten-man detachment alone. In fact that was exactly what she had planned to do until the short toad-like soldier with mismatched armour had started salivating whilst running towards her shouting, 'Ooooh big uns. Yes please, I get to search her first.' Well, at least he wouldn't be doing much groping in the near future. Not with two broken thumbs and a set of ear-height testicles.

Sod it. Dreenee stopped abruptly. A small detachment of cavalry were heading down the street towards her, pennants rippling bravely from their shiny steel lances, armour-clad and alert. They hadn't seen her yet but it was only a matter of seconds. With nowhere else to go Dreenee turned to the closest door, pulled it open and jumped in. Both Plob and Smegly looked up from the scrolled parchment that they were studying.

'Ah,' said Master Smegly. 'The beautiful maid.'

Chapter 6

It is rumoured that a time will come to pass when Evil begins to enjoy domination over good. The nights will grow longer, the days duller and the only vegetable that will grow will be the dreaded brussel sprout®.

But, it is said, mankind must not be overly perturbed because, when it seems that all hope is lost, then all of the past heroes of antiquity will arise from the grave and join together against the evil host and in one last great battle the face of Evil will be forever scoured from humanity's fair domain.

Many believe this.

Which just goes to show what complete pillocks many are. Stuff it - if you were dead would you arise from the grave and most probably be hacked to death all over again? No. I should hope not. You would simply lie there, getting nibbled by worms, or chewed on by badgers or doing whatever it is that corpses pass off as having a good time.

In reality Evil is pretty much always there and it's up to people like Plob, Smegly, you and me to fight the good fight. I know. You never realised how much responsibility you had until now. Bummer, huh? Sorry, but that's life

Now - on with our story.

Little Kleebles lay prostrate on the floor squealing in abject terror. At first Bill stared at him blankly, and then distastefully, and finally, he came to the conclusion that this was just a dream and so he could do anything that he felt like. So he raised the wrench up high, shrieked 'Be gone, oh p-p-porky and dislikeable child,' and brought the wrench crashing down on the back of little Kleebles' skull causing an instant cessation of said squealing as most of the contents shot out of his nose.

Evil went apoplectic with mirth.

'What do you mean "the beautiful maid"?' Dreenee gasped at Master Smegly, her breath coming in deep pants after her frantic dash.

Smegly blinked. Plob blinked as well. Only he did it with one eye at a time fearing that, if he closed both eyes at ones, this panting, dewy-skinned, flushed-cheek, heaving bosomed blonde substantiation of every teenage boy's insanely testosterone-driven fantasy, would disappear.

'The note,' said Smegly, drawing a blank look from Dreenee. 'On the door,' he added to another blank look. 'Beautiful maid wanted for quest.'

Dreenee's next blank look was interrupted by a gauntleted hammering on the front door.

'Open up in the name of King Mange the Partially Inept,' demanded a military sounding voice without. (No I'm not even going to get into the 'without what?' scenario. Substitute 'outside' if you prefer).

Dreenee's eyes flicked around the room in search of a weapon as her body tensed for action.

Like a startled fawn ready to flee in terror, thought Plob, as he took an involuntary step forward. Master Smegly, who was older and wiser and less testosterone driven, hurriedly took two steps back. Gods, he thought, she looks like a man-eating tigress about to savage a group of kindergarten children.

Dreenee turned to Master Smegly. 'Who are you?' she asked

'I am Smegly. Master magician and third in line to the head of the circle of mages and this sweat-soaked young lad here is my assistant.'

The banging on the door intensified.

Dreenee glanced swiftly at the door and then at Plob. 'Please,' she said. 'Make them go away. I don't want to hurt any more of them.'

Plob heard this as 'I don't want them to hurt me' but the true import of the words was not lost on Master Smegly as he nodded his affirmation to Plob who walked over to the door, slipped the bolts, and cracked it ajar.

'Can I help you, officer?' Plob asked.

'I certainly hope so, boy.' replied the armoured cavalry officer in his most officious manner. 'We search for a small blonde girl. A perpetrator of vile and treasonous actions against the king's guard. She was seen running in this direction. Have you seen her?'

'No, sir. She could not have come this way, but in fairness, even if she had we would probably not have noticed. Our doors and shutters remain tightly shut as is my master's habit.'

'Well, if you do happen to see a small, remarkably attractive women in a blood-splattered dress, be sure to contact the king's guard. There is certain to be a large reward.'

Plob nodded as he closed and latched the door.

Dreenee stared at him; her eyes had softened slightly from the 'man-eating-tigress-about-to-savage-group-of-kindergarten-children' look to 'Grizzly-bear-whose-honey-has-been-stolen-by-Winnie-the-Pooh' look.

She walked deliberately towards Plob. One foot in front of the other. Hip left - thrust. Hip right - thrust. Left - thrust. Right - thrust. Left. Right.

She lifted her tiny alabaster hands, held his face lightly and kissed Plob full on the lips, crushing her soft pliant hips up against his. 'Thank you,' she breathed into his mouth. The blood rushed from Plob's head, thundering into his nether regions, robbing his brain of oxygen and causing him to fall flat on his back. Dreenee, well accustomed to this sort of reaction, batted nary an eye. Looking at a grinning Master Smegly she asked, 'Now - could you please tell me what, exactly, is going on here?'

Interesting that, thought Bill as he stared at the Technicolor mashed-in mess that was the back of Kleebles' skull. And so realistic too. For a dream, that is.

The door swung open as Kleebles' mother walked in. Her eyes widened in shock and horror as they registered the scene laid before them. She opened her mouth to scream.

The wrench rose high…

It would have to go, thought Horgy. He would have to take it back to the blacksmith and get him to make two smaller suits and a nice range of heavy-based pots and pans from the leftover bits. He wouldn't take it off just yet though, not whilst still in public. Not after being so newly knighted. Not here. Not now. Anyway, he couldn't actually remember how the bloody release straps and buckles worked, so he would have to get home first and let the servants do it.

He lunged forward, arms outstretched ala 'mummy-from-the-forgotten-crypt' legs pumping mightily. Now, where was the mounting crane? Gods, he was hot.

'Valet,' Horgy screeched. His voice ricocheted around violently inside his suit tearing at his eardrums until it was finally absorbed by the spongy membranes of his inner skull. Ooh - important safety tip, thought Horgy, never shriek with visor down. He lifted up his visor and tried again. 'Valet.'

This time someone heard. A grossly obese valet came jiggling up.

'You wanted me, sir?'

'No,' replied Horgy sarcastically. 'I was shouting for King Pathet, the ruler of the far northern places.'

'Oh,' mumbled the valet. 'Sounded like valet to me. Sorry to have bothered you, sir knight,' he concluded as he joggled off.

'No, wait.' cried Horgy to no avail. So once again he filled his lungs and threw his head back, and as his visor clanged shut, once again screamed mightily into his suit of armour.

'Valet - ley -ley - ley - ley - ley,' careened around his suit causing his jaw to cramp, toes to curl and eyes to fold in on themselves like a pair of live oysters doused in lemon juice.

'I see,' breathed Dreenee. She tilted her head to one side. 'Beautiful maid required.' She arched one perfect eyebrow. 'How much?' she asked.

'How much what?' asked the master magician right back.

'Aardvarks,' she quipped.

'Shouldn't that be 'how many'?' Questioned Plob seriously. 'You know - how 'many' aardvarks?'

Smegly harrumphed. 'She's talking about money, Plob. How much money. The aardvark thing is just a sarky aside. Anyway it's a quest. One doesn't get paid for a quest. Well - not in monetary terms at least.'

Dreenee's lips assumed 'The Pout.' (At this point let me clarify. When one says 'The Pout' one doesn't mean a pout, one means THE POUT. As in The Pout that all others of the female race aspire to. The pout of pouts. An X-rated, lock your husbands up and cover the eyes of your first-born male child pout). She glided silkily towards Smegly looking like sex on ball-bearings, eyes artfully downcast.

'Please,' she whispered as she got up really close. 'Please, please, please, pleasepleaseplease,' she continued as she ground her hips up against Master Smegly. 'Pleeeeeeeeeeeezzuugh,' she finished as she threw her head back and stared up at him, tear-glazed eyes impossibly wide, wet ripe red lips parted, and breath coming in small hot pants.

'No,' said Smegly as he turned on his heel and strode off down the corridor.

Alas, poor Dreenee, for Smegly was a master magician and, as we all know, master magicians are totally immune to the wiles of even the sultriest of succubae.

Dreenee stiffened with shock. Her entire body registered its disbelief. She spun around, rushed over to Plob's side of the room and repeated the entire performance directly at him.

Plob's nervous system went paroxysmal. Saliva drooled, toes curled, hands formed claws, vocal cords issued alternate mooing and grunting sounds and, finally, he fell to the floor and lay there, heels drumming spasmodically on the stripped wooden planking.

Dreenee breathed a sigh of relief.

'Come along, children,' called Smegly as he walked back up the corridor. 'The quest is about to begin. Plob go and get the trunk whilst I hail a cab. Plob?' Smegly looked down at the prostrate and powerless, sweat-drenched teenager lying on the floor and moaning softly through a mouthful of Dreenee-induced drool. He shook his head. 'Tut tut, poor Plob. Really, my dear girl. Was this absolutely necessary? It's a little unfair on my unfortunate unsuspecting assistant, don't you think?'

Dreenee blushed fetchingly, and the glow of her cheeks threw the azureness of her eyes into a lush sparkling relief. 'I'm sorry, Master Smegly. Truly I am. It's just that, well, what with…and you didn't…and normally men, and sometimes even women just…I had to...sorry. It won't happen again. I promise.'

Smegly chuckled. 'Don't make promises that you can't keep, little one. Any road up, no permanent harm done, I'm sure. Go to the kitchen, it's over there, draw a pail of water and chuck it on him. After the steam has stopped rising, give him a kick in the ribs and tell him to fetch the trunk. We're on our way. Now I'll go and fetch that cab. Oh, and Dreenee.'

'Yes, Master Smegly.'

'Welcome to the Quest.'

Chapter 7

‘No, there is not,’ said Plob emphatically.

‘Is so.’

‘No. There is not,’ repeated Plob.

‘Well then,’ retorted the driver of the cab that Smegly had hailed. ‘What am I doing here, caught up in it as it were?’

‘Nothing,’ said Plob, sighing. ‘You are merely a mode of transport. You have nothing to do with the quest.’

‘I do so. There’s always a cabbic in a qucst.’

‘No there is not,’ repeated Plob yet again.

‘Yes. It’s a well documented fact,’ continued the cabbie relentlessly.

‘No it is not.’

‘Is so. What about *the chronicles of Glimburble*?’

‘There’s no cabbie in them. I should know. I’ve read them twenty-three times.’

The cabbie rolled his eyes. ‘Oh what a full and busy life you must lead. Anyways, in the second chronicle…’

‘Glimburble goes south,’ interrupted Plob.

‘Yes,’ agreed the cabbie. ‘In the third chapter, just after he’s had a meal at the inn, he walks outside and he hails a cab.’

‘Yes?’ questioned Plob.

‘Well there you go,’ finished the cabbie.

Plob snorted and shook his head. ‘No. You’ll have to do better than that.’

‘OK. What about *Poodlepot’s quest for the sacred orb*? A cabbie was extensively involved in that one.’

Plob pinched his bottom lip as he dug through his memory.

(Metaphorically speaking, of course. Not with an actual spade, pick and shovel. Yes I admit that it's a bit of a stupid expression but it was either that or 'rifled' through his memory, which is also pretty weak. I suppose that I could have tried a little harder, given the clichés a complete miss and gone all poetic, like - Plob went dashing through the shadowy vaulted corridors of his long-term memory waving his arms in the air and shouting, 'Poodlepot's quest for the sacred orb' to no avail - oh sod it).

Plob pinched his bottom lip as he thought. (Ha, that's better).

'No. I don't know that one.'

'Ooh you must. It's very famous. It involved lots of cabbies. Actually Poodlepot himself was a cabbie. Yes, that's it. The full name of the book was actually 'Poodlepot the cabby's quest for the sacred orb, whilst being helped by numerous other cabbies who are oft involved in quests often…quite a lot.'

Plob stared. 'Rubbish. You're just making this up as you go along.'

'Am not.'

'Are so.'

'Am not.'

'Are so.'

'Not not notnotnot.'

'Are are areareareareaaaarrrr.'

'Notnotnotnoooooooot,' raved Plob, once again astonishing himself at how easily the cabbie managed to cause his normally fairly high intelligence quotient to plummet like a plucked chicken in flight.

'Boys,' Dreenee interrupted.

'Yes,' they replied in unison as, given the perfect excuse, both heads turned to watch Dreenees magnificent front jiggle interestingly up and down with the motion of the cab.

'Eyes up,' she continued, 'now - QUIET.'
They obeyed.

Well bugger this for a lark, thought Horgy. There was no way out of it. He was stuck for sure. Well and truly stranded. Like a dung beetle on its back.

'Buggerbuggerbugger,' he shouted as he thrashed around inside his suit of armour.

It had all been going so well. He'd eventually found a valet who had cranked him up onto his noble steed, Kashfloh, and he had ridden off to vast cheering and much swooning by a clutch of female Xbltqwb Buttneys. The first league or two were also fine, being borne aloft by his exultation. Then the armour began to take its toll. Heavier and heavier. Each clip, every clop seemed to add another pound until, finally, his strength simply gave out and he slid off noble Kashfloh like an avalanche of so much old iron.

And that's where he'd stayed for the last two hours. Grunting, groaning, grimacing, growling, grumbling, gnarling, sweating and forsaking. Promising that if anybody rescued him he would abandon knighting forever and never again put on any metal clothing.

Horgy took a deep breath, followed it immediately with another and started to calm down. Now - let's think this through, he thought whilst thinking about how to think it through. Think, think, think. (Perfectly good word 'think.' That is until you say it over and over a few times - think, think, think, think, think – then it starts to ring false as if maybe it isn't a word, and you just made it up.

And now that you've repeated it a few more times it's starting to sound more and more like a word that you just made up. So you decide to substitute it with another word. A more real word. But then you realise that no other word describes the process, so you panic, get paranoid.

What if someone actually publishes this? And then someone actually reads it. Not Mum or Dad or the wife or kids but someone from the general populous. And they enjoy the first few chapters until they get to this point and come across the word 'think.'

'I say, Susan.'

'Yes, John.'

'Awfully good book this. Rather. Except for this word "think".'

'Thnock, dear?'

'No, no. Think.'

'That's not actually a word, dear.'

'Hmm. Thought not. What a pity. I reckon I'll chuck it then. Not really worth reading the rest of it then what?'

'No, dear. And while you're about it why don't you write to the newspapers and tell them about the 'thninck' word.'

'Think, dear.'

'Whatever.'

John writes to the newspapers, reporters pick up on it as a hot new story. Front-page news throughout the civilized world. I can no longer leave the house for fear of people pointing and laughing. Children jeering and chanting, 'he thought think was a word, he thought think was a word. Nyaah nya nya nyaarh naah.'

No I can't take the risk. I know. I'll substitute another word. That's it. Phew.

Strouge – yes – good word.

Horgy took a deep breath, followed it immediately with another and started to calm down.

Now let's strouge this through (yes, it's working) he thought while strouging about how to strouge it through (brilliant). Strouge, strouge, strouge. (Oh ye Gods. It's worse than 'think.' Anyway, my wife just walked in, read this and told me not to panic as no one will ever publish and if they do they'll cut out all of the stupid bits anyway. Thanks).

If I could just turn over, thought Horgy, then maybe I would stand a chance of levering myself up onto my knees. Then, once on my knees, the possibilities are endless. I could pray for help. I could beg for help. I could pray and beg. Maybe even shuffle homewards. Oh yes. Life would definitely be rosy if I were on my knees.

Here goes. Deep breathe. Relax the muscles. Wait. Wait…Turn.

Horgy put everything into it. Every muscle turned. Every thought turned. Every cash flow, every balance sheet and every tax return in his brain took the strain.

And - miraculously - Horgy turned.

Unfortunately his suit of armour did not.

So lay our intrepid knight. Back to front and face down in an oversized suit of armour.

It's at times like these that one truly realizes how mightily life can suck.

This dream's a little frantic, thought Bill, as he wandered down the street in a vague and puzzled fug, small nameless bits of Kleebles and his mother still splattered on his cheek and stuck to his wrench. People rushing about. Street vendors attempting to sell their wares. The odd travelling performer. It simply wasn't good enough. It was his dream and he was going to do something about it.

Bill's dream must play the way Bill wants it to. Not right now though. First a drink, Bill was thirsty. Odd to be thirsty in a dream but it was that sort of dream.

Bill's eyes wandered around the street seeking a pub. Ah – there, 'The Swans Pyjamas.' Bill loped over, opened the door and strode up to the counter. The barkeeper scurried over.

'Pint.'

The barkeeper slid over a pint of PJ's best bitter.

'That'll be four pennies, good sir.'

Bill raised his head, eyes burning insanely and cast a stare in the barkeeper's general direction. The unfortunate hireling broke out into a sweat of the cold and clammy variety.

'O-o-on the house, my lord. This one's o-on the house,' he haltingly muttered as he staggered back from the weight of Bill's ocular insanity.

That's better, thought Bill. Much better. Good dream this. He pulled deeply on his mug of PJ's best.

Yes - very good dream. He'd even managed to order a drink without stuttering. Excellent.

Since Dreenee's last command, the quest had been continuing in relative silence. The only sounds being the clop of hooves, the odd harrumph, an occasional 'is, is, isn't, is' and the almost imperceptible rustle of Dreenee's breasts rubbing against the thin cotton of her blouse as they bounced sympathetically with the motion of the cab. Well, when I say almost imperceptible, it was for all but Plob. To Plob, with his testosterone-enhanced hearing, it was as a roaring in his ears that threatened to rob him of his precarious teenage sanity.

'Look.' Dreenee leaned forward in her chair and pointed.

'Nipple!' shouted Plob.

All eyes, even the horse's, turned to look at Plob who had gone a violent shade of puce.

'Sorry. I meant to say "what",' he corrected as his entire body writhed and squirmed and threatened to implode with an onrush of teenage embarrassment. The cabbie gave him a lascivious wink.

‘Over there,’ continued Dreenee. ‘ It’s a suit of armour lying on the side of the road.’

Chapter 8

'Look, mate, that's no good to us,' said Hugo. 'We all know that the murders were caused by a blunt metal object being brought into violent impact with the skull. We all know that. What we do not know is what the metal object is. A length of pipe? A tyre iron? A poker? What?'

The coroner shrugged.

'Listen, mate,' shouted Terry in his best East End accent. 'If you don't stop shrugging and start coming up with some useful info then so help me, cop or not, I will become very upset. And you don't want that to happen do you, my china plate?'

The coroner, who actually was from the East End and thought that Terry was a complete and utter prat, turned to cast a world-weary gaze upon him. 'Firstly, guv, I am not your mate. Secondly, if you threaten me again, cop or not, I shall tear you a shiny new arsehole with my bare hands and, thirdly, if you don't stop conversing in that fake East End bovver-boy accent I shall never speak to you ever again. And you don't want that to happen do you, my little ray of sunshine?'

Terry swallowed hard. 'OK. Point taken. So, can you help us?'

The coroner, whose name was Phred. Phred Smythe. (Which just goes to show that even the most simple and honest of names like Fred Smith can be cocked up by having pretentious parents) stared at Terry for a while and then acquiesced with another shrug. 'I think that it's painted red. Bright red. Probably. Maybe. It's not much to go on,' he conceded. 'But at the moment that's all we've got.'

Terry nodded. 'Thanks, Phred. Every little bit helps.'

'What's that then?' asked the old man at Bill's side as he gestured towards the bright red wrench. Bill turned and stared.

'It's a wre…sceptre.'

'Oh,' nodded the old man. 'A receptor,' he nodded again. 'Ah.'

'No, you stupid daft old coot. Not a receptor, just a sceptre.'

'Hey bugger off,' growled the old man. 'What gives you the right to call me a stupid daft old coot?'

'This,' said Bill shaking the wrench in front of the old man's face.

'Why?'

'Cause. It means that I'm the king. King Bill.'

The old man stared blankly at Bill, his mouth hanging open as his age addled, less than agile mind tried desperately to keep up with Bill's mad reasoning.

Bill stared insanely at the old man. The old man stared back blankly. Insanely, blankly, insanely, blankly.

'Oh sod it,' exclaimed Bill, as he savagely backhanded the old man with the wrench causing him to somersault off his barstool and crash to the floor like a lightning-struck veteran golfer in an electrical storm.

Now, we've seen it all before. It's not the biggest kid in the playground. More often than not you can pick them by the 'constant slight sneer,' 'the left eye twitch' and the 'thousand-yard stare' as they lurch around by the sandpit or the swings attempting to rip off girls' pigtails, putting head locks on all the other kids and indiscriminately lashing out at innocent passers by.

And we all know what happens next - a group of basically decent kids get together and discipline the little psycho by clipping him sharply around his schizophrenic lughole and convincing him to no longer torment his peers in such an unseemly fashion.

In our dreams perhaps - in reality, the group of basically decent kids get together and join our budding young Genghis Kahn in his vile oppression of the general populace.

It's no good denying it. This is what happens. Perhaps not the playground, perchance the teenage bicycle gang, the office bully and his sycophantic lackeys, the lynch mobs in the Westerns, Kermit and his Muppets, or - Bill the plumber, his wrench and his soon-to-be expanding group of Hitleresque goons.

This was truly great fun. Far and away the best dream that Bill had ever had. He didn't stutter any more, he seemed to be able to do anything that he wanted and behave exactly as he felt like.

In fact, the worse he behaved the more his new friends cheered him on.

And a scurvier band of cut throats, vagabonds, camp followers, spin doctors and thoughtless racial stereotypes, one couldn't wish for.

They loved him.

And he hardly had to use the wrench anymore. He found that by raising it up on high to the striking position, stopped any approaching arguments or indiscipline in their tracks.

Lo, he had even discovered that oft times he merely had to point his bright red, drop forged all-steel wrench at the offending miscreant and his newfound friends would carry out a bit of severe reprimanding on his behalf.

His new live friends.

His people.

His true subjects.

Good old Bill the plumber.

Great Bill de Plumber.

King Bil dePlummer.

Chapter 8

And the forces of evil shall be legion.

And the armies of light shall consist of a cabbie, an accountant, a waitress, a teenager and an old magician.

Why? I do not know. But it's always like that, isn't it. Well -isn't it?

'Whoa there. Whoa.' Cabbie hauled back on the reins stopping his cab and snow-white horse next to the prone suit of armour.

'Come on, Plob my boy,' said Smegly. 'Jump off and have a quick butchers.'

Plob vaulted off the front of the cab and walked over to the pile of iron.

'It's a suit of armour,' he said.

Dreenee rolled her eyes. 'Obviously.'

'Looks like a Smithmaster series seven with the reinforced epaulettes and the multi-swivel knee joints,' said the cabbie. 'A real beauty. Got five stars in last month's issue of 'Axe & Armour.' Damn heavy though,' he continued. 'A real hernia fest. Well, open up the visor and see if anyone's at home.'

Plob tugged at the visor to no avail. It wouldn't budge.

'No, no,' urged the cabbie. 'Push that button on the side. That's right. Now grab the tip of the visor and pull.'

Plob did as instructed, pulling up the visor to expose…

'Cripes,' he yelled as he leapt back in shock.

'It's a werewolf,' screamed the cabbie pointing at the back of Horgy's head with a shaking digit.

'Calm down, Cabbie,' shouted Master Smegly. 'Show some control, damn it, man,' he continued as he clambered down off the cab and strode over to the armour

And then they all heard it. Echoing and vague. Like an exhausted whisper from a tomb so very far away -'Hello, hello. Is someone there? Anyone…help me…please…anyone.'

'The voice of the damned,' whispered the cabbie as he proscribed the complex, but totally ineffectual, warding sign of the small pink-headed god Oxtoclitris on his chest with a shaky finger.

'I think it's coming from in here,' said Plob pointing at the non-ambulatory Smithmaster series seven.

'Well of course it is,' agreed Smegly. 'Now let's see if we can prise that helmet off and attempt an educated guess at what in the gods' names is actually transpiring. Cabbie, get down here, you seem to know a fair bit about how these steel overcoats work.'

The cabbie shook his head.

'Come on, get down here,' repeated Smegly.

Another more vigorous shake.

Master Smegly seemed to grow in stature, lose his 'kindly-wise-old-man' look and replace it with the unfamiliar visage of a true Master of magiks in their prime.

'Now,' he commanded.

The cabbie all but flew off the driver's seat to Master Smegly's side.

'I live but to serve, Master,' he said nervously.

Smegly nodded. 'Right, how does one remove this helmet?'

'There,' the cabbie pointed at a small silver lever on the chest. 'You pull that out, then you swivel the helmet one third turn to the left and remove. It's quite simple really.'

Master Smegly looked at the cabbie thoughtfully. 'So you're pretty up with all this militaria are you, Cabbie?'

Cabbie shrugged. 'I don't recommend opening that,' he said. 'We don't know what manner of dire beast lies within.'

Smegly shook his head in seeming despair. 'It's a man, you pillock, Plob, remove the helmet.'

Plob knelt down again, toggled the lever, turned the helmet and pulled. 'The Master's right. It's a man. I think that he's broken his neck. His head's all twisted around.'

'Oh thank you, good sir. Thank you, thank you,' mumbled the twisted head.

'He's still alive,' said Plob in amazement.

'A miracle,' quoth the cabbie.

Smegly clipped him about the ear. 'We'll have no "quothing" by you, my friend Cabbie,' he said. 'Strictly higher mortals' word that. Now, turn him over and let's have a chat.'

Dreenee walked up for a closer look as Plob and the cabbie readied themselves to roll the prostrate iron suit over.

'Together now,' said Plob. 'One, two, three…Hunggh.'

And over it went.

And there he lay. Poor old Horgy. Hoarse from his hours of begging and pleading. Exhausted, dehydrated and back to front in the world's heaviest suit of armour.

And staring down at him – a magician, a cabbie a teenager and…

It was all too much for Horgy. Tears rolled freely down his face.

'I'm dead,' he blubbered. 'Buggeration, what a senseless waste of money.'

Smegly chuckled. 'You're not dead, my good man. Far from it. Plob, get the man some water.'

'But….' Horgy looked confused. 'The angel,' he said staring at Dreenee. 'How can it be that such poignant and ethereal beauty may walk the face of this poor and wretched land and not be heaven sent. My life has most surely seen its zenith and now all else shall pale in comparison.' He finished and started blubbering again.

Dreenee leant forward and kissed him lingeringly on the forehead. 'You sweet, sweet man,' she breathed.

For once Horgy was pleased that some areas of his suit allowed ample space for growth.

It had been a long day and they had only found an acceptable inn many hours after night had fallen. The quest members were sitting around a rough-hewn wooden table in the tap room, spearing chunks of rare venison off a large steaming platter set in the centre.

Plob was nursing a beer, his first ever, whilst simultaneously feeling both grown up and slightly nauseous. He'd heard that ale was an acquired taste that needed a little perseverance, and now he was wondering why anyone bothered. He forced another sip down and marvelled at the look of relish on the cabbie's face as he swigged down his fourth ale and then placed the empty tankard upside down on his head.

'Ye Gods,' shouted the cabbie. 'My drink's evaporated again and I am being cruelly left without by our less than attentive serving wench.' He stood up and did a jig over to the bar to rustle up another round returning quickly with more ale for all. Plob groaned.

'Come on, Plob,' ribbed Cabbie. 'It's not always easy drinking and having fun. There are times when I really just can't face it. But do I let that stop me? No. I show strength of character. Fortitude. Oft I have to force the first couple of ales down, and then try to stop me.'

Plob nodded politely and managed to brave a larger sip of his, by now, body-temperature ale.

'Here,' said the cabbie. 'I'll teach you a song. It's a good one. Goes like this. Concentrate now. You're gonna have to sing it yourself after I've taught you. OK.'

Plob nodded whilst taking down another gulp of ale.

'Right…Ahem…La, la, la,' the cabbie stood up and struck what he considered to be a suitably operatic pose. 'First verse -Ale, ale, ale, ale. Ale. Ale. Ale.' He paused for a breath, quaffed half of his ale, and continued. 'Second verse - Ale, ale, ale, ale. Ale. Ale. Ale. The end.'

The cabbie sat down to huge applause from the gathered quest members.

He polished off the rest of his ale and started singing again. 'That was a very good song. Sing us another one, just like that other one. Sing us another one -Plob.'

All eyes turned to the magician's assistant who, surprisingly, agreed. Plob raised his tankard to his lips for another quick sip only to find that it was empty. Cabbie pushed a full one into his hand. Plob drew deeply on it and launched forth. 'Ale, ale. Ale. Ale. Ale.'

'No,' said the cabbie irritably. 'You've got the words wrong. It's - Ale, ale, *ale*. Not Ale, ale. Ale. Ale. Ale. That's a completely different song. Try again.'

Plob assumed the position and gave song – 'Ale, ale, ale. Ale. Ale. Ale.'

'Yay,' the cabbie cheered. 'All together now,' he continued as he climbed up on his chair to conduct.

The quest members all joined in -'Ale, ale, ale.' Excepting for Plob who was now near the end of his third first ale (or first third ale), as it were, and had forgotten the words.

The hours passed quickly, as they do when you're having fun (or in a coma, but that's a different kettle of mice -or is that fish, I'm never quite sure)?

It was definitely the wee hours of the morning. Dreenee, Master Smegly and Horgy had all left and gone to bed, and that amber nectar, so capable of helping along with a good time, had now bitten the hand (or perhaps mouth) that drinks it. Both Plob and the cabbie had been through all of the phases. Incredibly happy and jovial (Ale, ale, ale), happy and serious (I am really having a good time. No seriously, guys, a really good time), happy and loving (I love you guys. Never before has anyone meant so much to me. Never), happy and weepy (Everyone else has gone to bed and left us. But we're still here. And we're still happy. Right?). Wrong -finally -not happy, just weepy. And morose. Weepy and morose.

The cabbie scrubbed his eyes with the back of his hand. 'I was a champion. One of the best. Agile, dextr…dextro..dextererereres..bloody good. No, really. There was no better with a sword and very few with a…a…long pointy thing.' He waved his hands in the air. '…wooden. Longish and pointyish….'

'Stick,' prompted Plob.

The cabbie stared at him blankly. 'Thash stooped. Is not a stick.'

'Could be,' said Plob. 'Sounds like a stick.'

The cabbie shook his head. 'Not stick. Sticks aren't pointy…or long…just wooden. And sticky.'

'Maybe it's a long pointy stick,' affirmed Plob.

The cabbie stared at him in drunken amazement. 'Thash brilliant. Yeah, you're right. There were very few better than me with a long pointy stick.'

Plob poured some ale in the general direction of his face, choking and spluttering as he inhaled a goodly amount into his sinuses. 'I can't believe that you were a knight,' he burbled through his ale. 'What was your praise name?'

'Can't say,' said the cabbie sadly.

'Oh,' nodded Plob understandingly. 'You've taken an oath.'

'No, I'm just too drunk to remember.'

'That's sad,' said Plob. 'So sad. It's alright thou. We'll all just call you Cabbie. Why did you give up?'

‘It’s a long tale containing much woe.’ Cabbie slumped forward onto the table. ‘Basically I developed an inferiority complex. You can’t be an inferior knight. It doesn’t work.’

‘Don’t be so hard on yourself,’ consoled Plob. ‘I’m sure we’ve all got some sort of inferiority complex about something.’

‘Probably,’ agreed Cabbie. ‘But other people’s inferiority complexes are better than mine. I have an inferior inferiority complex.’ His head fell forward into the pool of spilt ale on the table and he started weeping drunkenly and inconsolably, pausing every now and then to lick some ale off the table top.

‘So sad,’ repeated Plob as he slid off his chair onto the floor. ‘So very sad.’ He hit the floor with a thump. ‘Lance. It’s a lan….’

Plob had run out of deities to pray to.

He had woken up in his bed that morning (God knows how he got there) fully clothed, rumpled, bent, nauseous and gummy. Sporting a mouth that tasted like the moist parts of a vulture’s crotch.

And the thirst. It was as if some gigantic dishwashing type person had used him as a sponge to scour all the grease off the pots left over from a meal prepared by ‘the deep fried lard cooking convention’ and then wrung him out, leaving not a drop of usable moisture in his poor dehydrated body.

And the head ache. Ye Gods. He was convinced that some small burrowing creature had clambered into his cranium via his left ear and was proceeding to gnaw viciously on his spongy grey matter.

He would never drink again. Never. This he had solemnly sworn whilst kneeling in the latrine worshipping position and seemingly throwing up every meal he had ever eaten. Ever.

Cabbie had met him in the corridor on their way out and banged him chirpily on the back, looking no worse for wear than a vegetarian teetotaller after a Sunday afternoon sing song.

He had asked Plob not to mention the knight thing. Plob had readily agreed as, anyway, he could only vaguely recollect some discussion regarding knights and…pointy sticks?

Over breakfast, Master Smegly filled in the uninformed members of the quest regarding Bil dePlummer and the problem of the unknown evil as well as his short-to-medium-turn plans apropos the solving of said circumstances.

'I'm not sure that I understand,' said Horgy. 'We have to go and see the master?'

'Yes,' replied Smegly.

'But I thought that you were the master.'

'No, no. I'm merely a master magician. Well, in one way you're right. I am Plob's master.'

'Ah,' Horgy nodded. 'Two masters.'

'I'm only talking about my master,' continued Smegly.

'And is he also a master magician?' Horgy wanted to know.

'Oh yes,' affirmed Smegly, 'he's The master magician.'

'A sort of master magicians' masters' master. Three masters. Or would that be four masters', as it were?'

'Isn't that a boat,' Cabbie interjected. 'A four master.'

Horgy shook his head. 'No. You're thinking of a ketch aren't you?'

'That would be a two master,' said Dreenee. 'I saw one down at the docks once. I'm sure that a ketch has two masts.'

'Well a cutter then,' offered Horgy. 'That's got four masts.'

'I think that's a Man-of-war,' corrected Cabbie. 'A cutter's got six masts.'

'That's a midshipman,' said Plob, unable to keep out of the fast spiralling conversation despite his newly discovered brain tumour.

Every one turned to stare.

'A midshipman,' said Smegly. 'That's a person that works on a ship.'

'Yes,' agreed Plob. 'And he has six masters. There's the ship's master, the captain, the bosun, the navigator, the gunny and…and…the other one.'

'The sea,' offered Cabbie. 'The sea is a sailor's master.'

'No, no,' disagreed Horgy. 'The sea is a sailor's mistress, the sea's always a mistress. Anyway, a midshipman outranks a gunny. I think.'

'I thought that a gunny was a sack,' said Dreenee. 'You know, a gunny sack.'

Smegly sighed. 'The Gods help us.' He pointed forward. 'Let us be off, Cabbie, and show some haste.'

'It can't be a poker,' said Terry. 'No one paints a poker red. Could be a piece of piping, a red piece of pipe. Or a length of reinforcing rod.'

'A fire bucket,' suggested Hugo. 'That's red.'

'Yep,' agreed Terry. 'Or a toy fire engine. Or that red Tele-tubby. What's its name? Tinky-winky? Or little Red bloody Riding Hood. Or a red bicycle…or…or…just be real can't you, Hugo, a fire bucket. Geez.'

'Po.'

'What?'

'The red one is called Po. Tinky-winky's purple.'

Terry rolled his eyes skywards in frustration and disbelief.

They set off at a goodly pace as Cabbie had harnessed both his snow-white charger and the noble Kashfloh to the cab.

After a few hours they stopped for an al fresco lunch of ham, bread and cheese that Smegly had purchased from the inn that morning.

Plob's head was still thumping, although the nausea had stopped and he had finally managed to quench his outrageous thirst by putting the top of a water skin into his mouth and liberally squeezing a jet of about two gallons of water down his parched throat. This had left him re-hydrated but uncomfortably full. Also he sloshed when he moved - still, can't have everything. Cabbie had suggested he down another ale. 'Hair of the cur that had savaged him the night before.' Plob shuddered at the thought. Anyway, he still remembered his vow of abstinence taken at the latrine.

After the quick lunch they were back on the road. Smegly felt that there was some need for speed as they were all still unsure of how, and even what they were going to fight, and they still had to journey through the valley of 'Strange' and onwards still, over the dreaded mountains of 'Steve.'

Plob fervently hoped that the quest would involve little or no violence. Not that he was afraid, no, not our intrepid magician's assistant. There had never really been the need for Plob to be physically afraid of much. From as early as he could remember he had always been built like an aspiring blacksmith, and tall into the bargain. And the physical nature of his work with Master Smegly had honed all of his baby fat off and left him a fine figure of a teenage almost man.

It was simply that Plob didn't like violence. He thought it a silly, unnecessary and, usually, ineffective way of dealing with a situation. Mature thoughts from our hero. Wrong. But mature nonetheless.

I know that it's abhorrent, but let's be brutally honest (how brutal? Well, that's up to you. But nothing kinky, huh. OK). Violence is often silly and unnecessary but it is also often an extremely effective way of dealing with things. Especially if you're a bit thick. In fact violence is definitely the thicky's friend. Thickies unite for a violent world, one could say. Fortunately true violence is impossible for the thickies to achieve. To achieve real state of the art, world cock-up-type violence one needs to be bright. The brighter the better. Don't believe me? Well -tell that to Einstein, $E=MC^2$ I rest my case.

Also Plob was experiencing a few reservations regarding Horgy, nice guy that he was. Although he was definitely a knight and, most probably very noble, Plob really would have preferred a knight that would be able to fight in his armour as opposed to next to it.

Dreenee was great, what with her being the quintessential beauty and all. It was just that, far be it for him to complain, but she wasn't quite right. Weren't the beautiful maids in quests meant to be demure, shy, reticent and ever so slightly nervous? The only thing that Dreenee was nervous about was that she might kill someone by mistake. Being in possession of freakish strength, coupled with an extremely volatile character and the world's shortest temper meant she was less of a beautiful maid and more of a small blonde, succulent wrecking machine.

And they didn't have a thief. Plob was sure that a thief was essential.

And then there was Cabbie. Best leave thinking about him for later.

At least there was no doubt as to the master magician and the master magician's assistant. So that was a plus.

Plob sighed.

'Why the sigh, Plob?' enquired Dreenee as she leant forward to touch his arm. Her head tilted enquiringly to one side, lips slightly apart, her thin cotton dress betraying her impossibly lush figure which had been thrown into stark relief by the now sinking sun.

Plob paused before he answered. Not because he was thinking of what to say, he was more thinking of what not to say, the 'Nipple' incident still fresh in his mind. He knew that he would never be able to live down another inadvertent body part blurtation. And who knows which specific part he might mention next.

No it didn't bear thinking about. Bear. Bare. Bare Dreenee. Bare naked Dreenee. Oh Gods, Plob fought for control and, admirably, attainted it, although the nausea and great thirst were now back with a vengeance.

'Oh, nothing,' he replied, thinking it better to deflect the situation.

Dreenee slid over to his seat, sat next to him and laid her head on his shoulder. 'You worry too much,' she said, with what sounded like real concern. 'Don't. You're too young to be so unduly perturbed. There's a time for worrying and a time for relaxing. This is a good time for relaxing, start your worrying in your twenties. I promise you there'll still be plenty to go around.'

Fat chance, thought Plob. How can I not worry with this vision of loveliness nestled up against me, the mouth, the long eyelashes, and the soft smell of her recently washed, thick blonde tresses? Who knows what will betray me first – my body or my mind.

Dreenee snuggled a little closer to Plob and gently drifted into slumber. Plob held his breath until, with surprise, he realised that not only was his body not overreacting uncontrollably but his mind was also almost totally devoid of any inappropriate or lascivious thoughts (I say almost because it is impossible for any young man's mind to be totally devoid of inappropriate or lascivious thoughts). Plob grinned to himself. Amazing, he thought. I do seem to have some control over my hormones. Brilliant. He put his arm around Dreenee's shoulders and also proceeded to trundle off to the land of nod.

That night they stopped off at another inn that was much like the one from the night before. As they sat in the cosy taproom, eating a hearty warm lamb stew with hunks of newly baked buttered bread, Plob found himself with a tankard of ale in his hands. He shrugged and reckoned that perhaps oaths don't count when taken under duress, for in all honesty he had thought that he was going to die that morning.

He at least had enough sense to retire fairly early after only two or three tankards and spent a couple of hours studying one of his master's weighty tomes on wild magic and its effect on human biology.

They rose early the next morning and Master Smegly, normally so staid and calm of demeanour, seemed a little out of sorts. After they had been travelling for a couple of hours he called to Cabbie to halt and pull off the road into a glade of silver-green ash trees that straddled a fast flowing stream of cold, clear water.

'Right.' He surveyed the quest members with a stern eye. 'Up until now this whole thing has been a bit of a lark. We all have our own private reasons for coming and now will be a good time to review them. From this moment on we will begin to travel further and further into the realms of nightmares. I have no knowledge of Bil de Plummer but, over the past few decades, I have both studied and fought Evil in almost all its misbegotten forms and guises. And this one thing I can promise you – it's no bloody picnic.'

Smegly paused for a while and then turned his gaze to Dreenee. 'My girl. You are no longer in danger from the king's men. We have travelled far from their magisterial district and, if I were you, I would go back to the last village that we passed through, get a job, settle down and live a long and, perhaps, happy life.'

Dreenee held Master Smegly's iron gaze until it was too much for her and then she turned her head aside. 'Work as a waitress,' she said in a flat voice. 'Do you think that's all I'm good for?'

'You, all of you, are worth what you decide. Except Plob, of course, I'm his master so I will decide both his worth and his fate. And at the moment his fate is to stick with the quest. Anyway, it was his idea after all.'

'I'm staying,' said Dreenee. 'You're my friends. I don't leave my friends.'

Smegly turned questioningly to Horgy.

'I'm a knight,' Horgy said. 'Questing is what I do. It's pretty much my middle name. Sir "questing" Horgelbund - the pheasant killer. Oh, if I could tell you all of the quests that I've been on well I'd…I'd…tell you…about them.' Horgy looked down embarrassedly at the ground. 'Friends?' He glanced at Dreenee. 'It's unusual for accounta…knights to have friends. And this knighting lark has cost me an absolute bucket so far. I might as well stick with it and try to show some return on capital invested. Count me in.'

They all turned to Cabbie who laughed out loud. 'Well obviously I'm staying. I have to. What's a quest without a Cabbie? There has to be a Cabbie.' He winked at Plob. 'Doesn't there?'

Plob grinned widely and nodded. 'Yep, Cabbie, there surely does.'

'It's settled then,' quoth Smegly. 'Right, Plob, break out the travelling oven, the anvil and the number three hammer. Cabbie, start a fire over there. Dreenee, collect some water and, Horgy.'

Yes,' answered Horgy.

'Keep guard. Now hurry along, people, I'll explain the whys and wherefores as we proceed. Come, come,' he continued, clapping his hands together. 'We have many complex and difficult spells to forge before the sun sets.'

Plob enjoyed mass spell forging. Smegly prepared the spells and cast them, glittering and writhing, into the oven. Cabbie kept a brisk fire going with use of both wood and bellows. Plob removed the newly forged spells from the oven with his tongs, hammering them into shape on the anvil using the medium-weight number three hammer and passed them on to Dreenee who quenched them in a bowl of water, before wrapping them in their protective vellum skins.

At the same time as they worked Master Smegly explained what he was doing.

'As Plob knows there are two types of spells. Those created from common "air" magic and those forged from the powerful "earth" magic. Simple spells such as creating small quantities of light, starting fires, placing minor curses on people and the curing of certain trifling afflictions, are all common magic or "air" spells. These can be cast on the spot by using various incantations, gestures and breathing techniques.

'The more demanding spells – general protection, calling up storms, the casting of lightning bolts and so on fall into the powerful magic or "earth" spell camp. Now, the essence of these spells has to be prepared beforehand, cast, forged into shape and kept ready for use. Upon release they are channelled, via the aforementioned incantations etcetera, into the specific guise that we are looking for at the time. For instance, a thunderbolt, a fireball, or a small hailstorm would be cast from the same forged spell. It is on release that the magician decides which form that particular spell will take.

Remember, however, that a protection forging cannot be used for an attack spell and vice versa.

'When Plob and I discuss spells, we will always refer to them as air spells or earth spells followed by their designation, such as "earth, attack, thunderbolt", "earth, protect, shield wall", or "air, light". Get used to those terms so as to avoid possible confusion in moments of extremis.'

Master Smegly stopped his casting for a moment and went over to the small pile of vellum-wrapped spells. He drew a number of rolls of ribbon from his pocket and started tying the various colours around the different types of spells. Yellow ribbons for protective spells and red for attack spells. After this he took over from Plob for a while and spent almost an hour forging one spell himself. As he held onto the raw superheated magic with the tongs and hammered away he used both mental and physical force to bend the earth power into the semblance of the spell that he wanted. He then wrapped it in a double layer of vellum and tied it in a white ribbon onto which he inscribed many detailed and complex runes. The forging of this spell seemed to exhaust the master and he sat down next to the fire with a colossal sigh.

Dreenee went over to the cab, opened the dickey boot and took out a small cask of ale that they had purchased from the inn that morning before they had left. She carried it over to the fire, broached it with her tiny fist, and drew Master Smegly a tankard full.

Smegly looked up appreciatively as she brought it to him. 'Thank you, my girl,' he said. 'You're an angel.'

'I know,' said Dreenee as she giggled. 'Horgy already told me so, remember.'

She walked on back to the cab. 'All right, chaps. Why don't you all clear up, put the tools away and have a bit of a wash. I'll prepare dinner.'

Dinner wasn't half bad. Dreenee knocked up a thick soup of ham, potatoes and dried peas, cooked in ale and flavoured with some peppery herb that she had noticed growing in abundance next to the small stream.

Using air magic Smegly cast a warning perimeter around the campsite, then they all wrapped themselves in their blankets and promptly fell asleep.

The next day was almost a carbon copy of the day before. They rode all day, stopping for a quick bite at lunch and, that evening, they stopped for the night at an old, slightly shabby, inn.

The last available inn before entering the valley of Strange.

They drew up into the forecourt at the front of the inn to be greeted by a wizened old hunchback with perhaps the thinnest neck that Plob had ever seen. It made his head look like a half-deflated pink balloon tied to a lollipop stick. He nodded and bobbed up to the cab.

'Ah, masters, masters, masters. So good to have you here,' he gurgled, head wobbling back and forth.

'No. Just one master,' corrected Horgy. 'He's an assistant, I'm a Knight there's the cabbie and here,' he gestured towards Dreenee, 'our very own angel of prettiness.'

The old man stared incomprehensibly at Horgy. 'Master?' he questioned.

'No,' repeated Horgy. 'I'm the knight. He is the master,' he affirmed, pointing at Smegly. 'Concentrate now. Master, knight, cabbie, assistant, beautiful maid. One master. Only one.'

'Yes. Like a yacht,' interjected Cabbie helpfully. 'Only one mast. A single master as it were.'

The old man's head started to vibrate in confusion as it whipped frantically from one quest member to the other, his brain working feverishly as he continued to silently mouth the words 'masters' under his breath.

Fortunately he was saved from a total mental collapse by the timely appearance of the innkeeper who bustled up busily, wiping his hands on his apron and shaking his head in annoyance.

'Come along now, Mister Hobgoblinsson, stop bothering the good masters and take their horses off to the stable to be fed and watered.'

'One,' said the old man in a confused voice.

The innkeeper looked at him irritably. 'What?'

'Just one,' repeated the old man, raising a single spindly digit skywards in proclamation. 'Like a boat,' he continued. 'Exactly like a boat.'

He dithered over to the horses and started unhitching them, a constant low level muttering issuing forth with the minimum of help from his decrepit old vocal cords.

'Sorry about him,' apologised the innkeeper. 'It's simply that it's almost impossible to find decent help this close to the valley. Here, good masters, let me help you with your bags.'

'No…' started Horgy.

'Leave it,' snapped Smegly. 'For God's sake leave it.'

Their baggage was carried in and they were shown to their various dusty, seedy rooms. After they had changed out of their travelling clothes into more comfortable attire they met in the taproom.

Cabbie was busy raving at the innkeeper.

'What do you mean you don't have any ale? What sort of wretched establishment doesn't keep ale? How is a man supposed to recover from a hard day's journey without the help of a tankard or four of good, dark ale, or mediocre ale, or even bad ale, any ale? But no ale? This is a disaster. A travesty. It's deplorable. And cruel, yes, mainly it's cruel. You should have a sign outside saying 'No Bloody Ale at

This Inn,' then you wouldn't get people fixing their taste buds for ale only to be offered a choice of either bugger all ale or none whatsoever ale. What's the name of this ale-free establishment?'

'The Pigs Garters, sir,' replied the innkeeper.

'Right,' continued Cabbie. 'From now on it shall be known as "The ale less cruel and deplorable buggery pig's garters and no bloody ale place" inn.' Cabbie paused for a breath.

'We have red wine, sir,' interjected the keeper quickly whilst he had a chance.

'Oh,' exclaimed Cabbie as he was brought up short in mid rant. 'Well bring forth a flagon of your best red then, my good man. Quickly now as I grow weary of your constant chatter regarding your ale free existence and I may soon expire due to a build up an excessive amount of blood in my alcohol stream.'

The keeper rushed off at top speed with a suitably chastened expression adorning his plump and sweaty face.

'Oh stop being so mean, Cabbie,' said Dreenee with a smile. 'You can live without ale for a night or two. I'm more concerned with the state of the rooms. I don't think that I've ever seen so much dust in one place. I suspect that the innkeeper collects it as a hobby.'

'Either that or he has a dust fetish,' retorted Cabbie seriously.

'Can you?' asked Plob. 'I mean can one have a dust fetish? It's just that that seems a bit weird. Even for this neck of the woods.'

'Of course,' affirmed Cabbie knowledgably. 'When it comes to fetishes the weirder the better I always say. I knew a girl once, had a foot fetish.'

'Well that's pretty normal, isn't it? As far as fetishes go at any rate,' commented Dreenee.

‘Chicken’s feet,’ countered Cabbie.

Dreenee shuddered.

‘Ah happy days.’ Cabbie clapped as the keeper returned with a large flagon of red wine and mugs enough for all.

‘Well, Plob,’ said Cabbie. ‘As I’ve always said,’ he continued as he picked up a brimful mug of red. ‘This is the answer. It’s the question that’s the bugger to find. Here you go.’ He passed the mug over and Plob quickly applied himself to some serious self-medication.

The innkeeper trundled back in with another flagon of wine and a huge platter of sausages, onions and potatoes that he placed on a dumb waiter next to the table. Hobgoblinsson followed with a pile of mismatched cutlery and crockery.

After they had suitably savaged the contents of the platter, Smegly called for some brandy and lit up a large dark cigar.

‘Tomorrow’s the day, gentlepeople,’ puffed he. ‘We should enter the valley sometime before midday. I wish that we could travel around it but with the “sea of tantrums” on the one side and the “chasm of Brad” on the other we have no choices open to us. It should take us no more than two days to pass through, perhaps three if we are held up a little, and I am hoping that we all make it relatively unscathed.’

‘Half a mo,’ interjected Cabbie. ‘I’m just the Cabbie. I don’t want to be relatively unscathed. I don’t want to be scathed at all. I want to be part of a scathe-free existence.’

‘You can’t be scathed, Cabbie,’ said Horgy. ‘It’s not a word.’

Cabbie shook his head in disagreement. ‘If you can be unscathed then you can definitely be scathed. In fact I would be extremely gruntled if I remained completely free of all scathing type activity as from now on.’

‘You can’t be gruntled either,’ argued Horgy. (As it happens he was wrong, on both counts, so there).

‘Look, chaps,’ interrupted Smegly. ‘We’ve made our decisions. The time for turning back has gone. From now on we follow the quest, complete with scathing, gruntling and any other form of -ing that may or may not take place’

‘Like maiming,’ said Plob.

‘Or hurting,’ added Dreenee.

‘Or killing, torturing, dying, burning, screaming…’

‘Plob,’ shouted Smegly, interrupting our youthful apprentice in mid -ing. ‘That is enough. I suggest that we all retire, for tomorrow is sure to be a full day.’

‘Yeah,’ said Cabbie. ‘Full of -ings. Goodnight.’

And with that our team hit the hay.

Bil couldn’t ride a horse. He’d never learned. Well how could he, being brought up in Milton Keynes and then moving to Islington and all where there’s not much call for equine assisted plumbers. So they had made him a litter on which he was dragged. Resplendent in his blue boiler suit and bedspread cloak, red wrench held aloft for his disciples to see. Not quite the golden coach of legend what with it being so close to the ground and all and being rather dusty, and silly looking. But this silliness of look was nought to King Bil. For he was beloved and obeyed. And him, and his now formidable group of societal flotsam and jetsam, were drawing ever nearer to the palace, for an impending showdown with King Mange the pretender.

For Bil would be more than a king in name only. He would be a king in deed. With a castle. And a throne. And a bigger litter, drawn by four horses. And other stuff too. Lots of it.

King Mange stood on the balcony surveying Bil’s personal rabble collection milling around below. His royal bodyguards kept a close eye on him least he forget that he couldn’t fly and stepped off for a quick float around, or death inducing crash to the cobblestones, as reality would have it.

'Why, oh why are theeth nathty unwashed typth milling around below and offering up profanities and inthults to me?' he asked his chief bodyguard. 'Do they not know that I am their king?'

'I am sure that they are aware of that, my liege,' reassured the said guarder of the king. 'I feel that is why, in all probability, they are chanting "death to King Mange the usurper" and hurling rocks in your general direction.'

'Well get rid of them. They're noisy and ugly and poor. And they're upsetting Mucous.'

'Of course, my king. What do you suggest? Perhaps a good shouting should make them go away. One hopes that this will be sufficient as most of the royal guard are still out scouring the countryside for a small blonde girl that seems to have offended the royal family in some way.'

King Mange made a pretence at thought. Not a very good pretence, mind you, as he didn't have anything to actually base his performance on. 'Yeth. Go ahead then. I believe a good thouting would be in order. Wait until I'm inside though as all thith noith ith upthetting me awfully. Oh yeth, and while I'm inside boil up thome oil and pour it all over them.' Not so stupid after all, our Mangy King.

The chief bodyguard shook his head. 'Let them eat deep fried cake,' he said to himself as he discounted the Kings suggestion almost immediately. Not through any thoughts of humanity but merely because he knew that the castle lamp oil deliveries arrived every second Thursday of the month, or tomorrow, and present stocks were almost non existent. Oh well perhaps we can try boiling water. At least it'll give the buggers a much-needed wash.

Down below him things were heating up. Bill had gathered his people around him and commanded that they cut down a tree for use as a battering ram and, once inside, that they tie King Mange to a stake and burn him. Unfortunately, due to the generally low IQ of his cohorts, some had cut a tree down but others had already set fire to it.

It was promising to be a pretty protracted siege.

Chapter 9

‘Behold,’ said Master Smegly as he gestured flamboyantly. ‘The valley of Strange.’

A less than pleasant vista lay before them. Unfriendly, stumpily treed, craggy and blasted. If it were at all possible for a rural setting to suffer from urban decay then this was it. A housing project of a forest. A veritable ghetto of a valley.

‘It is here,’ he continued, ‘that the Trogres live. A shunned tribe of the progeny that have sprung forth from the interbreeding of Troll and Ogre. A simple, warlike species that have developed their own set of rules for their own unique environment. If we are lucky then we might pass through their neighbourhood unmolested. If unlucky we be, well, we have the spells. Right, troops, let’s go.’

Cabbie urged the horses forward. As they got deeper into the valley the stunted trees started to loom larger and the road shrunk to a path that became narrower and more treacherous underfoot. The general feeling amongst the quest members was one of wariness and distraction. Each large boulder or tall tree next to the path looked a perfect place for an ambush. It seemed as every copse contained an army, every turn in the path concealed a pitfall. Nerves were drawn tendon tight. At this rate they would be knackered by nightfall.

And they were. As the day drew to a close, Smegly ordered camp in a small clearing surrounded by boulders. Plob and Horgy collected a huge pile of wood and started a goodly sized fire. The wood was warped and knotted, but it was hard, so it burnt well. They prepared a dinner of bread and bacon and, although Plob knew that he must be hungry, the tension of the day had cramped his stomach and he didn’t much feel like eating.

‘Only another couple of days of this,’ said Horgy, ‘if all continues to go well. We’ll need to keep watch. I suggest four watches of two hours each. I'll take first shift. Plob you next, then Master Smegly and lastly Cabbie.'

Dreenee looked up. 'What about me?' she questioned.

'I've given that some thought and, well, there's the question of danger.'

Dreenee bristled.

'No, no. Hear me out,' continued Horgy. 'From what I've heard about the Trogres not every meeting ends in fighting. There are times, few though they may be, that bloodshed has been averted by the simple actions of proffering a small bribe together with some first-class pleading and whining. You, my dear, whilst being imminently qualified for stunning people with beauty and, or, smashing the blobby bits out of their cranium through their ears with your bare hands, you are not huge on either subtlety or pleading.'

'He's right, Dreenee,' said Plob. 'You're too dangerous to have on guard.'

'What about me?' asked Cabbie. 'I'm beautiful and dangerous. Can I also be excused from duty?'

'OK,' said Horgy. 'Go on over and give Dreenee a salacious kiss coupled with an inappropriate comment or two. If she lets you get away with it I'll admit that you are definitely both beautiful and dangerous.'

'Last shift for me it is then,' confirmed Cabbie as he rolled himself up in his blanket.

Plob threw another log on the fire before he followed Cabbie's example. Dreenee poured Master Smegly a cup of tea before she, and then finally Horgy, went to their separate bedrolls.

'Plob.'

Plob slammed awake to Smegly's call and, as he did, he became aware of the music. A savage drum-like thumping with a bass line of vocal accompaniment. He looked up and saw that they were surrounded by the shimmering veil of an 'earth, protect, shield wall' spell that had been cast by his master.

'Come on over here, my boy,' Smegly called. 'I need you to construct a scrying spell whilst I maintain the structure of the protection wall. We need to know how many of them there are out there.'

Plob wove the intricate designs of the air spell with his fingers as he recited the formulas. He spun round once, releasing and spreading the spell out in circle around him. It echoed off the surroundings and bounced back to him.

'It feels as if there are seven of them. I can't be sure because they're not human. I don't know how to adjust the spell for Trogres,' Plob shouted.

Horgy and Dreenee ran up. 'What's going on?' Dreenee asked. 'Are we under attack?'

'Not yet,' answered Smegly. 'I've warded us just in case but with seven possibles out there I'm not sure how long I'll be able to hold the spell in place. Horgy and Dreenee, arm yourselves and wake up Cabbie. We may need to make a speedy strategic withdrawal. Plob, ready yourself with an 'earth, attack, thunderbolt' and keep the other spells close to hand.'

Plob ran to the cab and brought back the vellum-wrapped enchantments. He unwrapped an 'earth, attack' spell and held it at the ready. Out of the corner of his eye he saw Dreenee pour the cold pot of tea over Cabbie in a desperate attempt to wake him. He jerked upright, spluttering and sneezing.

'Mom?' he asked, looking around. He took in the scene and came instantly awake. 'The horses.' He jumped up and started hitching the horses to the cab.

At the perimeter of the wall Plob could make out the vast shadowy shapes of the Trogres lumbering around. The music was louder now and he could see that it was issuing from a set of drums on a small platform that one vast individual was carrying on his one shoulder. On top of these drums was a goblin that was frantically playing a thumping solo whilst vocalising a throbbing bass back beat to the whole thing. Every now and then the Trogre would shout out something and punch his arm in the air.

'One time…Respect…For da people…Westside.' He shambled off to one side and stared at the shimmering perimeter. Then suddenly and without warning he leant forward and struck the wall a tremendous blow with a wheelbarrow-sized fist.

Smegly staggered back, a light sweat forming on his forehead. 'Right, Plob,' he grunted. 'On three I'm going to drop the wall for a second and I want you to hurl an 'earth, attack, thunderbolt' at the big one with the portable music goblin. Two, three.'

Plob released the spell and hurled it forth. A massive crack rent the air combined with the reek of sulphur and singed hair. The huge Trogre was rocked backwards as the thunderbolt exploded on his upper chest, blackening his skin and decimating his goblin system.

'Hey,' he roared. 'You guys has broked my goblin blaster. Dats unfair. I only buyed it yesterday. Got it cheap too 'cause it fell off the back of a wagon.'

'He picked it up for a song,' interjected Cabbie with a skull-like grin on his tense visage.

The Trogre rubbed his chest. 'That hurts. Hey you guys is good. This is gonna be fun.' He rushed at the wall again, unleashing another titanic blow causing Smegly to grunt painfully. The other Trogres had all gathered around the huge one and were egging him on as Plob prepared another earth attack spell. This time an 'earth, attack, hailstorm.'

'Ready, Plob,' shouted Smegly. 'Two, three.'

Plob released a storm of fist-sized hailstones at the group of Trogres, knocking all but the big one to the ground, as Smegly hastily restructured the wall. The big one ran around picking the others up and encouraging them by smacking them on the tops of their heads with a huge flat hand.

'Gets up, you muthas. You gots no cohones. You's is some kind of fragile if you can gets knocked over by some bits of flying ice. Come on let's all hit this wall at once,' he shouted, clenched fist raised up.

Smegly groaned in anticipation. 'Quickly, Dreenee, Cabbie and Horgy. Fetch the suit of armour and bring it over here. No questions, just do it. Plob, go and get the white wrapped spell from my trunk.' As he finished, all seven of the Trogres struck the wall in unison. Smegly doubled over in pain. Master magician or not, he could not take another one of those.

Dreenee, Cabbie and Horgy came stumbling over with Horgy's massive metal suit and dumped it at Smegly's feet. At the same time Plob arrived with the spell.

'OK, Plob,' grunted Smegly. 'You take over this protection wall. Hold hard and concentrate; these bastards are seriously strong.'

Plob opened his mind and felt the control structure slide into him. He tensed up and concentrated on keeping it firmly in place. Meanwhile Smegly unwrapped the spell and laid it on the chest of the suit of armour. Then he turned to Horgy, Cabbie and Dreenee.

'Right. Cabbie, I need your help. This is an animation spell, I am going to use it to animate the iron and command the suit to attack the Trogres. Unfortunately I cannot impart the knowledge of combat to it. For that I need you, I am going to harness your fighting skills and transfer them, temporarily, to the suit. Are you ready?'

'No wait,' begged Cabbie. 'You've got the wrong guy. I'm no knight. Ask Horgy. Leave me out of this.' Horgy nodded and stepped forward drawing his sword.

'No, Horgy. Cabbie, we haven't time for this. Horgy, I'm sorry. I'll explain later.'

Smegly beckoned to Cabbie who knelt beside the supine suit. Smegly took Cabbie's hand in his, muttered an incantation and banged the spell into the suit with his free hand. Instantly the suit sprang up, grabbed up a large corded log of wood and ran at the wall.

'Plob, drop the wall,' commanded Master Smegly.

Plob released the spell, and the suit, powered by Smegly's spell and driven by Cabbie's alleged knowledge of battle tactics, piled into the group of Trogres. Four of them were down and out before they had even reacted. The suit spun and ducked, bobbed and weaved, the log blurred like a hummingbird's wings such was the speed at which it was being wielded. Two more Trogres went down and then only the biggest one was left.

Brute strength against skill. And what skill. The quest members were stunned into silence, mouths hanging open like feeding chicks. The Trogre rumbled forward, swinging wildly and catching the suit a glancing blow, knocking it to the ground. But the suit rolled forward, spun around and caught the Trogre a massive blow on the back of his head. The Trogre reacted by picking up a large boulder and hurling it at the suit, the suit deflected it with its corded log, dropped down on one knee and swiped mightily at the Trogre's shins. The Trogre yelped in pain and hobbled backwards tripping over a small bush and falling over, cracking his head on a rock and lying still. The suit's job completed, it collapsed to the ground.

'Quickly,' commanded Smegly. 'Get some rope and let's tie these buggers up before they recover.'

Plob stoked up the fire and threw a few more logs on. The Trogres lay in a big pile, firmly trussed, snorting, grunting and twitching in their sleep like a mountain of massive dreaming dogs.

'It looks like some sort of explanation is in order,' said Horgy gesturing at Cabbie. 'If that suit was running on Cabbie's expertise then someone has been keeping something from us.'

Cabbie sat on a log staring intently into the flames of the now roaring fire.

'He's a knight…or was, I think,' blurted out Plob.

Cabbie glared at him, causing Plob to look down uncomfortably and shuffle his feet from side to side, building up a small hummock of blasted sand between them.

Smegly stood up and walked over to Cabbie, placing a comforting hand on his shoulder. 'We're all friends here, Cabbie. I don't think it would be right to keep secrets from each other. Of course I've known who you are from when first we met, secrets and master magicians don't mix. It's not for me to tell the others - but I do feel that you should.'

Cabbie cleared his throat uncomfortably. 'I've got a name,' he started. 'I mean, well obviously, everybody has. It's just that I prefer to be known as Cabbie. It's less complicated, easier with nothing to live up to. When people know who I am…was…it's…well, harder. I don't do it anymore.' He picked up a stick and poked at the fire.

Dreenee came over to him, sat down and put her arm around his shoulders. 'Go on,' she encouraged.

Cabbie stood up and threw his shoulders back. All were suddenly struck by his heroic stature. Head held high, broad of shoulder and lean of flank, firelight flickering across his unshaven jaw. 'My name is Tarlek Honourusson son of Glimburble Honourus son of Swain Honour. Tarlek

Honourusson "the Dragonslayer", knight at arms and keeper of the sword of the nation.'

Dreenee's hands flew to her mouth as she exclaimed out loud, Plob dropped the log he was carrying to the fire onto his foot and didn't even notice and Horgy all but passed out in amazement. Smegly stood quietly with a slightly amused smile on his face.

'Hey, no wonder yous guys is so good,' rumbled the big Trogre who had just come to. 'You gots yourselves a Tarlek. He's one mean mutha. Hey wake up, you uselessneses,' he shouted at the other Trogres 'look whom we's got here. It's that Tarlek guy. Da one dat killed that dragon over in the mountain of Bert where our cousins live.'

Another Trogre woke up and looked at Cabbie. 'Hey Tarlek how yous doing, brudda. Respect.'

'Do you know these…er…people?' Plob asked Cabbie.

'No,' replied Cabbie. 'They know of me, that's all. I've fought lots of them before so they know of me.'

'Everybody knows you,' said Dreenee accusingly. 'I can't believe that I didn't recognise you.'

'No one recognises me anymore. That's the whole point of being a cabbie, I don't want to be recognised.'

All of the Trogres were awake now and seemed to be very exited that they had been bested by the skill of both a well-known master magician and Tarlek Honourusson, sword of the nation etcetera.

'Hey, Tarlek,' rumbled the ex-goblin blaster owner. 'Dis is a real honour, man. I wants to shake you by the hand.' He stood up and walked over to Cabbie, his hand outstretched, the ropes that had bound him parted like cotton candy. There was a moment of consternation until they all realised that he meant them no harm and genuinely just wanted to shake Cabbie's hand. The other Trogres followed suit, forming a queue like they were at a royal line up. Cabbie had a short chat to each of them and told them to sit down.

And there they sat. A master magician, an ex-accountant become knight, a waitress, a knight become Cabbie, a teenage assistant and seven monstrous Trogres.

The Trogres introduced themselves. The large one went by the moniker of Biggest and the others, in true Trogre fashion, continued along in the same vein. Huge, Large, Great, Massive, Broad and Jock. Mother had apparently run out of variations on the theme with the youngest.

They listened carefully as Smegly told them the tale of the quest.

'Well dis plummer dude, he sounds like one sick puppy. Dis is not right, if anyones gonna be evil it is us,' said Biggest. The others agreed, nodding their heads and making loud 'Oogoorah' sounds. 'Yep,' continued Biggest. 'We's one bad group of muthas.'

'Brothers,' corrected Plob.

'What you want, Plob my man?' acknowledged Biggest.

'You're brothers, not mothers.'

There was a pause as the quest members collectively held their breath and Plob, having realised his potentially terminal social gaffe, desperately tried to think of a suitable apology.

Biggest laughed out loud. 'Right on, you is correct. We is one bad group of muthas, brothers.'

The Trogres growled their agreement and they all raised their clenched fists in the air and shouted in unison, 'Brothers.' Then they all gathered around in a huddle and had a hurried conflab following which they broke up sporting extremely pleased looks on their vast hairy visages.

'Yo, Master Smegly,' continued Biggest. 'My brothers and I have decided that I will accompany you on your quest in order to provide you with some extra muscle as well as a bit of well-needed cool.'

Smegly nodded and graciously accepted.

Horgy looked a little worried as he whispered to Cabbie, 'He won't fit in the cab.'

'No worries,' said Cabbie. 'He'll run beside us.'

Horgy looked impressed. 'They can do that?' he asked.

'Sure,' confirmed Biggest, who had overheard. 'We's can run for days, no problem. Us Trogres is a very athletic bunch of muthas, brothers.'

When Plob awoke the next morning the sun was fairly high in the sky as most of them had overslept, what with the battle fatigue and then talking late into the night with the Trogres. To his surprise Plob found that he liked Biggest and his brothers. They were straightforward and uncomplicated on one level, but obtuse and complex on another. They hid a lot of their intellect behind their hammy otherwise way of talking, but they didn't miss much. Also they all had incredibly infectious laughs, notwithstanding the fact that if one didn't laugh with them Biggest would lean across, grab you by the arm and rumble 'laugh, you mutha, it's funny.'

The group of brothers decided that they would accompany the cab to the edge of the valley and then would say their farewells, leaving Biggest to continue as the newest member of the quest.

The rest of that day was uneventful and they made very good time as the seven Trogres ran in front of the cab, kicking any loose boulders or rocks out of the way and flattening the path so that the horses could run along at a fair clip.

They camped that night in a small depression off to the side of the trail, protected from the wind and with some good grazing for the horses. Two of the Trogres had run on ahead of the group, done a little hunting and set up camp. So when the rest of the group got to the camp site a huge fire was going and two whole stags were sizzling on spits suspended over the flames. They ate their full and drank a little of the Trogres' fiery cane spirit or 'blutop' that all of the brothers carried with them.

The next day, at around noon, they reached the end of the valley of Strange. The Trogres took their leave amidst much high-fives, mean muthas, brothers and yo's.

Chapter 10

The boiling water ploy hadn't worked very well; in fact all it had done was doused the burning battering ram that Bil's intelligence deficient followers had erroneously set fire to. Bil was now trying to urge his followers to pick up the tree and run at the castle gates with it. Now, this is easier said than done.

It's one thing for thirty, totally inept, people to pick up a twenty-eight-foot, one-and-a-half-ton tree trunk still complete with branches and leaves. It's another completely different thing to get them to run in a coordinated fashion, at high speed, across a narrow bridge and into a huge oaken gate whilst maintaining enough aggression, under fire, to actually knock the gate down. This sort of exercise takes training - and lots of it.

The tree made its erratic way forward, zigging and zagging, partly due to the fact that some of the rammers were facing the wrong way and partly because the rest of them couldn't see through the thick foliage that Bil had neglected to tell them to trim from the trunk. Some carriers had pulled off small branches in error and were running around with their own little miniature battering rams. After almost ten minutes of this farcical progress they finally made it the moat, and fell in. At least the log floated well so only two or three of them drowned.

Bravad, the chief of the guard, stared down at the rabble doggy paddling around in the moat, shook his head almost sadly, raised his arm up and then brought it slashing down. On his signal, his small group of soldiers picked four metal tubs up off the large fire over which they were heating and upended their contents of red-hot rocks over the battlements. They fell hissing indiscriminately into the moat, striking the water, the tree and various heads with equal vigour. The cries of pain and outrage could be heard across the city.

'Unfair, unfair,' shouted Bill. 'You bloody buggeries.' He then sounded the retreat by screaming 'run away, run away' at the top of his voice. It was time for his cohorts to regroup and rethink, or at least start to think.

The chief of the guard propped his shield up against the wall and leant back on it. This wasn't right, he thought. Defending the castle against a rag-tag bunch of halfwits wasn't exactly what he'd been trained for. When he'd joined up he wanted to fight proper battles filled with brave acts and feats of honour against well-armed and vicious evil troops. He sighed, although he needn't have, for Bravad r Us, chief of the royal bodyguard and keenly aspiring hero, was about to get his wish. Which just goes to prove the old adage 'be careful what you wish for, it just might come to pass.'

'What's that? Over there.' Terry pointed at the top corner of the large, close-up full-colour photograph of the caved-in side of the dyed-blonde girl's cranium.

Hugo leaned forward and squinted. 'Bits of skin? Bone?'

'No. Not that,' he pointed again. 'That. It looks like some sort of squiggly bit.'

'Yes. You're right,' Hugo agreed. 'A spiral.'

'OK. What's painted red, heavy, made out of metal and has a twisty squiggly spiral thingy on it?'

'I give up,' conceded Hugo. 'What?'

'That, my dear upper-class twit, is the million-quid question,' answered Terry as they both returned to studying the unpleasant photo.

It was a sort of no-man's-land between the valley of Strange and the mountains of Steve. This is not to say that no one lived there, they did. In fact there were a few small villages complete with the ubiquitous church, dry goods store and inn with a suitably grandiose sounding name.

Plob had always wondered why that was so.

It always seemed that the smaller the town the bigger the church and the grander the name of the solitary inn. In the capital city of Maudlin, where Plob and Smegly lived and worked, there were perhaps fifty or sixty inns, most of them with pretty unique names but, as far as Plob could remember, no Royals or Imperials. Unlike the shabby, three-bedroom run-down building at the centre of this tiny hamlet, which went by the unlikely name of 'The Grand Royal Imperial Inn, Eatery and Stables.'

It appeared to Plob that all the residents of the little villages that they had been travelling through seemed dull and lacklustre. Their movements slow and energy less, their expressions slack and their general demeanour to be one of unhappiness. He commented on this to Master Smegly.

'Yes, Plob. It has been thus for many years in all of the areas surrounding the mountains of Steve. There is a great evil that lurks in the heart of the range and it leaches the spirit out of all who live within sight of its peaks.'

'Why don't they leave? Go somewhere else, start up again.'

'They can't be bothered,' replied Smegly. 'The lassitude has become too great for them. They know that life could, and should, be better but they no longer have the energy or inclination to change. So they just live out their dull, grey existence in these small hamlets within sight of Steve.'

Smegly faced the rest of the group. 'I'm glad Plob brought this up,' he continued. 'This lassitude that I've been talking about is contagious. We must all guard against negative thoughts. We must be strong and keep the quest uppermost in our minds lest we too fall into depression and listlessness. And remember, the closer we get to the mountains the harder it will become to resist.'

With that Cabbie flicked his whip and drove the horses forward through the hamlet and onwards to the mountains of Steve.

As the day drew on, a squally biting wind picked up, carrying with it a smattering of unpleasant cold rain. They made camp that night at the foothills of Steve on a bare patch of ground with little or no protection from the elements. To top it all, only a limited amount of wood was available and what there was proved to be either damp or rotten resulting in a tiny fire that provided more smoke than heat.

Biggest was sharing his large flask of Blutop and, as they passed it around, each member could feel the spirit-induced warmth spread through their bodies like a slow fire. Biggest spat a mouthful of spirit onto the struggling fire. There was a 'woomph' as a small fireball rose heavenward and the fire started to crackle merrily.

Biggest chuckled. 'Dat's one good drink dat. You can use it to start fires, polish metal, sterilise wounds, cure colic, and it's also great poured over fruit. Yep, life wouldn't be the da same without Blutop. Probably da best cane spirit in da world.' He looked fondly at his flask and then passed it on.

Horgy took some into his mouth and tried to do the same as Biggest, spraying a mouthful at the fire. The flame leapt up the stream of highly flammable fluid like a bolt from a crossbow, burning Horgy's lips and causing his three-day growth of facial hair to burst into flames. Dreenee responded by stripping her skirt off and wrapping it around Horgy's face to smother the flames.

Biggest rose to his feet and applauded. 'Good reactions, girlfriend,' he shouted. Then he paused to look Dreenee up and down. His eyebrows both raised skywards like a pair of shaggy black sails. 'Damn,' he said staring at Dreenee's half naked form. 'You is built like a brick house, women. Whooee.'

'Well thank you kindly, my good Trogre. Now will you please look the other way before I tear your raggedy-ass pointy ears off.' Bigger laughed hugely, loving the fact that he had been insulted in the vernacular, although he did have the sense to look away.

Plob, however, couldn't move. It was proving a physical impossibility to tear his eyes away from the exposed, milky white, lower half of his quest member's perfect body. To be fair he was trying, it was just that his body would not react to the commands his brain was frantically issuing. In short, he was suffering from a total visual sensory overload. Dreenee unwound her skirt from Horgy's now flame-free face and stepped into it, flapping it back into shape. Plob's body finally caught up with his brain and he quickly turned to look the other way.

'A little late don't you think, Plob?' remarked Dreenee as she inspected Horgy's face.

Plob mumbled an apology under his breath.

'I don't actually mind,' said Dreenee. 'You're a nice boy and I can see that it was hard for you. I thought your eyes were going to fall out but you were trying really hard to look away. Next time try a little harder, OK?'

Plob nodded jerkily and wished that Dreenee would stop saying hard over and over like that. As it was he had had to sit down next to the fire and knew it would be a while before he could stand up, as it were, without causing some embarrassment. Biggest passed him the Blutop with a knowing grin. Plob thanked him and slugged back a solid mouthful. The alcohol sprinted through his nervous system and brought some semblance of normality back to his extremities.

With the fun over they retired to their blankets and fell quickly asleep. All except for Plob who was driven oft awake by teenage dreams of perfectly proportioned porcelain white thighs, in various positions, flashing through his mind.

The next morning they awoke with a feeling of despair lying thickly on all of them. All except for Master Smegly who was his usual intractable self. Plob was irritable from lack of sleep and the rest of the quest members looked both restless and despondent. Cabbie knocked the kettle into the fire when he was making the tea and Dreenee sniped at him for being an idiot, so he got the sulks and went and sat in the cab by himself whilst the others struck camp.

Biggest looked wistfully at his huge half-empty flask of Blutop and then accused Horgy of taking some during the night when they had all slept. Horgy denied this saying that it was typical of a Trogre to think that everyone was as light-fingered as they were. Biggest stood up threateningly and, at that point, Smegly decided to put a stop to it all.

'Listen to yourselves,' he said. 'Didn't I warn you of this only yesterday? And we're only in the foothills of Steve. Do you honestly think that we can make it through the whole range if you've already begun to forget both your bonds of friendship and the needs of the quest?' He stared at them each individually, a stern look on his face. 'What I see disgusts me. Now snap out of it or go home. You're acting like a bunch of spoilt gnomes.'

The quest members looked sheepishly at each other and then there was much apologising, hugging, slapping of backs and shaking of hands although Dreenee did put a stop to the hugging when Cabbie came around for the fifth time.

After a while on the road, the trail took a number of complicated turns and forks but Smegly appeared to know the way so they continued to make good time. They stopped next to the track for a quick bite of lunch and Biggest amused them by telling them some stories about his childhood.

'I's da eldest of a big family,' he told them. 'My mammy had herself nine kids, all boys, but only seven of us survived cause Mammy ate the twins at birth. Oh yeh, dose were the days. Before society got all pinko-liberal and decided dat twins should be allowed to live. It's unnatural and I'm just not for it.'

Smegly nodded in agreement but the rest of the group were shocked.

Biggest saw their expressions and carried on. 'You see, a female Trogre is only capable of feeding one offspring at a time. She don't produce enough milk for two so, if she tries, then normally both kids die. So one of the kids has gots to be put down. Well the council of elders decided that it was too heavy a burden to make a mammy choose a child so they solved it by saying dat dey both gots to go. Problem solved.' He chuckled unrepentantly.

'But all in all I hads me a good childhood. We was poor, but what we lacked for in money we made up for in aggression. As my daddy always said, "it's not whether you win or lose, it's just beating up on the other guys that's important." Our favourite game was military chairs, every night my mammy used to set six places at the table and then we'd all wallop on each other until one brother couldn't get up, so that night he didn't eat. I'm proud to say dat I never missed myself a meal in my life. Our pappy used to wop on us every morning to punish us for all the wrong doings that we was going to get up to that day, so just to make sure that we weren't punished for nuthin we used to commit at least two felonious acts a day. I still remember when I came of age and turned twelve, I came down stairs and joined the line for the morning whipping and when it gots to be my turn my pappy turned me away saying that I was a man now and no longer needed a daily whippin'. I was so happy that day that my daddy stopped beating me. Of course he kicked me out of the den that afternoon and tole me I hads to go make my own life now. Still, them was happy carefree days.'

Plob liked Biggest. It was hard not to like someone whose concept of luxury was not being beaten every day. He helped Dreenee clear up the lunch leftovers, packed up the crockery and they were on their way once again. Biggest stopped his biographical musings when they got going and concentrated on keeping up with the cab.

'I believe that a person's life as a child is the gods' ways of paying you back for all sins committed in any past lives,' said Horgy. 'Children are put on this earth to be bullied by their peers, humiliated by their parents and totally ignored by all members of the opposite sex. And then you become an adult, and your parents die and life becomes just that little bit more bearable. And if you're wealthy, and can afford good physicians, then maybe all the kids that bullied you die off too. And then finally the girls.'

'Or you become a knight, huh, Horgy,' interjected Cabbie. 'You showed them. I bet those bullies wouldn't dare now, hey?'

Horgy stared at Cabbie. 'Oh, be serious, Cabbie. I can't even stand up in a suit of armour, let alone swing a two-handed broadsword in battle. I bought my knighthood. I'm a fraud. A phoney.'

'Man,' rumbled Biggest. 'You've got some serious self-respect issues, my man. You's got to learn to be comfortable with yourself. Dis self-flagellation is mega unhealthy. In fact it's starting to make me feel bummed off.'

'Horgy.' Dreenee lent closer to the ersatz knight. 'You are the only man that I've ever met that looks at my eyes when I speak. You're both kind and courteous. You never knowingly talk down to people, you never shirk a duty and you're also the cleverest man that I know. You may not call yourself a knight but I think that you are. You are my knight. Sir Horgy. Sir Horgelbund the courteous.' She moved over and kissed Sir Horgy on the lips causing his face to light up like a bonfire on the king's jubilee night and causing the other quest members to think things like 'there's none so strange as folk' etcetera.

The day continued on event-free, with small talk and the odd pause to water the horses. But as they progressed, Plob began to feel more and more depressed. Every thought that came into his mind seemed to bring the prickle of tears to his eyes and he started wondering why they were all wasting their time in this desolate unhappy place.

He was feeling too self-absorbed to notice that the other quest members, including the master, were looking similarly disaffected. Dreenee was actually crying quietly to herself and ringing her hands together, not even bothering to wipe away the tears that were running freely down her face.

They stopped to pitch camp as the light was beginning to fade, Biggest having run on ahead and brought down a small antelope for supper. But no one had bothered to dress the animal and the sight of the carcass lying next to the fire had depressed them all even further.

Before they went to sleep that night Master Smegly listlessly warded the camp with an 'air, alarm' spell. 'Just a precaution,' he mumbled as they were now smack bang in the centre of the mountains of Steve.

Sometime, close to the middle of the night, Plob was shaken awake by Cabbie. Plob woke up and, commendably, didn't go through the standard 'what-who-where-am-I' routine.

'There's something out there,' whispered Cabbie.

‘Impossible,’ answered Plob. ‘If someone was out there the ward would pick them up and sound the alarm.’

‘I didn’t say someone,’ corrected Cabbie. ‘I said something. Look.’

Plob could make out a sort of murky graveyard glimmer, about the same size as Biggest, swirling around the perimeter of the camp. ‘Wait,’ he said as he formed an ‘air, identify’ spell and let it loose at the incoherent shape. It sounded back through Plob imparting its information. ‘Well that didn’t help much,’ mumbled Plob. ‘Although it has confirmed that it’s bad, very bad.’ He shuddered.

‘Hey, I could have told you that without the spell,’ said Cabbie. ‘Come, quickly, we’d better wake the master.’

They both ran across to Smegly only to find him already awake and contemplating the entity with a puzzled expression on his face.

‘What is it?’ whispered Plob. ‘Should we raise an “earth, protect, shield wall”?’

‘It wouldn’t do any good,’ answered Smegly. ‘I can’t be one hundred percent certain but I think that it’s the essence of the mountain. The spirit of Steve. Wake the others up and tell them to gather round. I’m not sure how we’re going to handle this but we have to get rid of it. If it attacks and possesses any of us it is quite possible that that person will die of despair and depression .’

‘What do you mean? They throw themselves on the own spoon, that sort of thing?’ asked Cabbie.

Smegly shook his head. ‘No, they would just drown in a torrent of doubt and self-pity.’

Plob woke up the quest members and they all came and stood around Smegly who was still staring at the misty being and releasing the odd explosive ‘Harrumph.’

‘So,’ asked Biggest, ‘has we gots to fight this thing? ’Cause if we does I’m not sure how to do it. It don’t got no substance.' He left the group and walked a little way towards the spirit of Steve. 'Yo. Ethereal boy. Your mama, you misty shred of glowing ectoplasm, come here and fight, you bodiless freakazoid.'

The misty form suddenly glowed brighter and the earth that they were standing on shook violently throwing them all to the ground. Without thinking Plob tore open an Earth spell and launched an 'Earth, attack, thunderbolt' straight at the entity The air crackled with power and the group were left feeling slightly breathless as the burning spell leeched the oxygen out of the atmosphere around them. As the thunderbolt struck the entity it was merely absorbed and Steve and got bigger and brighter still.

'Stop,' shouted Smegly. 'It's feeding off of our violence. The more aggression that we show the more powerful it becomes. Everybody calm down. Gather round me, hold hands and try to relax. Banish all thoughts of battle.'

'Yeah, bros,' rumbled Biggest. 'Let's chill out.'

As they gathered in a circle, Plob noticed that Horgy wasn't with them. He looked around to see him striding purposefully towards the spirit of Steve. 'Horgy, no,' he shouted and started to follow him, but Dreenee laid a restraining hand on his shoulder.

'Leave him,' she said softly. 'He knows what he's doing.'

The group collectively held its breath as Horgy walked right into the swirling, glowing miasmic form and threw his arms wide. The mist contracted swiftly and Horgy was driven to his knees, a scream of pain tearing from his throat. And then, Plob thought that Horgy was crying, but as they watched and listened, it became obvious that he was laughing. Painfully and breathlessly, but sounds of mirth nonetheless were issuing forth.

'Is that the best you can do,' he said laughingly. 'Do you call that despair? Do you call that depression? You pathetic whinger.'

The mist contracted again but the light didn't glow as brightly as the time before. Horgy doubled over in agony but still his apparent glee continued. 'What was that?' he asked. 'An insult? You clueless non-entity. You're meant to be the very essence of despair. You've caused whole villages to live in darkness and depression for generations, but you're nothing compared to one mealtime with my family. You really haven't a clue, have you? Do you want to hear about failure, depression, fear?' And with that Horgy proceeded to go on a rant about his childhood starting from when he was born and the physician took one look at him and slapped his mother, to how his parents went on holiday and forgot him at home. Shunned by his peers for being too clever and rejected by his father for not being clever enough. Days spent locked in the under stairs cupboard for only getting ninety-eight percent for his school exams. The ritual humiliation of the bi-yearly school balls, and so on, and so on, and on and on and on.

Slowly the light drained from the spirit of Steve as, faced with a despair overload, it struggled to maintain its form. Eventually it stopped enveloping Horgy and seemed to sit down next to him, nodding what could have been its head and groaning echoingly in agreement. After half an hour or so Horgy's aching soliloquy dribbled to an end. The spirit of Steve had grown completely dull, lifeless and wispy. As if bereft of the desire to maintain its form and slowly, ever so slowly, the mist evaporated into the ether and disappeared - never to be seen again.

Horgy stood up and started back to the group, limping slightly from the after effects of the pain that he had gone through. Spontaneously the group started clapping and cheering wildly as our conquering hero approached.

Biggest took out his flask of Blutop and proffered it to Horgy. 'Man,' he said. 'You is one seriously depressing mutha. You done good, my bro,' he finished and pummelled Horgy enthusiastically on the back.

The rest of the group joined in the congratulations wholeheartedly, laughing and shouting. Not realising until now, how great a pall of despair had been hanging over them until Horgy had defeated the dismal spirit of Steve.

Although it was still the middle of the night Plob and Cabbie skinned and dressed the antelope that Biggest had hunted down that evening whilst Dreenee built up the fire. They cut up a pile of thick steaks which they laid on the coals and sat around the fire until the wee hours eating, drinking and telling jokes.

Life was good once more.

Chapter 11

Bil was standing on an upended beer barrel, regaling his cohorts that were gathered about him. Wrench held aloft, bedspread billowing dramatically from his shoulders. Every inch the leader, every inch the king – every inch some insane prat with a wrench.

'Who's bad?' he screeched at the crowd.

'We're bad,' came back the unified response.

'We're all bad,' continued Bil, shouting at the top of his voice. 'Give me a B.'

'B,' the crowd responded.

'Give me an A.'

'A.'

'Give me a D.'

'D.'

'What does it spell?'

An embarrassed shuffling of feet and studying of shoes ensued as the cohorts tried desperately to get their minds around advanced spelling. Eventually a huge, moustached man at the back dressed in a leather cloak and carrying a club put up his hand.

'Yes?' screamed Bil.

'Uh…Duck?' ventured the large club-endowed one.

Bil shrieked in rage and swung his wrench around him in a tight circle. It came to rest with a satisfying crunch on the cranium of his now ex-second in command. 'Bad, bad, bad,' he squealed.

'Yeah, I know. It's bad of us, very bad. Sorry, boss,' replied the moustached one. 'We'll try harder next time.'

Bil threw himself to the ground and flayed about for a while, banging his head on the sod, chewing on the turf and generally putting forward yet more proof of his growing world class insanity.

Meanwhile, as Bil worked towards putting the finishing touches on his rampant paranoid schizophrenia, a group of fifty or so of his followers were scouring the town for daggers, swords, crossbows, catapults and siege engines. Those weapons of destruction that they came across were duly confiscated and transported to the camp of King Bil to be readied for war.

Already a large group of troops had been issued with crossbows and were receiving their first training session in the art of loading and firing the said weapon. The self-appointed sergeant-at-arms, a twice jailed poacher of the king's deer, was explaining the rudiments of the weapon.

'This is a crossbow,' he yelled, holding it up above his head.

'This is a crossbow,' reiterated the crowd, enthusiastically doing the same.

The poacher held a bolt aloft. 'This is a bolt.'

'This is a bolt,' responded the vocal crowd of misfits.

'This is the drawstring,' shouted the poacher, holding same up high.

'This is the drawstring,' repeated the crowd at full volume.

The newly self-appointed sergeant looked well chuffed with himself as he surveyed his motley crew.

'What is this?' he cried as he held his crossbow aloft once again.

'What is this?' came the thunderous response from the troops.

The sergeant fell to his knees and wept.

Master Smegly climbed off the cab and strode up to the door of the humungous sprawling residence. The rest of the group did likewise and straggled behind him.

As he raised his hand to the knocker, the door opened on its own volition and a disembodied voice asked them politely to enter. This they all did and, as they got inside, the door closed behind them. A small bright green light appeared, floating in the air in front of them. The voice asked them to follow it.

They meandered down dusty badly lit corridors, up flights of wooden stairs and down long stone ramps that appeared to be cut into the living rock on which the house was built. Eventually they were all so confused and lost that, if their lives depended on it, they could not have found the way out.

'I thought that you had been here before,' said Cabbie, addressing Master Smegly.

'I have, often.'

'Well how come you don't know the way?' asked Cabbie.

'It's always different. You'll see. Tomorrow the building won't be the same as today. Different corridors, different décor, sometimes the whole structure moves a little to the right or left.'

'Or backwards or forwards I suppose,' added Cabbie.

'Don't be ridiculous,' said Smegly. 'Why on earth would it do that?' He shook his head in disbelief. 'Pwah. Some people's children,' he muttered.

Cabbie managed to look even more confused than he actually was.

Finally, after what seemed an age, the corridor widened, the lighting improved and they were led out into a spacious central courtyard that was roofed in with a moving riotous palette of different stained glasses that fractured the sunlight into a myriad of seemingly ever-changing colours like a schizophrenic rainbow.

And in the centre of the room, next to a massive indoor waterfall surrounded by exotic plants, crossed legged and floating some six-foot above the floor was the mage that they had all come to see. The mage of mages. The master of masters. The man. He slowly swivelled in the air and wafted, leaf-like, down to the level that normal people perambulated.

'Ah, Wegly-woo, my boy,' he greeted Smegly. His voice sounded like a chorus of knowledge, voice overlapping voice as if he were speaking with the vocal cords of all the members of the mages circle. This, plus the fact that his eyes were pure white, right put the wind up the questers apart from Smegly and, oddly enough, Plob, who was staring open-mouthed at his master.

'Wegly-woo,' he said, shaking his head in astonishment. 'Wegly-woo,' he repeated. 'Is that your real name, Master?' he questioned disbelievingly.

Smegly harrumphed and told Plob to shut it.

The master's masters, magician's master's master (Master) faced each quest member in turn. 'Ah, the magician's assistant. I bid welcome to a fellow mage.' Plob nodded his thanks, well chuffed to be included in such esteemed company. 'The beautiful maid,' he chorused, looking at Dreenee. 'And a right stonker you are too, my girl. If I were four hundred years younger,' he paused. 'Well then I'd still be about seven hundred and forty-two, but still. Unga-bunga.' He then addressed Cabbie. 'Greetings, oh courageous knight.' He bowed and totally ignored Cabbie's murmured protestations about him being a humble Cabbie and Horgy being the knight and, and, and. He walked forward, clasping Horgy by the arm. 'The noble thief,' he said. 'Greetings and salutations, oh great pilfering one.'

Horgy looked aghast. 'I'm no thief,' he protested.

The master's masters etcetera stared at him for a while. 'Not yet, my talented friend. Not yet.'

Finally he strode over to Biggest. 'Yo, my bro,' he shouted, throwing Biggest a high five and then crossing his arms in front of his chest. 'How's it hanging, you mutha humpin' jive monkey?'

A huge grin split Biggest's hairy visage exposing his massive canines to full effect. 'I's hanging fine, multiple master man, just fine,' he answered, hunching his shoulders and bopping from side to side.

'Come with me all,' invited the master's master magician's master's master as he walked to the far end of the courtyard. 'Before we discuss the reasons for your welcomed visit, let us first partake of this splendid repast laid before us by my excellent servants.' He gestured at a huge trestle laden with a veritable mountain of splendid and varied victuals, much out of season and even some hereto unseen and uneaten by mortal man (or Trogre).

'Hot damn,' exclaimed Cabbie, licking his lips.

'Over there,' responded the master's master, pointing at an array of silver tureens.

'What?' questioned Cabbie in much puzzlement.

'Hot damn,' answered the masters squared. 'We have the full range of damn. Hot damn, pickled damn, damn pate and even the rarely seen damn sushi complete with a side of hot-diggerty-damn.'

Cabbie stared blankly and then helped himself to a wedge of cheese and a flagon of ale as he tried to work out what the damn food was. Biggest picked up a whole suckling pig on a stick, complete with toffee apple in its mouth and a grape in each ear.

Horgy leant over and tentatively tried a small piece of pickled damn. His eyebrows lifted in surprise and he ladled a goodly helping of it onto a plate. 'Damn good,' he muttered.

‘Pig good too,’ responded Biggest.

Cabbie looked at Horgy and raised his tankard. ‘Ale good, cheese good.’

Horgy stared at both of them. ‘Why are guys talking so funny?’

‘Well you started it,’ replied Cabbie, downing his remaining ale.

After they had all piled their platters high with sundry comestibles they retired to a set of divans that the many mastered one had conjured up for them to sit upon. Biggest lay back on a special extra large recliner with suckling pig in each hand, the others reposed likewise amidst much smacking of chops, rubbing of tummies and voicing of yummy sounds.

The mage of many masters stood up, centre stage as it were, and took the floor. ‘My dear quest members,’ he started. ‘First let me assure you. I know why you are all here and I have spent many a slumber-free nocturnal sojourn a-contemplating and divining. This Bil de Plummer, the unknown evil, is now known to me. He is not of this world coming from a far-off place of complications and politicians. A corrupt world of actors, inventions and political correctness. And in coming here he has upset the balance of that finely tuned see-saw on which the children of good and evil both ride. And now evil’s big brother has come to play and good has not sufficient weight to participate in the game. My friends, if we do not right this imbalance then all is lost, and I mean all. This is the big one, the full Monty, the last roll of the dice, sphincter tightening time, the do-or-die moment, last will and testament time, the small-faced moment, balls to the wall…’ (He continued longer in this vein using more last ditch-type analogies than this author could ever hope, or bother, to think up).

‘So, my noble questarians, what do we plan to do about it? And I ask this in a rhetorical fashion as how could you know the reply when I have not yet gifted you with the correct answer, what with me being the master magician’s master’s masters master’s master (master?) and all. This, my dear friends, noble questers, fellow mages and stonking little blondes with huge…Trogres as companions (Hah, got you), is the answer. You must go forth and correct the imbalance. Right the wrongs. Do the deeds of good. Crush the bad, protect the weak and help the needy. When you have in some way helped to correct the imbalances, and caused Bil and his evils to become weaker and you and your goodness to have grown in stature, then, and only then might you have the power to succeed.’

Well if the masterly endowed one was expecting a happy response to this revelation then he was much mistaken, or would have been if he had, but he didn’t, so he wasn’t, so we needn’t have worried. For he was a master magician’s masters buggery and so on and he knew exactly how they would respond, and they did, so he was right, as he knew he would be.

‘Bloody hell,’ expleted Cabbie. ‘Why don’t you just tell us to save the world whilst you’re about it?’

The mega mastered mage stared at Cabbie. ‘My dear knight,’ he assured, ‘that is precisely what I have told you to do. Or weren’t you listening? Wegly-woo, you have all had a long and tiring trip thus far. I recommend a room to retiring for the knight, and the others, and we will continue said discussions tomorrow. Believe me, things will all seem better by the light of the new day.’

And with that the master full one disappeared to be replaced by the bobbing green light of before which led them to their separate, large and luxurious rooms.

That night Plob's sleep was once again disturbed by teenage fantasies involving a skirt-less Dreenee, indoor waterfalls, peeled grapes and a suckling pig with an apple in its mouth (don't ask). He awoke the next morning ragged and worried and more than a little guilty over the whole pig incident that took place in the previous night's nocturnal mental wanderings. (I said don't ask).

They were all led by the green light back to the courtyard and, true to Master Smegly's warnings, the master magician's masters by many had subtly changed their environ. Corridors were longer, stairs were shorter and the courtyard was now roofed over with a glittering cover of translucent mother of pearl.

The many mastered one greeted them and showed them to a large black marble table. Here they were served up a huge traditional breakfast including bacon, sausages, mushrooms (magic and otherwise), tomatoes, eggs (Scrambled, fried sunny side up and over easy, poached, boiled both hard and soft, omeletted, benedictined, florentined, stuffed, deviled, buttered, addled, dropped, shirred, souffled, nogged, in a blanket and raw). Plob avoided the bacon.

After their splendid fast-breaking meal, Master Smegly addressed the multiple mastered one. 'Master,' he started. 'I spent many an hour last night pondering the import of your advice and I must admit to a modicum of concern. How do you propose that we go about our quest, what with it being of a save the world through good deeds type of thing? I was wondering would it be done via helping old ladies across the road ala Boy Scout troop manner, or are we talking a little more esoteric here, as in cross-legged contemplation and oneness with the universe? Or perhaps even riding forth with unsheathed swords, banners aloft wreaking bloody vengeance upon all doers of evil and badness?' Smegly paused waiting for an answer.

The master magician's yah dee dah dee smiled and nodded. 'Yes.'

'Yes?' inquired Smegly and Plob simultaneously.

'All of the above. But be not downcast and depressed at the seemingly unattainable nature of your quest. The knowledge and know-how lies already within all of you. In fact you have already achieved far more than you all realise.'

Master Smegly seemed puzzled.

'Oh yes,' continued the one of the many-mastered moniker, 'Horgy's victory over the spirit of Steve has helped countless people that before lived under that shadow. As we speak the pall has been lifted, former Stevarians smile and walk with a purpose. Their lives are brighter and happier, albeit they have started from an extremely low base, and now begin to have true meaning.

This, added to the hereto unheard of companionship between Trogre and human, has made a deep and happy impact on the whole area of both Strange and Steve.

Already Biggest's brothers have decided to no longer kill humans for sport, unless they really, really feel the need, and so passage through the valley of Strange has become that much more bearable.

But do not overanalyse this quest lest you become stilted in your approach. Just do as you feel you should do and do it to the best of your ability. And now, without further ado (beedoobeedoo) - it is time for you to leave. You will find your belongings are already in the cab along with a good supply of victuals and beverages. The light will show you the way out but, before you go, I would make a gift to each of you to help in your forthcoming ordeals.'

The mastered one gestured and a large onyx box appeared on the table in front of them. He dipped inside and withdrew a long, leather-wrapped package that he handed to Cabbie. Cabbie unrolled the leather covering to reveal a two-handed broadsword sheathed in a deep blue metal scabbard.

'Ooh,' said Plob. 'A magic sword.'

'Well, not quite,' quoth the masterful one. 'It does stay permanently sharp and will never tarnish but, apart from that, it is to all intents and purposes a normal sword. The magic will come from Tarlek, the greatest swordsman in the world.'

Although Cabbie was less than pleased with the gift he knew it would be churlish to refuse it and he thanked the master blaster, bowing deeply as he did so.

The next gift to be produced was a golden flask that was handed to Biggest. This turned out to be a never emptying flask of Blutop; a gift which Biggest considered to be princely beyond all imagining and his thanks were profuse.

Dreenee was the recipient of an exquisitely jewelled bracelet which was both ornamental and practical as it could be used to ward off physical attack by erecting an instant shield wall capable of covering her and one other person.

To Horgy a present of a coat of shifting colours was gifted and, when he put it on, the colours shifted into a facsimile of the background causing him to be nigh on invisible, or at least very hard to see, sort of, apart from his head, and feet, and the other parts that were uncovered by the cloak. Also, it was warm.

Master Smegly was given a small cube-shaped crystal which he explained to all was a spell enhancer that could be used once to greatly expand the power of any single chosen spell.

Finally the numerously mastered master gave Plob what appeared to be a small telescope. Plob looked at it in puzzlement until the master man told him to gaze upon someone through the glass. Plob did so, holding it to his eye and looking at Dreenee. Plob went instantly bright red and then pale as his breathing stopped and his pulse went into overdrive.

'What is it?' asked Dreenee as she took the glass and looked him up and down through it. 'You little bugger,' she cried, spinning around and smacking Plob a ringing blow on the side of the head.

'It's not my fault,' responded Plob, ducking away. 'How was I supposed to know that it sees through clothing? He didn't warn me.'

'I'm sorry, master of my master's master,' Dreenee said. 'There's no way Plob can have this. Look at him,' she gestured at the pale-faced, sweating, guilty looking teenager. 'We can't risk the strain on his heart. Or his head if I catch him using that pervert's looking glass again. Anyway, he's too young, although…' She raised the glass to her eye once more and a slow grin spread across Dreenee's elvin face 'some parts of him are extremely grown up at the moment,' she finished, arching one perfect eyebrow suggestively at Plob.

Plob's hands flew to cover his groin and, as he went purple with embarrassment, Dreenee cast the glass back into the box with a throaty chuckle.

The master magician's multi master laughed. 'Never fear, good Plob. I have here a substitute gift that will more than compensate. Although I can't be sure,' he said staring at Dreenee and leering comically.

'Oh bugger off, you thousand-year-old perv,' joshed Dreenee, still chuckling. Which just goes to show that pretty girls can always get away with saying things that the most respected of men wouldn't dare to utter. Such as joshing a thousand-year-old master magician's masters master master, master (master?)

The aforementioned-mastered one drew a small pouch from his cloak and handed it to Plob with a fanfare and a flourish. The fanfare coming from twenty golden trumpets that had just appeared out of thin air and the flourish coming from one of the servants that was clearing up the breakfast.

'Thank you, good master,' Plob said. 'I shall treasure this always. What is it?' he queried.

'It is a spell miniaturiser,' explained Smegly's master. 'You can feed up to thirty full-size earth spells into that small pouch, it both miniaturises them and nullifies their weight (for as we all know, earth spells are extremely heavy. Or did I forget to mention that? Well everybody else knew) and, when you remove them, they revert to their actual size and weight again ready for use.'

Plob reaffirmed his thanks and turned to follow the green guiding light with his friends but, as he was leaving, the several mastered one bade him stay a short while.

'I have one more gift for you, my young friend,' he told the apprentice. 'It is in the form of advice. The proof that you seek regarding your paternal grandfather does exist and, when you chance across the spell that will show it, you will then, and only then, see clearly the reasoning and logic behind his disappearance. Remember, never lose heart, and always eat at least two pieces of fruit a day to keep yourself regular. Now be off with you.'

The quest members boarded the cab and, with Biggest bringing up the rear, they set off into the future and to the second part of their quest.

Chapter 12

Bil's newly sort-of-trained, unwashed, eager and unbelievably slow-witted troops were once again drawn up in front of him for a quick pre-battle rant.

'You are the uncouth.'

Cheer from the troops.

'The flotsam and jetsam.'

Cheer, cheer.

'The detritus.'

Cheer, cheer, cheer.

'The socially unacceptable.'

Cheer, cheer.

'The mentally challenged.'

Cheer.

'The ignoble and insincere.'

Cheer?

'The scurvy, the putrid and the unliked.'

Huh?

'The scum.'

… ?

'But you are my scum.'

Cheer, cheer.

'My own cohort of personal human filth and - You Are Bad.'

Huge cheers, except for some who were desperately trying to remember how to spell 'bad' in case Bil went in for the old give us a 'B' routine again.

Bil de Plummer beckoned for his lieutenants to come forward in order to have his masterful plan of attack explained in detail to them. This took about seven seconds as, true to the habit of most insane generals, (i.e. all of them) the attack consisted of a frontal assault, with maybe a pincer movement of a leftal and rightal assault if the frontal went well.

Bil pointed castlewards with his wrench screeching, ‘Chaaaaaaaarge,’ using the full capacity of his mentally unstable lungs.

The rabble ran forward waving swords, firing crossbows in the air and pushing covered rams and siege catapults before them.

King Mange’s captain of the guards waited patiently with his small detachment of fourteen skilled, highly trained, multi-talented soldiers at arms. They were all sporting the latest in lightweight, series ten, multi-swivel cross-riveted body armour and carrying a four-foot longbow complete with quiver of yard-long pitch-soaked arrows.

As the ranting, raving rabble drew closer, the captain placed a flame-full brazier in front of his archers and instructed them each to notch up an arrow and continue waiting.

When Bil’s minions had approached the two hundred pace mark, the captain raised his arm above his head. In response, the archers touched the tips of their flammable arrows to the flame causing them to burst instantly into a hot and vicious blaze. The captain’s arm chopped down and fourteen longbows were drawn and discharged. The flaming yard-long arrows traced blazing arcs overhead like a flock of burning seagulls and before they had even reached their zenith, the captain’s men had fired again, and again, and again.

By the time the first flight of flaming death had hit Bil’s unorganised barely trained rabble there were already another fifty fiery messengers of mortality on their way. The arrow storm marched through their ranks like some psychotic cremator, leaving fully thirty dead, as many again wounded and two of the precious siege engines merrily ablaze, flickering and crackling like Christmas trees at a pyromaniacs convention.

Bil sounded the run away again.

Master Smegly had decided to take the long way home. When asked why, he had explained to all that it would allow them more time to do the right things, whatever and wherever they might be.

This new route would take them fifty leagues further north leaving the mountains of Steve directly behind them as they rode through the strip of land flanked by the Sea of Tantrums and the Chasm of Brad until they would come eventually to the ruined city of Sloth where they would turn east and start their long semicircular return back home to Maudlin to confront Bil de Plummer and his minions. (No - I'm not going to provide you with a map. If you're so enamoured with the bloody things then draw your own, you juvenile *dungeons-and-dragons* train-spotting anorak wearer).

At present, Horgy, being of a fiscal nature, was expressing concern to Master Smegly vis-à-vis their financial soundness as a group, notwithstanding the fact that he may be able to write off a large part of their expenditure as tax deductible. He was also worried that Master Smegly's seemingly endless purse was, in fact, not endless and, more to the point, almost ended.

Smegly chuckled. 'Never fear, my good man,' he reassured Horgy. 'To all intents and purposes my purse is endless.'

Horgy, who was a man of not insubstantial wealth himself, looked duly impressed and said as much.

'Don't be,' said Smegly. 'I have very little actual money, as such. I merely have an unlimited source of payment.' Smegly pulled out his purse and wafted it at Horgy. It was, as he had feared, flat, floppy and well and truly devoid of coinage.

Horgy slapped his ex-accountant's, ex-knight's, newly-appointed-thief's forehead and swore. 'I knew it. We're skint.' He grasped Smegly's forearm. 'Tell me that we have money. Tell me that we're not undercapitalised. Reassure me regarding our cash flow, or at least our ability to raise funds in the market.'

'Sorry, Horgy,' apologised Smegly. 'I can do none of the above. However I can assure you, once again, that I have an unlimited source of payment. Panic not and be not overwrought for I am, after all, the master magician.'

Horgy groaned and looked imploringly at Plob, who was, in turn, regarding his master with a mixture of respect and disbelief on his honest, marginally attractive face.

'You've worked it out,' he said, addressing Smegly. 'Master, you've done it.' Plob whooped in excitement and jumped up banging his head on the roof of the cab. Smegly smiled the huge smile of the happily self-impressed and nodded. 'When?' continued Plob. 'How? Is it air or earth? Tell me, tell me.'

'Air,' replied Smegly.

'What are you guys talking about?' asked Horgy exasperatedly.

'It's a spell,' answered Plob. 'Blundelberry's eternal intensifier. Its alleged existence has been common knowledge for over two hundred years but, after Blundelberry's death, no one has been able to actually perform it as he never left any instructions. People were eventually starting to think that it was Master Blundelberry's idea of a practical joke.'

'OK. But why the excitement? I mean, I'm sure it's a very nice spell and all but, how does it help our financial strife? Unless you can turn stone into gold or such what then

I don't see how it can help.' Horgy paused as both Plob and Smegly laughed out loud. 'You can't, can you?' Horgy asked breathlessly.

Master Smegly shook his head. 'Afraid not, Horgy old man. We mages discovered long ago that transmutation is impossible; something to do with the base memory of matter, whatever, it's very complicated. I can, however, do the next best thing, well for our purposes it will suffice.' He took out his wealth-free purse and proffered it to Horgy. 'As you can see there is nil in this purse. What I would like you to do is place some small object in it for me, anything, a pebble, wood chip, something of that sort.'

Horgy called out to Biggest who bent down in mid stride and picked up a pile of stones which he passed over to him. Horgy placed three of them in Smegly's purse. The master hunched over the purse and muttered a string of incantations weaving his hands in intricate patterns and breathing in a measured fashion. He straightened up and passed the pouch back to Horgy. 'There you go,' he said. 'Done. Now look inside.'

Horgy opened the purse and spilled out three gold sovereigns onto the palm of his hand. He looked up incredulously. 'You turned the three pebbles into golden sovereigns. But I thought you said that you couldn't.'

'He hasn't,' said Plob. 'They're still pebbles. You just think that you can see sovereigns. The master has changed the perception of the stones. From now on all who see them will perceive them as golden sovereigns. Blundelberry's eternal intensifier.'

Dreenee clapped her appreciation and Cabbie whistled and shouted money, money, money, money, money loudly. Horgy, however, looked shocked. 'But that's forgery,' he said. 'It's illegal, in fact it carries a life sentence, or a death sentence, or both. I'd go as far as to call it a life and death issue.'

Smegly shook his head in disagreement. 'No forgery has taken place. I am not attempting to pass off base metal as gold and I am not counterfeiting the king's visage in any way. I am merely convincing a few small rocks to look like money, forever.'

With an accountant's inherent respect for coinage Horgy didn't look convinced. 'That's just legal frippery. What you're doing amounts to the same thing - it's immoral. And I'm sure that it will devalue the sovereign if we flood the market with bits of wood and rock that go around telling everyone that they're now a precious metal.'

Smegly stared at Horgy. 'Well, maybe you're right. It may be immoral, why don't we use your money, I hear that you are a man of means.'

Horgy flinched. 'That's immoral.'

'Yes,' said Smegly who was starting to get a little irritable. 'You've already said so.'

'No, not that. Using my money is immoral, I'm very attached to it, you see. I'll tell you what, let's go with the clever bits of wood and stone and all agree not to attempt to kidnap Horgy's own personal wealth that he has, over time, grown very attached to and admits to loving in an almost creepy way that only other accountants would understand.'

'Done,' agreed Master Smegly.

'Nutcase,' said Cabbie.

'Shut up,' said Dreenee.

'Giddy up,' said Cabbie, and they continued on their way.

The nameless strip of land nestled in between the chasm of Brad and the Sea of Tantrums provided for pleasant journeying. It was fertile, mild and fairly well populated with both farms and market towns. The region was also well known for its marvellous range of ales and hence was well endowed with inns, pubs and many informal roadside drinking establishments. It was early evening and the team had stopped in at one such establishment and were waiting for a tray of ales that Cabbie had just ordered from a pleasant looking, impossibly buxom young wench of the serving variety.

‘Well, well,’ said Cabbie. ‘What do you think of that hey, Plob,’ he continued, gesturing at the receding waitress. ‘I wouldn’t mind a butchers through that magic lens at that one. Wooah,’ Cabbie held his two hands out in front of his chest in the universal gesture of male appreciation of female well endowment.

‘Oh stop it, Cabbie,’ said Dreenee. ‘It’s not funny.’

‘Yeah, you’re right,’ said Cabbie, sighing. ‘I mustn’t tease the poor girl what with her problematically small feet and all.’

‘Why do you think she’s got problematically small feet?’ asked Plob.

‘She must have, nothing grows in the shade. Hey, hey. Budda-bing budda-boom.’

Dreenee punched Cabbie hard on the shoulder.

‘Ow!’ he rubbed himself ruefully. ‘OK, no more boob jokes. If Dreenee keeps hitting me I’ll be writing cheques that my body can’t cash.’

The serving girl returned with their ales and placed the tray on the table, leaning unnecessarily close to Plob and brushing his ear with her aforementioned assets. Cabbie winked at Plob and licked his lips lasciviously. ‘Ow! Dreenee, stop it. That hurts.’ He rubbed his arm again.

‘So,’ inquired the larger-breasted serving lass (Ow!) ‘You shall be staying the night, shall you?’

'Yes,' agreed Smegly. 'We have informed the bearded gentleman over there who said that he will make our rooms ready and organise for the luggage to be carried up.'

'Oh good,' replied the buxom one. 'I'll make sure that you are all made to be very comfortable,' she said, staring boldly at Plob. 'Now, let me bring you some sustenance of the edible variety. We have an exceptional chef and today he's done his special chicken dish, Breast Supreme.' Cabbie choked and then said Ow as Dreenee whacked him again. 'It's delicious,' the forward thinking lass continued. 'A mountain of large plump breasts, slathered in hot butter and served on a steaming platter with a side order of nice round dumplings and, to finish it all off, a huge helping of my favourite dessert, Spotted Dick.'

Cabbie punched himself in the shoulder to save Dreenee the trouble and then left the table to go and check on the horses.

The meal was every bit as good as promised and after two or four post-dinner ales they all retired to their rooms.

Later on that evening Plob was awoken by a soft knocking at his door. He climbed out of bed and opened it to reveal none other than the Miss Breast Supreme serving wench herself. Before Plob could voice any surprise she pushed her way into the room and locked the door behind her.

Plob did not dream that night. He didn't need to.

Kashfloh flicked his head to the side whilst Cabbie was hitching him up to the cab and snapped the leather harness causing Cabbie to swear vehemently and cuff the gelding about the ears. 'Damn,' he turned to the others. 'I'll have to get this stitched by a cobbler. Bugger, come on, Plob let's go and question the locals as to where we can seek one out.'

Biggest stretched and yawned. ‘I’ll come along too,’ he said. ‘It’ll be boring sitting here and doing nothing and I need to stretch my legs. I feel like I slept on pile of rocks last night.’

The three of them set off on their way straight after getting a handful of post-pebble and woodchip sovereigns from Master Smegly. On the way out the serving wench waved at Plob and blew him a kiss.

‘Hello, big boy,’ she shouted and flicked her skirt at him as she turned to serve a table their bacon, eggs and breakfast ales. Plob grinned and waved back.

Cabbie laughed. ‘That’s enough of that for now, big boy we’ve got work to do.’

Biggest laughed with him, clenched his fist in front of him and made ‘wooaagh’ sounds. Plob had the decency to look a little embarrassed, although he did so in a Cheshire cat fallen into a vat of cream fashion. They proceeded out of the establishment and turned right, walking down the main road towards the centre of the village.

‘So,’ said Cabbie, looking sideways at Plob. ‘Did we, or did we not have fun last night, big boy?’

Plob smiled once again and nodded.

‘Ah yes,’ continued Cabbie. ‘A nice girl our breastful waitress. Full of the milk of human kindness. Still, don’t read too much into, my friend. You’re a young, less than ugly lad with an acceptable body and a prestigious profession. You’ll find that many such offers will pitch up as we travel the byways of life, it wouldn’t be wise to attach oneself to any one girl. No matter how nice you think that she’d be, slathered in butter and served on a warm platter with nice round dumplings and a large spotted dick.’

Biggest laughed hugely. ‘Hey, cab-man you’s have got filthy ways with words.’

Cabbie chuckled in agreement. 'That I do, my good Trogre, that I do. You get the picture though?' he continued to Plob.

Plob nodded. 'There's no need to worry, Cabbie. She's a great girl and built like a brick outhouse but I do realise that she's not one for a lifelong commitment, buttered breasts or not.'

'Good man, Plob. Still, she's a nice girl and well worth remembering in your thoughts. Often.'

As they walked Plob remembered vividly for a while.

It was a well-built village, wide streets, freshly painted houses and scrubbed doorsteps. They stopped to ask directions to the local cobbler and were shown down a small side street to a two-storey shop with a large gilded sign outside reading: 'Cobblers - the Biggest and the best.'

'This whole bloody town is one huge double entedre,' complained Cabbie as they entered the shop. 'It's just too easy, takes all of the fun out of it, don't you know.' He rang a small sliver bell that was lying on the counter and they waited for assistance.

Assistance arrived in the form of a bespectacled man of indeterminate to late middle age, sporting a work apron with the words 'cobblers do it with leather' embroidered on it, and he looked like the sort of person that actually found that a remarkably daring thing to display.

Cabbie looked around for a 'you don't have to be mad to work here but it does help' sign. Thankfully there wasn't one.

The man approached them nervously; eyes flicking from side to side, although Biggest seem to make him particularly shifty. 'I'm sorry,' he said. 'I know that it's late but I've been having cash flow problems what with the tannery putting their prices up and the new minimum wage laws. I promise that I'll pay in full by the end of the week, just please don't hurt me. Please.'

Cabbie took a step towards the man who held his hands up to his face and cringed. 'Apologies, mate,' said Cabbie. 'I'm afraid that we have no idea what you're talking about. We only came here to get this fixed,' he finished, holding up the broken halter.

A look of relief washed over the cobbler's face. 'Oh. Thank you kindly, good sirs. Here, let me sort that out for you.' He took the length of leather from Cabbie's outstretched hand and went through to the workshop at the back.

'What was all that about?' asked Plob as the cobbler disappeared.

'Insurance,' rumbled Biggest. 'You pay a monthly premium to a local firm of bully boys or you meet with a personal disfiguring accident. Dis is not an honest way to make money. Far better you approach someone openly and with intent, biff dem onna head and take their cashola. Painful, but over with quickly. Dis insurance racket makes people live in fear all the time, month in and month out.'

The cobbler returned from the back room with the newly stitched halter. 'Here you go, sirs,' he said, proffering the item to them. 'As good as the day it was first bought.'

Cabbie inspected it and declared the cobbler to be correct. 'What do I owe you, my good man?' he asked.

'Two copper pennies, sir,' replied the craftsman of the cobbling variety as

Cabbie placed an intensified gold sovereign on the counter. 'I'm terribly sorry, noble sir,' apologised the cobbler, his eyes bulging at the seldom-seen gold coin on the worktop. 'I don't posses sufficient quantities of cash to make change for you.'

'No problem,' said Cabbie. 'You can keep the lot.' The cobbler's hand streaked, snake quick, to grab the sovereign but as he clasped it Cabbie snared his wrist in a vice-like grip. ‘For a little information of course,’ continued Cabbie still holding tight. ‘Tell us about this alleged protection racket that seems to be going on here.’

The cobbler’s eyes flicked around the room and his tongue darted nervously from between dry lips. ‘I don’t know anything,’ he croaked, looking wistfully at the golden coin.

‘Oh, I think we can do better than that,’ prompted Cabbie. ‘We’re not going to hurt you. We’re just looking for a little harmless information and then we’ll be on our way.’ He slid another ersatz coin across the counter.

Avarice finally overcame fear and words began to tumble from the cobbler’s mouth, falling over each other in their haste to get out. ‘It’s a racket run by the local magician and his henchmen. There’s about twenty of them they live on the old manor house on the hill and demand bi-monthly payments from everyone in the village and if you can’t pay they bash your face in or hurt your family or burn your place down and he’s a very powerful mage and I wouldn’t double cross him and I didn’t tell you any of this and can I really have the money or are you all going to beat up on me now and I hope that my work has been to your liking please don’t hurt me and…’ the cobbler finally ran out of air.

Cabbie cursed violently under his breath. Plob turned to look and was surprised to see a wave of intense anger cross his face. For a moment Cabbie seemed to have been replaced completely with Tarlek, tall, lean, frightening – and very pissed off. ‘Only the worst sort of filth would run that type of protection racket,’ he shook his head. ‘No, I won’t stand for this. This will be stopped or my name is not…is not…Cabbie,’ he ended lamely. ‘Come on, gentlemen, let’s away.’

They walked out of the shop leaving behind one by extremely puzzled, newly well off, cobbler.

Smegly sat in contemplation, ruminating over the information that Cabbie, Plob and Biggest had just imparted. He produced a cigar from a fold in his cloak, stood up and strode over to the fire at the end of the taproom to light up. He turned to face the team, smoke billowing out of his mouth like a peat-fired charcoal burner. 'I think it's pretty obvious that this is one of those not good things that we're supposed to stamp out.' Everyone murmured their agreement. 'The question is – how? Any suggestions?'

Horgy shrugged. 'Economic sanctions,' he proposed.

'No way, man,' Biggest disagreed. 'Dis one's simple. We just finds where dis manor house is, we all go over there and bash their brains out of their heads by means of acute violence. Then we drag their bodies down to the town square, tell everyone that we has saved their sorry asses and we proceed on our way.'

Smegly nodded. 'Cabbie, Plob, what do you think?'

'I'm inclined to agree,' affirmed Cabbie and Plob nodded.

'Dreenee?' inquired Master Smegly.

'Might as well, there's only twenty or so of them so they should find themselves reasonably outnumbered. I think that we should march up to the house, knock on the door, and then smash up everybody inside.'

'What about the powerful Mage that's supposed to be their leader?' asked Horgy.

Master Smegly laced his fingers together and stretched, cracking his knuckles as he did so. 'I'll take care of that,' he said in a voice dripping with distain. 'Powerful mage, my buttocks. Plob, load your miniaturising pouch up with all the left over earth spells, there's no time like the present, let us to battle.'

Chapter 13

Well it was only a matter of time, thought the king's captain at arms. Even one as obviously mentally challenged as the nutcase out there waving that red sort of bent knobbly thing in the air was certain to eventually work it out.

Bil de Plummer had placed his catapults and siege onagers in a line opposite the gates and out of range of the dreaded longbows that had previously so riddled them with death. The minions of Bil were gathering huge piles of stones and rocks which they were placing next to the siege engines and, at any moment the bombardment was about to ensue. The captain had ordered scores of buckets of water to be placed strategically around the castle, just in case the metal wielding moron outside discovered fire and started lobbing burning pitch-soaked hay bales at them.

There was a cheer from the rabble as the first catapult smacked against its restraints and the first boulder arced through the air and landed in the moat. The next one hit the huge oaken castle gate bang in the middle and, with the range now established, all the engines opened up at once.

Not long now, figured the captain, three, four, five days at most and the door would give. Then time for heroics. He smiled grimly to himself.

'Hold hard, Plob. Hold hard,' shouted Master Smegly.

Plob was dripping with sweat as he strained to keep the 'earth, protect, shield wall' in place against the barrage of thunderbolts, ice storms and fireballs that were careening up against it. Smegly was busy casting a series of complicated 'air, seeker' spells as he attempted to find exactly what they were up against. Plob gasped as a particularly large fireball smashed up against the wall. Dreenee stood behind him, massaging his shoulders and whispering words of encouragement into his ear. Biggest had his flask out and, every now and then, he tipped a medicinal amount of Blutop into Plob's mouth.

'Got it,' said Smegly in a satisfied voice. 'There's four of them. All middle order mages. Three of them are in that tower over there,' he said, pointing, 'and the other one is in that room there on the second floor,' he continued.

'You'd better do something about dem pretty soon, master man,' said Biggest. 'Your boy here's taking himself a pounding. A man cannot survive by Blutop alone and at the moment I suspects that dat's de only thing keeping him upright.'

'He'll survive,' reassured Smegly. 'He has to. And anyway, they're only a pack of middle-order mages. We wouldn't be in this predicament if our intelligence reports had been a little more accurate though,' he finished, looking accusingly at Cabbie.

Cabbie mumbled an apology.

Smegly approached Plob and placed his hands on his shoulders, staring into his eyes. 'Are you all right, my boy?' he asked, his face showing more concern than his voice allowed.

Plob groaned an affirmative and nodded jerkily.

'Right, this is what we're going to do. I'm going to combine our last three 'earth, attack, thunderbolt' spells and use them against the tower.'

Plob shook his head. 'Too dangerous,' he grunted. 'There could be feedback with so much power being released at once.'

'That's true,' confirmed Master Smegly. 'So that is where you come in. As I cast the combi-spell I want you to throw this protection wall after it and envelop the tower, thus holding the feedback in a contained area. If you can do it, and

I know that you can, it should reduce the tower and its contents to a mixture of mage and stone vapour. Are you ready?'

Plob shrugged, too exhausted to care and anyway, he trusted his master. If Smegly said that he could do it then he was sure that he could.

Smegly wasn't always right – but this time he was bang on the money. His triple 'earth, attack, thunderbolt' combi-spell screamed through the intervening space, superheating the air, singing eyebrows and sucking the moisture from everything around them.

Plob mentally tore the shield wall away from them and hurled it after the searing mega-thunderbolt. Their timing was perfect, the shield arriving a split second after the thunderbolt and, true to Smegly's plan, the tower seemed to merely cease to exist. The concentrated fire storm inside the shield wall surrounding the tower vaporised everything within.

Plob sank to his knees and then fell forward in a faint of total exhaustion. As he did so the shield wall, no longer being maintained by him, winked out of existence. The mother of all thunderbolts was now free to expand unhindered across the manor house, and this it did in a horrifyingly spectacular way.

Master Smegly fumbled at Plob's spell pouch as he pulled out an 'earth, protect' spell and hurriedly erected a shield wall around them. 'Quickly,' he shouted. 'Get in as close as you can so that I can draw the wall in tighter. The smaller it is, the stronger the protection.' They all huddled around Plob's prostrate body as Smegly clasped the protection wall around them and took the strain.

The festival of thunderbolts was busy rampaging across the manor house tearing the roof off and ripping the insides asunder with a huge fiery malignance. Red-hot clay roof tiles and burning beams of wood crashed down on Smegly's shield wall as the house was literally torn to molten shreds.

Finally, after the house, the stables, the outbuildings, the folly and all of the vegetation within a hundred paces, had been completely eliminated, the 'earth, attack, thunderbolt' combi-spell turned on itself and slowly guttered out leaving a huge, sulphuric smelling circle of charred earth as its last will and testament.

Smegly released his hold on the shield wall and drew a deep lungful of air. Plob was still out cold, his head in Dreenee's lap and his breath coming in short ragged gasps.

Biggest stood up from the crouch that he had assumed when Smegly had told them to huddle together. He stretched and looked at the field of devastation before him. 'Now that's what I calls kicking ass.' He punched his fist in the air and shuffled round in a circle. 'Who's the man? Smegly's the man. He's bad, he's mean. Hey, hey. Hey, hey.' He stopped to take a massive swig of Blutop from his magic flask and then offered it around.

Plob, who was finally coming to, got the first sip. He raised his head from Dreenee's lap and surveyed the results of their handiwork. 'Well,' he said, his voice still hoarse from exhaustion. 'tha-tha-that's all, folks.'

Biggest carried the exhausted Plob into his room when they got back and laid him on his bed, Dreenee helped strip him off , covered him with a blanket and stoked the fire up until it was crackling away with a warm merry little blaze. The serving wench slid into the room later that evening but, after taking a look at Plob's haggard sleeping face, gave him a kiss on the forehead and went off to molest some other lucky patron. (A girl of large and varied appetite our Supreme Breasted lass).

The next morning the team arose at a much later hour than usual. They all met in Plob's room and were pleased to see that youth and fitness had largely conquered his extreme fatigue and had replaced it with a ravenous hunger.

As they trooped down into the hall, readying themselves for a large breakfast, they were all but bowled over by the humungous round of applause that greeted them. The serving wench, looking like a dead heat in a zeppelin race, rushed up to hug Plob to plant a stupendously sensual kiss on his more than slightly surprised mug.

The quest members were shown to a hugely laden table in the centre of the room and, whilst they were eating, the crowd gathered round, eager to hear exactly what had transpired the evening before. They were not disappointed as Cabbie, breakfast ale in hand, regaled them with an impossibly exaggerated account of stupendous acts of valour, bravery and heroism heretofore never been seen by the likes of man.

The battle was fought against a gathering of master sorcerers from mid afternoon until way past sundown. Legions of enemy knights were put to the sword and vile enemies from other dimensions were slaughtered in their scores before Master Smegly and Plob finally brought down the wrath of the heavens upon the dastardly scourge.

Smegly finally brought a close to Cabbie's vast imaginings when he stood up and gave a short speech of thanks for the people's generosity and told them that they would soon be on their way.

As they left the hall, Biggest turned to the crowd with a warning. 'We has done some good and you'se will now be able to live in peace and prosperity. But if this sort of thing starts up again I want you'se to take care of it your selfs. If you'se don't then I is gonna think that you have wimped out on us and I'll come back with a whole can of whip ass which

I will apply liberally to you folks. So - stand up for your sorry selves. Death before dishonour, cause if me and my posse has to come back here, then no more Mister Nice Guy. Bye now, you all has a nice day.' He turned on his heel and left the room.

'Really, Biggest,' said Dreenee. 'Was that entirely necessary?' she asked.

'Entirely,' rumbled Biggest. 'We won't always be here for these folks so theys gots to learn to stand up for themselves. Sometimes you gots to be cruel to be kind. Only sometimes though, mainly you've got to be kind to be kind. Usually if you're cruel it's to be cruel, but dis is different and if I keeps on explaining myself I's gonna get confused, so stop it.'

They rode out of the town of Flobby to a trio of hip-hoorays and much waving of hankies and strewing of rose petals in the path of. Plob's waitress waved frantically with both arms and almost knocked herself out in the process.

The team felt great. They felt, as Biggest put it, like righteous sons of bitches. And it was good.

Chapter 14

The land changed abruptly as they left the strip between the sea and the chasm. It flattened out and opened to up reveal hectare upon hectare of rolling grasslands interspaced with the odd wheat field and dissected by lines of fast growing pines and poplars, planted as windbreaks. It was cattle country and cows were everywhere, as was the oddly fresh smell of bovine flatulence and newly chewed grass.

That afternoon they stopped to pitch camp a little early as Master Smegly wanted to forge a new batch of spells to load into Plob's magic pouch. Plob selected a number five heavy hammer and wielded it with a deftness and skill that both surprised and impressed Smegly. He smiled as he watched Plob work the spells, an assistant who was becoming a master, a boy who was becoming a man.

After they had forged and loaded the enchantments, Horgy and Dreenee prepared supper and Smegly sat down with Plob to discuss spells. Master Smegly could feel the power growing in Plob and now was a time for careful instruction lest Plob become careless through overconfidence.

They discussed the more intricate air spell weaves and Plob put forward the theory of combined weaves, using the power of Earth and the subtlety of Air to create a precision spell that could be cast over long distances. Smegly agreed that, in theory, it could be done but no one had been able to master the combination thus far. If they could, then it would be possible to communicate over long distances with individual people and the mage that could do that could make a fortune selling his services to both businessmen and families. Anyway, Master Smegly argued, when combining Air and Earth a great deal of mental participation was needed and they faced the very real danger of the resultant spell leaching off the caster's mental capacity or, perhaps, even their physical being. Plob disagreed and thus they talked shop late into the night, long after the others had gone to sleep and Smegly stayed up for longer, even after Plob had fallen to the soft snare of slumber.

The next day brought with it, surprise surprise, more cattle. Even Biggest got bored looking at them and making yummy sounds whenever he saw a particularly plump one.

Later that afternoon they happened upon the town of Hefereen, a large sprawling cattle market of a town surrounded by acres of fenced-in paddocks. After asking around they were shown to the town's best inn for, as Master Smegly said as he hefted his stone-filled purse, why bother with the price, it's only money. (Isn't it?)

The rooms that they were shown to were magnificent, four-poster beds, silken drapes, thick woollen carpets and, opposite the bed in each room, a large copper bathing tub three quarters filled with steaming lavender-scented water.

They all stayed in the rooms a little longer than necessary, soaking away the grime of the trail and steaming the tension out of cramped muscles. Whilst Plob was bathing, a servant took his clothes away and, a short while later, they arrived back, washed, dried and pressed with any small tears and frays neatly mended. After he had shaved he went downstairs to the drinking lounge (nothing as crass as a taproom here) to meet with the others.

They were all already on their second ale by the time Dreenee arrived. In deference to the surroundings she had taken extra special care in preparing herself for dinner and, as she walked down the stairs, every person in the room was struck dumb by her extravagant sensuality.

She reached the bottom of the stairs and seemed to glide over to the group, her silky soft hair glittered and shimmered like a halo of fine spun golden thread and, as her eyes swept the crowded room igniting fires of passion in all present, every person there seemed convinced that her bold steamy gaze was for them alone.

Cabbie bowed deeply when she reached them and leaned forward to lift her hand to his lips. 'Princess,' he greeted her as he kissed her palm. 'You honour us with your divine presence.'

Dreenee laughed. 'The last time I asked I definitely wasn't a royal and I'm hardly a divinity, my good Tarlek, but thanks to you nonetheless.' She grabbed his ale and downed what remained of it in one go. And with that the spell was broken, conversations were resumed, drinks were drunk and dinners consumed. The quest members showed themselves to a table and sat down.

They were treated to a meal that surpassed everything that they had thus far been served, including their repast at the manifold mastered one's abode. Platters of small roasted game fowls, smoked sausages, exotic vegetables, honeyed sweetmeats and gallons of wine and ale.

As they settled down to brandy and Master Smegly lit up his ubiquitous cigar, they were approached by a wan young girl dressed in a simple dress of the finest red cotton and a soft tan leather jacket.

She approached Master Smegly and curtsied gracefully. 'I hope that you will forgive me for my impertinent interruption, good people, but may I, a simple farm girl, trouble you with a question?'

Smegly nodded. 'Fire away, my girl,' he answered.

'Rumour has it that you are the brave saviours of the town of Flobby, if this is true may I be seated and assail you with my poor sad tale?'

Smegly nodded and Plob drew up a chair for the pale faced girl who sat down and smoothed her red dress before beginning. 'My name is Prado, daughter of Munge the vegetable farmer. I am the chosen representative of a small group of farming folk who are being driven off their land by an unscrupulous landowner who goes by the name of Gordo. He has already taken over most of the farms in the area and if something is not done very soon we, the last small group of farmers in the area that still resist, will be swallowed up by Gordo's conglomerate. Please, noble sirs, please help my poor family and friends in our dastardly plight.'

Plob stood up. 'This is outrageous; something must and will be done. Fear not kind Prado your plight is now our own and we…'

'Sit down, Plob,' ordered Master Smegly as he pointed at the chair. 'Now.' He turned to face the girl and surveyed her beneath hooded eyes. After a moment he seemed to come to a conclusion. He called Horgy over and whispered some instructions in his ear. Horgy nodded, gestured to Biggest and the two of them left the room together. Smegly faced the girl again. 'Forgive my rudeness, dear child, I had to send our two companions off on an errand of great urgency, but worry not for they shall soon return. Now, my dear, would you like a drink? We have just finished a bottle of the Flobby seventy-three and were about to order some brandy, unless of course you could recommend something a little more sophisticated.'

Prado cocked her head to one side and thought for a while. 'Yes,' she said. 'I think a bottle of the Chasm Bin Number nineteen would suit your palate, if your purse will stretch that far.'

'That, my dear, will never be a problem,' reassured Smegly as he ordered a bottle of same from the waitress.

They waited in uncomfortable silence whilst the waitress went off to the cellar to fetch their wine. Every time Plob, Cabbie or Dreenee attempted to start a conversation they were halted by a stern look from the master. When the waitress returned and opened the bottle, Master Smegly asked Prado to taste it as she was the one most familiar with the region. She did so, swilling the wine in her glass, sniffing it, holding it to the light and then, finally, tasting it. She declared it to be fit and glasses were poured all round.

Smegly held his newly filled glass up. 'A toast,' he said. 'To truth.'

'To truth,' repeated all except Cabbie who had downed his glass and was busy refilling.

'Good bit of muck this,' he said, slurping noisily from the tankard that he had now substituted for the glass. 'Better order another.' He gestured to the hovering waitress, pointed to the bottle, held up two fingers and then made running motions with his arms. The waitress scuttled off at speed to fulfil the order.

Once again they sat in silence waiting for the waitress. After a while she returned and, under Cabbie's instructions, opened both bottles and left them on the table. Shortly afterwards Horgy and Biggest returned, Horgy nodded at Smegly and they sat down. Cabbie poured some wine for both of them, Horgy sniffed it and then took an appreciative sip. Biggest took out his flask, added a slug of Blutop to his, slurped up a mouthful and nodded in approval.

'Well, gentlemen and ladies,' said Smegly. 'All seated comfortably? Good, good. Now let me begin.' He stared intently at Prado, his eyes glistening with seldom revealed power, and she shifted uncomfortably in her seat. 'I think that your name probably is Prado,' Smegly started. 'But as for the rest of your badly woven tissue of vague half truths I cannot be completely sure.'

'Master,' Plob objected. 'Please, this poor girl has come to us for help.'

Smegly raised an eyebrow at Plob. 'Girl? Yes, that goes without saying. Poor? I seriously doubt it, my dear Plob. The tailor-made dress, the expensive jacket, the fact that she is obviously quite at home ordering bottles of wine that cost over three golden sovereigns each.'

Cabbie choked violently and Biggest pounded him on the back, knocking him off his chair and driving him to his knees. He held his hands above his head. 'All right, I surrender. Stop hitting me. Please. I promise not to cough again. Ever.' He climbed back onto his chair and picked his tankard full of wine back up, staring at it reverently and muttered 'three' under his breath a few times before he had another large swig.

'Truth, as the toast went, my girl. Truth is what we want and we want it all and we want it now.'

Prado flicked her head back and looked at them all disdainfully. 'I believe I am wasting my time here, gentlemen, I think that it's my prerogative to leave.'

She made to stand up and, as she did so, Plob wove a quick 'air, restraint' spell which held her to her chair. 'If you scoundrels don't let me go I shall scream,' she threatened, causing Plob to follow up with another 'air, restraint' around her mouth. Prado sat in silence staring daggers at them all, especially Plob.

'Well, Horgy,' said Smegly. 'What did you manage to find out?'

'Not a huge amount,' admitted Horgy, 'but enough to confirm your suspicions.'

'What suspicions?' asked Plob. 'What in the gods' names is going on? I've tied up Prado and I don't even know why. Will somebody please tell me what's going on before one of us dies.'

'From the moment Prado introduced herself I knew that something didn't ring true,' explained Smegly. 'Her bearing, her clothes, her manner. It all smacked of play acting. So I asked our good friend Horgy here to take Biggest and go on a little fact finding mission regarding our well-dressed peasant girl. So, Horgy my good man, tell all.'

Horgy cleared his throat. 'Her name is Prado; that much is true. Oddly enough her father is actually a vegetable farmer, the largest vegetable farmer this side of the valley of Strange. He also owns the wholesalers, packaging plants and a large number of the retail outlets. In short, he is a man of quite stupendous wealth, or so it would seem.'

Cabbie leant forward. 'What do you mean, "or so it would seem"?'

'Well, I spoke to a couple of seed and fertiliser merchants that supply Mister Munge and it seems as if he's beginning to backslide a bit on his payments. He's also having some trouble with his labour, mostly peasants who are refusing to work. As well as this he's offering huge discounts to garner early payments from his customers. Put that all together and you get a financial empire that's right on the verge of total collapse. If I was an investor I wouldn't touch him with an eight-foot broadsword.'

Master Smegly turned to Prado. 'Does that about sum the situation up? Just nod, we'll allow you to talk later.'

Prado nodded reluctantly and Smegly stood up. 'Gentle folk, I think we should go upstairs to my suite and continue this discussion in more private surroundings. Plob, support Prado and make sure that she gets up the stairs without coming to any harm.'

They left the room with Cabbie holding the two opened wine bottles and Plob half carrying Prado up the stairs. When they got to Master Smegly's suite, Plob released the spells that bound the pretend peasant and helped her to a chair.

Smegly lit up a cigar. 'Right, my girl. What's the real story? Why are you actually here and what do you really want us to do?'

Prado asked Cabbie to pour her a glass of wine and, after he had obliged, she faced the group. 'Your Mister Horgy is right,' she confirmed. 'My father's empire is literally on the bones of its buttocks. We've had a few bad seasons, there are massive labour problems and cash flow has become an absolute nightmare. We somehow limp from day to day with borrowings and early payments but I'm not sure how much longer we can continue. Last month, however, a land baron by the name of Gordo started showing a lot of interest in the local property and began to buy up a lot of peasants' smallholdings for bargain basement prices. My father and I figured that, if we could persuade you to stop him buying from the peasants then they would be forced to look for work. Then the property prices would become artificially inflated and we could unload a large portion of our holdings to Gordo thus sorting out both our labour and cash flow problems at the same time. I had no idea that you'd see through me so quickly, to tell the truth, from what I'd heard you just sounded like a group of uncouth roughnecks and conjurers spoiling for a fight. I'm sorry. It appears that I was desperately wrong.'

Smegly nodded his acceptance of her apology. 'It sounds as if you're in trouble. Now this would not normally be the sort of thing that we'd get involved in but, I have the glimmerings of a plan that may be advantageous to all of us. Gentlemen we need to caucus. Prado, thank you for an entertaining evening, I'm sure that you know your way out. Meet us back here tomorrow after breakfast and then I think that you should take us all to see your father.'

They stayed up late into the night as Master Smegly explained his idea and both he and Horgy hammered out the details.

The next morning Plob wandered into the dining hall to be greeted by Cabbie in full complaint.

‘No, come on now. That’s not breakfast,’ he said, pointing at a huge spread of foods laid out before them. ‘It’s just bread and jams and fruit and cheese and cold meats and stuff.’

‘It’s supposed to be fancy,’ assured Smegly. ‘That’s how it’s done this side of the valley. It’s called a Northern-ental breakfast.’

Cabbie shook his head. ‘It’s not breakfast. I mean look, it’s basically just bread. See, look,’ he continued poking at various rolls, croissants, breads, ryes, pumpernickels, ashcakes and baps with an accusing digit. ‘How’s a man supposed to face the day with only a gut full of bread in him?’ as he grabbed the horrified looking waiter by the collar. ‘Listen, friend, I demand fried eggs and fried bacon and fried sausage and fried tomatoes and fried mushrooms. And here,’ Cabbie thrust a piece of bread at him, ‘get the chef to fry this up as well, and just for luck tell him to put an extra portion of deep fried lard on a side plate. And beans, baked in tomato sauce, better fry them as well just to be on the safe side. Move it; chop, chop.’ Cabbie shuddered. ‘Bread and fruit for breakfast. Gods, what ever will they think of next?’

After they had all eaten and Cabbie had gobbled up his deep-fried cholesterol frenzy, with an ale just to settle the stomach, Prado arrived in a large gilt encrusted carriage drawn by four horses. They all got in and were transported to her father’s offices where Master Smegly and Horgy put forward their plan to him.

Chapter 15

The captain offered up appreciation to his deities once again. Thank the gods for moronic enemies. It was seven days since Bil's bombardment had started and still the gates held. This was partly to do with the huge mound of stone that the captain had piled against the door, courtesy of the king's ex-stables that had been torn down to provide building material, and partly due to the complete and utter ineptitude of Bil and his followers.

Bil ranted around his camp countermanding previous orders and replacing them with new conflicting ones only to reissue them in another format minutes later. His wobbly leadership structure was also constantly changing as second in commands became third in commands and third in commands became latrine diggers, latrine diggers were promoted to generals and vice versa.

Every now and then drunken fights broke out amongst the rabble, although Bil put these down swiftly and severely with a quick swing of his wrench.

All in all there was nothing for the captain and his men to do except wait, and this they did. Their strained nervous boredom was relieved every so often when one of the minions strayed into bow shot and was summarily dispatched by one of the king's archers, although even this would soon have to stop as they were running low on arrows.

Sit and wait, and then the hand-to-hand combat. Well at least that should relieve the boredom, the captain thought as he sighed and settled back against the wall. Not long now.

'Are you insane?' Munge stood up and banged the table with both fists, his gross stomach wobbling unpleasantly with emotion as his eyes protruded from his head in disbelief.

Biggest leaned over, placed a huge paw on the merchant's head and slammed him back into his chair. 'Watch your tone of voice, mutha, show some respect to my main man Master Smegly here or you is going to meet with some grievous bodily harm.'

Smegly leaned back in his chair and, ostentatiously, lit his cigar with a bright green flame that he had conjured out of thin air. 'Perhaps I didn't explain things adequately,' he conceded. 'Horgy is actually the financial wiz so mayhap he will make more sense.'

Horgy cleared his throat and assumed centre stage. 'It's quite simple really. As we all know Munge vegetable industries is experiencing two major worries: a lack of willing labour and a growing cash flow problem. What we propose is solving both problems with what is essentially the same solution. You encourage all of the surrounding peasants to sell off their property to the land baron Gordo, perhaps by forming a consortium of some sort in order to drive the prices up, and then you offer to sell fifty percent of your company to the newly formed peasant consortium for an agreed price which will be sufficient to cover your cash shortfalls. In return they become contractually obligated to work for Munge vegetable industries and, due to the fact that they are now equal partners, you are sure to have a highly-motivated, hassle free labour force at your constant disposal. Not only that, it'll allow the peasants to start living an acceptable calibre of life as opposed to the atrocious way you've treated them thus far. It's a win-win situation. I'm only surprised that you didn't think of it before. My father, may he never rise from the grave, had been doing similar deals for many years and in the process managed to accumulate more money than the gods.'

Smegly pursed his lips and blew a huge smoke ring which wafted around the room lazily. 'Any road,' the master added. 'It's basically irrelevant whether you like the idea or not as you've got Hobson's choice.'

'That's where you're wrong,' stated Munge as he assumed a fatly superior expression. 'All I need to do is hire myself a group of mercenaries, ride roughshod over the peasants forcing them to work for me, make sure that anyone who sells to Gordo meets with a terminal farming accident and then, when Gordo is a little more desperate, sell off a few acres of my land at inflated prices.' Munge clasped his hands together over his more than adequate belly and looked smugly at Master Smegly.

The master shook his head sadly. 'Biggest,' he called the Trogre over.

'Yes, boss?' enquired Biggest.

Smegly pointed at Munge. 'Break two of the fingers on his right hand.'

'Yes, boss,' Biggest's arm whipped out with astonishing speed and even Munge's scream couldn't cover the three staccato pops his fingers made as Biggest bent them back beyond the point of no return. Biggest turned to look sheepishly at Smegly. 'Sorry, boss, in my boundless enthusiasm I seem to have busted three. I'll try harder to be more precise next time.'

Munge had fallen off his chair and was cradling his new look bendy fingers to his chest whilst squealing and sobbing like a banshee in the mating season.

Smegly gestured to the Trogre once more. 'Biggest, be a good chap and if the vegetable farmer here doesn't shut up within two seconds break both of his thumbs.'

The ensuing immediate silence was deafening.

Smegly wove an 'air, lift' spell and used it to drag Munge off the floor into a standing position. He strode up to him (in a higher mortal way) and held his face close to the merchant farmer. 'Listen to me, you flabby ungrateful horrible overweight broken-fingered vegetable farmer. We are not here to negotiate deals. We are on a mission of such importance that your paltry little problems are as nought to us in the scheme of things. However, by forming this alliance with the peasants you will be helping to right at least some past injustices and that will constitute as a good deed. Now I don't expect you to understand any of this as you are a socially reprehensible obese maggot but you will do as we have told you. We will spend two days with you to get things in motion, Horgy here will be in charge and I hope that any future bone breaking and other unpleasantness can be avoided. Horgy, take over,' he commanded and then he turned on his heel and left the room.

A stunned silence followed as the quest members adjusted their thinking to encompass this newly revealed vicious side of their normally mellow master.

'Well,' said Horgy. 'Let's get started.'

Chapter 16

With a vast tearing and splintering the castle doors collapsed inwards to open the way for the screaming minions of Bil de Plummer, the evil one.

The captain's small force stood in a line in the courtyard, longbows drawn, ready to make their last few arrows count. As the horde came spilling over the rubble that still partially blocked the entrance, the captain gave the order.

The men fired once, twice, thrice and then the enemy were upon them. Swords were pulled from scabbards, war axes hefted, shields held to hand and, as each of the King's men voiced their own personal battle cry, the last stand commenced.

It was the stuff of legends, and clichés, the battle would be impossible to explain without a good helping of all of the hackneyed old expressions such as fortitude and valour and windrows of fallen dead and cutting down like so much wheat and into the valley of death's etcetera and so on and so forth and yahdee yahdee.

But really, it was an absolute cracker of a battle, the captain and his highly trained troops stood firm showing great fortitude and valour, shields overlapped and weapons swinging freely. The windrows of fallen dead piled up at their feet as they cut them down like so much wheat and, finally, Bil's minions retreated as they no longer had the courage to continue into that personal valley of death and so on and so forth and yahdee yahdee.

The captain and his now slightly smaller group let free a yell and rushed forward to hurry the unorganised rout on its way.

But they were experienced troops, and they knew that soon, very soon, the enemy would be back.

Horgy stood up in front of the gathering. 'Good people, I give to you, Munge and Peasants vegetable industries.'

A polite smattering of applause greeted this announcement (except from Munge whose newly strapped fingers were still of the non-clap variety).

And then a large bearded man in the front stood up. 'You can't call it that. We're not peasants any more, we're a consortium of newly indoctrinated middle-class socio-economically empowered, previously disadvantaged, co-owning, capitalist farming merchants.'

Horgy shook his head. 'It doesn't work, I mean really, chaps – Munge and a consortium of newly indoctrinated, middle-class, socio-economically empowered, previously disadvantaged co-owning, capitalist farming merchants vegetable industries – it sounds stupid.'

The bearded member of the consortium of newly indoctrinated middle class socio-economically empowered previously disadvantaged co-owning capitalist farming merchants didn't look convinced. 'We could shorten it, you know? Like use initials or something.'

'What, like Munge and the ONIMICSOECOEMPREDCOCAPFAME's? Still sounds bloody stupid.'

Prado put her hand up. 'What about Munge and Partners vegetable industries?'

The bearded ONIMICSOECOEMPREDCOCAPFAME scratched his head and said 'Ooooh,' in an I'm so impressed way.

'I still prefer peasant,' said Munge.

'Up your peasant, capitalist pig dog,' shouted someone in the middle of the crowd. 'Don't ever say that word again.' There was a general murmur of agreement.

‘I like ONIMICSOECOEMPREDCOCAPFAME’ said a small, dungy smelling man at the back. ‘It’s got a nice ring to it.’

‘Your bum,’ said a woman next to him.

‘Yeah,’ shouted a fat man in a checked shirt. ‘That’s a good one. Munge and the your bum ONIMICSOECOEMPREDCOCAPFAME’s’

‘No, you idiot,’ shouted the woman. ‘I meant his bum,’ she continued pointing at the manure redolent, small man.

‘I have got a name,’ complained poo smell.

‘Well we’ve never met,’ argued the women. ‘How am I supposed to know it?’

‘Well you could have asked,’ dungy replied sulkily. ‘Anyway, it’s Manderball.’

‘Oh shut up,’ shouted the women.

‘You started it,’ accused dungy and the fat man as one.

‘Morons.’

‘Bitch.’

‘Dung pile.’

‘Fatty.’

‘Peasant.’

There was a stunned silence as the conglomerate of ex-dirt farmers paused to seek out who had uttered the ‘P’ word.

‘It wasn’t me,’ shouted the bearded man. ‘I didn’t say peasant. And anyway, I said it by mistake.’

Plob didn’t see who threw the first punch but it wasn’t long before a mighty brawl had ensued. Later that night they all partied hard and there was much hugging, patting of backs, crying and swearing of allegiance and everlasting friendships.

By midmorning of the next day the team were once more on their questing way. They took a little longer than expected to get out of town, as on the way out they came across an old lady dithering next to the road. Biggest, determined to do another good deed, had grabbed the octogenarian and half dragged, half carried her across the street, clapped her on the back and wished her a happy day.

A group of passing wagon drivers had misunderstood Biggest's intentions and decided to sternly reprimand him. Two of them escorted the old lady back to the other side of the road and the other five attempted to brutalise the Trogre. After Biggest had politely pointed out their mistake he went back across the road, dispatched the other two drivers and carried the old lady back, kicking the prostrate drivers' twitching bodies out of the way as he did so. They resumed their travels with Biggest beaming hugely as he jogged next to the cab.

Plob looked back and noticed the ancient women slowly shuffle her way slowly back across the street, take out a set of keys and let herself into her house. He didn't say anything to Biggest so as not to ruin the massively chuffed look that the Trogre had stretched across his furry face.

'Well,' said Biggest. 'Once again we has done folks a power of good. We is a bunch of fuggin Samaritans. Hoo-eee. All together now - Hooooo-eeeeee.' He punched the air with a humungous clenched fist. The team responded shouting and punching the air together.

And there were grins aplenty all round, and they felt good.

The captain didn't feel quite as good. He'd torn a strip off his tunic to staunch his head wound and his second in command had strapped the captain's marred and split shield to his badly cut and bruised left arm so he could continue to hold it up by himself. There were only seven of them left and, although they had exacted a monumental toll on the enemy, they were tired beyond belief. They slammed and barred the door to the prison tower that they had been forced to retreat into and the captain took stock.

Weapons, including crossbows and bolts, weren't a problem as they had their pick from the heaps of fallen enemy. Amazingly, morale was still high although no one was bereft enough to believe that this could end in any other way beside total heroic annihilation. He ordered the men to pile everything that they could find against the tower door and then proceed upstairs so that they could start shooting at the rabble from above.

It had been twelve days since the first attack. Twelve glorious battle-filled days. The captain grinned to himself - yep, this is why he joined up. He held his sword above his head. 'Hoo-eeee.' The captain turned to his men. 'Altogether now - Hooooo-eeeee.' His men responded shouting and thrusting their weapons into the air together. And outside, Bil's minions felt the hair on the back of their necks rise, and they marvelled at the courage of the doomed detachment.

And there were grins aplenty all round, and the doomed detachment felt good.

The captain and his men had thus far achieved the impossible. And I mean it, seriously, it is a physical impossibility for so few men to fight off so many with so little. But the impossible had come to pass for, like the mega mastered one had predicted, as the questers did more good and the balance between good and evil slowly righted itself in good's favour, so too did heroic acts such as those performed by the doomed detachment, become more and more possible.

For good shall conquer, in the end, eventually, ultimately, probably.

I hope.

Terry Block held the bright red, dropped-forged steel plumber's wrench above his head as he strode into the office that he shared with Hugo Prendergast. 'Look, Prendy my mukka.'

Hugo looked, and was duly puzzled. 'What in God's name is that?'

'What's it look like, my toffy friend?'

'Looks like a bright red thing with a knobble and a squiggly bit.'

'A squiggly twisty spiral bit?' asked Terry in a smug voice as he held the wrench up against the photograph of the girl's smashed-in skull, displaying that it was an almost perfect match.

'Jesus,' exclaimed Hugo. 'They were killed with a…a…what the hell is that thing?'

'This, my upper-class friend, is what we working-class stiffs call a tool. It's a device used by tradesmen to fix things. This particular one is called an adjustable plumber's wrench.'

Hugo nodded, even though he would never be so crass as to admit it, he was impressed.

Chapter 17

Clipitty cloppitty clip clop clip. They had been riding at a fairly brisk pace now since the morning. The last night had been relatively unpleasant, as far as nights spent outdoors go. A thin drizzle had started up yesterday afternoon and had definitely decided to take up long-term residence resulting in weather of the dull, wet and dreary school of thought.

Weather affects your moods and feelings, or so we're told. Personally this isn't a point of view that I give much truck to. Well, when the sun's up and it's hot, I feel warm. When it's raining and chilly I feel cold and wet. However, I suspect that this isn't what the touchy-feely brigade mean when they talk moods and feelings. They're talking emotions, affections, sentiment and so on. So, when it's sunny you are meant to feel excitement, titillation, exhilaration, stimulation and general all-round feelings of happiness and irritating bunny-huggedness.

When it's dark and dingy then these same 'I'm so happy-happy' people seem to agree that this gives you the right to act like a total prat. It's dull so I can be dissatisfied, wretched, bitter and twisted and, in the process, do half the amount of work that I could reasonably be expected to do as the bulk of my productive time will be taken up whingeing, whining and discussing SADS (I don't know, something to do with lack of sunshine or something. **S**tupid **A**rseholes **D**emand **S**un. Who knows?) as if it was an actual disease and, once contracted, gives you the right to ponce around acting like a malcontent nauseate.

Well get a life. What about people who live underground, or in maximum security prisons, or in a small cupboard under the stairs. They don't see the sun and I'm sure that they're all perfectly happy. Actually - come to think of it - they're probably not, but anyway, I'm sure that you see what I'm getting at. What this country needs is the reintroduction of national service and the death penalty and corporal punishment. And stoning. And being turned into pillars of salt, and then being sold to a large beef farming syndicate and used as a salt lick. Unless it rained and you just melted away into a puddle of salty water. OK - so maybe these 'rain makes me depressed' dudes are onto something, but only if hugely extenuating circumstances are involved.

'I hate this rain,' said Horgy. 'It's making me feel dissatisfied, wretched, bitter and twisted and, in the process, I'll probably do half the amount of work that I could reasonably be expected to do.' (He didn't mention SADS as no one had got bored enough to invent it yet).

'Oh buck up,' said Master Smegly. 'Stop being such a whingeing whiner.'

So Horgy did. 'Thanks, Master Smegly, I feel much better now.' He sat up straighter and his demeanour definitely seemed brighter. (Which just goes to show, doesn't it?)

'It must be time for lunch,' said Plob. 'Do you think that there's any chance of coming across an inn or some manner of eating establishment?' There was a general shrugging as it was anyone's guess.

'I don't know,' said Cabbie. 'It's anyone's guess isn't it?'

As Cabbie finished speaking the irksome drizzle changed its character slightly to become an offensive patter. It obviously decided that this was a good career choice so it quickly stepped up the ante to an obnoxious rainfall and finally, after a little practice, a torturously vengeful downpour of almost biblical proportions.

Thoroughly impressed with itself by now it added an aural and visual assault of gargantuan explosions of thunder and an army of bright white oak-cleaving bolts of lightning. This was the life, it thought, and so it settled itself in for the long haul.

'We've got to get out of this and find respite of some sort,' shouted Smegly above the banshee howl of the wind. 'Cabbie, let's get off the road into the trees, we're too exposed out here, much more of this and we could literally be drowned. Biggest, scout on ahead for some shelter, anything will do. Come on, people let's go.'

Cabbie turned off into the forest and Plob and Horgy jumped off the cab and helped guide it through the morass of muddy matter next to the track. Unbelievably, the storm managed to increase in intensity, hammering and screeching at them like a crowd of women at a rapist's stoning.

Biggest came trotting back out of the soaking darkness. 'There's a cave up front,' he pointed. 'That side of the hill.' He jogged off, leading the way. The cab lurched along behind him with Plob, Horgy and the horses snorting and spluttering damply as they heaved and pulled through the sodden night together.

'All effort now, gentlemen, all effort,' encouraged Smegly as he peered into the wringing wet gloom ahead. 'There's something eldritch about this squall and the sooner we can get to the cave and safely under cover the better.'

The eyeball etching flashes of lightning lit their way and, as they rounded the bottom of the hill, the smallish entrance to the cave was plainly in sight.

Together with Biggest's help they manhandled the cab over the rock-strewn entrance and into the cavern itself. As they proceeded into the subterranean retreat the sound of the stridently violent storm outside subsided unnaturally quickly to a barely perceptible murmur. They carried on into the cavern which swiftly expanded into a cathedral-sized interior underground abode where the team stood silently staring in awe at the massive rock expanse.

It was Plob that noticed it first. 'It's bigger,' he said waving his arm at the emptiness. 'Bigger than the outside. There's no way that the hill we entered could ever accommodate a cavern this size.'

'Look.' Biggest pointed to the end of the cave. 'There seems to be a door. Over there at the back.'

And it was. A huge black wooden door, with studs in and a mammoth brass handle in the shape of a rampant unicorn and a three-hundred-pound steel knocker cast in the facsimile of a pod of whales (Yes, a pod. Look it up - I did). A proper door. The way large wooden doors at the back of mysteriously huge caverns discovered in the night at the height of eldritch storms should be.

A door of note.

'Gentlemen, and Dreenee,' quoth Master Smegly. 'That is the reason we are here.'

'What,' asked Cabbie. 'We've been brought here by a door?' Cabbie wasn't impressed. Even by a door as overwhelmingly impressive as this one obviously was.

'Yes,' replied Smegly. 'Although that's not exactly what I meant. That storm was not natural; it was created by otherworldly forces. Forces which I suspect lie beyond that door at the end of this so conveniently discovered, larger inside than outside, cavern that we have entered to shelter from the force of that supernatural tempest.' He harrumphed, which Plob knew was not a good sign. 'People, let us proceed to the door and enter, for we have been summoned.'

Dreenee, Smegly and Cabbie descended from the cab and, together with the rest of the quest members, they proceeded. As they approached the door it opened of its own volition, smoothly and silently, with no hint of squeak or groan to mar its eerie stealth. Yes, this door was definitely living up to all of the standard idiosyncrasies expected of a substratum otherworldly entrance.

They trooped inside, Biggest taking the point and Cabbie at the rear leading the horses and cab.

The door swung closed behind them with a horribly intimidating crash causing them all to start violently and, as they watched, it disappeared, merging into the surrounding foliage as if it had never been. Cabbie soothed the horses as everyone looked around at the newly entered environment.

It was obvious to all that the small hillock outside had absolutely no bearing on the size of the place they were now in. To say that it was huge would be meaningless. A town is big, a mountain is huge. But a land? A continent? It would be like calling the ocean wet.

They had entered another world.

And then, approaching them from the middle distance, was a woman. Tall of stature, green and silver of garb and achingly graceful of bearing.

As she got nearer Plob could see that she was beyond any shard of doubt the most resplendently beautiful creature that he had ever had the privilege of seeing. Although not in the way that Dreenee was, there was no hint of sexuality, no touch of the seductress or coquet. Nothing so crass. Her pulchritude was beyond such base animal thoughts and instincts and, although she was very obviously a woman, her visual perfection was almost androgynous.

She stopped but a few paces away and cast her magnificent gaze upon them and, as she stood, her thick calf-length sable hair swirled around her like a cloak of nocturnal silk framing her exquisite countenance and exposing flashes of her perfectly pointed elvin ears.

Dreenee curtsied and Master Smegly bowed deeply. Both Horgy and Cabbie fell to their knees as they gawped at the ravishing elvish vision before them. Plob fought the compulsion to prostrate himself before the terribly beautiful elf women and, remembering that magicians kneel before nought, he gathered his wits and bowed long and sincerely.

'Welcome, good travellers,' she greeted, her voice as a shimmering of glass and a fluttering of feathers, at once both entreating and commanding. 'My name is Sitar. Follow me and I shall lead you to shelter and sustenance.'

They followed without thought or question.

As they walked, Master Smegly came up alongside Plob. 'Beware,' he whispered. 'Elves are not always what they are thought to be. Although exquisite of countenance and bearing they are oft vain, self-serving and cruel. Keep your wits about you and remember to show at all times the utmost of respect. We have been brought here for reasons of their own. Warn the others when you get the chance.'

Plob spread Smegly's caution amongst the group.

After an hour's or so walk through the emerald landscape they came to a forest of tall straight trees, awe inspiring in their height and girth. Their exquisite companion showed them to a broad path that led into the ancient forest and through the trees they followed. Shortly they came to a large shaded glade surrounded by the vastest of trees atop and within which were countless wooden elvish dwellings.

She turned to them. 'Behold,' she gestured. 'And welcome to the city of Ideldanglydilldohwillnothavahapydeyfahlatidosowat, or Danglydill-Doh as it is called in the common tongue.'

Oohs and aahs resounded amongst the quest members as they surveyed the legendary city of Danglydill-Doh. Post oohing they were greeted by a male of the species, golden of hair and eye and comely of character. He was Sitar's mate and went by the name of Istar.

'Come, good friends,' he said after hands were shaken and introductions were done. 'We have been expecting you and have prepared a banquet of quite stupendous proportions in your honour.'

He led them out of the central glade to an adjoining dell filled with trestles and foods, chairs and bunting, ale and elves, and the scene smacked of such beauty and munificence as to bring tears to the eyes of mere mortals.

There was much clapping and huzzahs as the team were shown to their seats at the head of the gathering in between Sitar and Istar. And Istar did command and the feast was begun.

Food was eaten in abundance and drink was imbibed in copious quantities and dancing was done and singing was sung and fun was had by all.

Afterwards Istar and Sitar explained why they had climatically commanded the quest to their land.

Chapter 18

At first the doomed detachment had taken turns holding back the enemy on the stairway at the entrance to the turret, two on two off, but slowly, as their numbers got whittled down it was left to the captain and two other survivors to battle constantly and without rest.

And then the captain and one other.

And then the captain - alone.

He was exhausted. Tired beyond all caring and belief. The only thing that kept him going was training and the stubborn refusal to fall to an enemy that was not worthy of him.

Finally, coming up the stairs three at a time, a huge man, moustached, armoured in black, carrying a short, wide-bladed stabbing spear and a small round shield with a heavy brass boss on the front. He came up alone, shouldering the smaller lesser men aside in his eagerness to get to the captain.

At last, a worthy opponent. One would never be able to say that it was a fight of legends. The combatants didn't rage back and forth hurling insults and clashing like titans roaring in bloodlust and anger.

What did happen was the huge man in black broached the turret entrance and ran full tilt into the smaller, severely wounded captain. The captain staggered back swinging his chipped and blunted sword overhand and lopping an ear off the howling spear carrier whilst screaming. 'What took you so long? I nearly died of boredom waiting for someone who could fight.'

And the man had at him, and Bravad r Us, the king's captain, parrying in clumsy exhaustion, drained from lack of sleep, loss of blood and constant pain, fell back. And the man in black ran him through, and picked him up and threw him off the tower to come crashing down onto the flagstones far below.

And that was the end of that.

It had been a long night. Beyond long. The sun had risen on a slumberless party of questers and still they were not completely up to speed with the elvish narrative that had been put forward.

'Right,' said Plob. 'Let's see if I've got this right. You, as in the Elves, are losing time. Yeah?' Istar shook his fair-haired locks in denial. 'I'm sorry,' apologised Plob. 'Run this scenario by us again. Please.'

'Dear Plob,' started the golden elf. 'As we have explained, time cannot be lost. It exists in an exterritorial fashion, flowing from one place to another outside of all rules but never getting lost. It can only be used. One uses time and we, the Elves, are using up extra increments of our time on an alternative existence, a hereto unrecognised branch of the future that may be. Unfortunately time is not ours to give away like a pair of stockings on a birthday, it is a precious commodity that can only be lent, never given. So - we are lending time.'

'OK,' ventured Plob. 'I think I'm getting it. You are lending time?' Istar nodded in agreement. 'Thus, if I'm getting this right, someone must be borrowing this time.' The bullion-hued elf showed the affirmative with a nod of his perfectly contoured head. 'Fine,' continued Plob. 'So - who is borrowing this time? Is it us?'

Istar voiced his denial. 'No, my dear friends. It is not you. It is, as I have alleged numerous times before on this good night,' continued the noble Elf with Herculean patience, 'the captain of the guard of King Mange the partially inept. He is living on our time or, to put it bluntly, the captain of the guards is living on borrowed time, time borrowed from us and, like all debts, this will have to be paid back.'

Smegly leant forward in his chair, his now almost ever-present cigar smoking in his hand. 'This is the same captain of the guards that you and your Elvish folk have claimed to be essential to the continuation of our world as we know it?' he asked.

'The self same one,' agreed Istar. 'Our auguries have shown - no captain, no time. As in the cessation of time. Nada, nil, null, nought, kaput, void, the end, zero, cipher, non-existent, devoid, non-subsistent, napoo, phut, gone to leave not a rack behind. The last in the series of etcetera - finished. If he dies we all go down the long drop of fate. The End.'

Smegly stared. 'This is not good,' he said, showing his hereto undisclosed gift for complete understatement.

'You mentioned debt and repayment thereof,' said Horgy, his accountant's mindset coming to the fore. 'Tell us a little regarding this liability and all and any reimbursement structures, strictures and codicils contained therein. Pray, good elf, be brief but to the point as I have a feeling that our group is destined to be very tightly bound to this debt-ridden contract of which we now speak.'

'Your perception is correct,' confirmed Istar. 'As you are now the official questarians all debts, dues, duties, obligations and responsibilities both moral and physical fall to the said official quest party, or parties, and such obligations and or debts must be met on demand by any other involved party, or parties, upon presentation of proof of debt, either natural or supernatural, by…er…by…well, I've forgotten the rest but I'm sure that you get the picture.'

'Yes,' confirmed Smegly. 'I'm sure that we do. However, there does seem to remain the small matter of proof...'

'Either natural or supernatural,' interjected Istar.

'Whatever,' said Smegly. 'Proof seems to be both necessary and demanded.'

'Of course,' agreed Istar as he stood up. 'Please, allow me to lead the way,' he gestured to the group who stood and followed.

The elf led the way to a low-roofed, leaf-covered wooden structure. They trooped inside to see what appeared to be a small rock pool that was fed by four tiny trickling springs of water, two of them clear, crystal and sparkling, one as black as bereavement and the fourth deep red and viscous as cold blood.

Istar told them to gather round the pool and look into the surface. 'This is an elven scrying pool,' he told them. 'It can be used to look into the past, to show us the present and, if the scryer is particularly gifted, to obtain brief glimpses of the future.' Istar linked his fingers together and stretched his arms above his head, cracking his knuckles as he did so. 'First, a brief synopsis of what our courageous captain has been up to thus far.'

The elf leaned forward and spread his hands out over the pool. The ripples on the surface shimmered and then slowly smoothed out until, finally, the pool grew cloudy and then hardened over like a sheet of frosted glass. 'Behold,' intoned Istar as he stood back from the scrying pool.

In short sharp précised form the group was treated to a thorough account of the captain's recent past from the moment that the first boulder hit the castle door to the final moment that the captain's body hit the castle floor. Then the pool went misty once more.

'Well I'd say we're in some serious strife here,' said Cabbie. 'Our erstwhile captain has ceased to be. Dead, deceased, departed, no more, he has been claimed by the old floorer and has paid that debt which cancels all others. So -

we are definitely up the proverbial whiffy creek without a punting pole.'

Istar shook his curly gilded locks in denial. 'Watch - then comment further.'

The ensemble of night had clothed the castle and the captain lay in the shadow of the turret from which he had been cast down and left for dead. He carefully raised his head to check if he was being observed and, noting to the contrary, he started leopard crawling towards a sally port at the side of the keep.

As he crawled he pondered as to what weird phenomenon was occurring. To be sure he had been stabbed before and lived to recount the saga; he was, after all, a professional soldier. He had also fallen from high places to low places, such as the time he had fallen from a tree whilst attempting to sight out the lay of the land before a minor scuffle with a renegade band of outlaws two years before. Apart from a dislocated shoulder he suffered no permanent injury so he knew that it was possible to be stabbed and descend vertically for some distance and not be everlastingly damaged.

But to be run through with a broad-bladed stabbing spear and cast from a hundred-foot-high tower onto a paving of cobbles and then still to live and, by the feel of it, to already be almost completely healed, apart from the pain caused by breathing, thinking, crawling and generally staying conscious and alert, well it was uncanny in the extreme.

He reached the sally port and, after a short rest, slipped through into the all encompassing murk.

'Well I'll be buggered,' cursed Cabbie. 'So that's what you mean about living on borrowed time. Amazing.'

'Dat is one seriously death defying, valiant sum-bitch,' rumbled Biggest. 'Who needs an army when you've got that stern faced mutha on your side. Whooee – don't that dude know the meaning of defeat?' He flicked his paw in the air and snapped his fingers together. 'Respect.'

The group nodded in agreement, all except for Dreenee who was sitting there with such a look of yearning juvenile infatuation and hero worship that she brought all conversation to a halt. Noticing the combined gazes of the group she quickly snapped out of her lovelorn reverie. 'What?' she snapped.

Cabbie chuckled. 'Dreenee's got a boyfriend, nyah nyah nyah nyah nayh. Dreenee loves the captain, ya yonkee ya ya.'

'Oh shut it, Cabbie,' responded the sensual one. 'That's enough. I'm serious. Unless of course you want some extensive facial restructuring.' Then she blushed, stood up and stormed out of the scrying room mumbling under her breath, ruining her dramatic exit only slightly by tripping over a small hummock of grass in the entrance and sprawling face first onto the spongy emerald turf.

'All right,' conceded Smegly. 'We accept the scrying vision as proof and we acknowledge the fact that we will have to pay for the time that the elves are lending to Bravad r Us, the king's captain. Now, how do we settle up this debt? I'm sure we're not talking money here.'

Istar nodded his agreement. 'That assumption is correct, oh Master Mage. We have but one request - that you take my son,' he glanced at Sitar. 'Our son - with you on your quest.'

'No problem,' assured Cabbie. 'Tell him to pack his bags and let's get going. After a petite fried morning repast and some small quantity of breakfast ale.'

Smegly agreed. 'That all seems to be in order. By what name does your son go and where is he that we may speak to him ere we depart together.'

'Ah, well, you see, um…' mumbled Istar. 'Therein lies the problem.'

'What?' interjected Cabbie. 'You don't know his name? Well that's ridiculous, I mean, after all, he is your son.'

'His name is Legles,' whispered Sitar.

'There you go,' said Cabbie. 'That wasn't so difficult, was it? All it took was a little…Half a mo. You do know his name but you don't know where he is.'

'We think that we do,' declared Sitar. 'You may, or may not know, but, in times most recent, we elves have strayed less and less from our inner land of sanctuary. We have become less knowledgeable of the customs and vagaries of the outside world and, as a result, our magiks and powers in the outside have waned to the point that all that we can control is the weather in a small area around the entrance to our world.

Some two weeks ago our son, Legles, decided that he wanted to take a look at the world outside for himself. Both Istar and I forbade him to do so as he has yet to come into adulthood, a mere seventy-five years of age, still a full twenty-five years before his centenarian celebration. But, like so many children, he disobeyed. He left and did not return.

After some while we sent scouts out to spy the land and two days ago we discovered that an elf of Legles' description has been captured by a band of dwarven outlaws and wastrels that terrorise much of the surrounding area and has been taken to their base camp which lies in the ruined city of Sloth.

We beseech thee, oh noble questarians, to please rescue our boy, take him on your journey and, after, return him safely to us.'

'Let's have us some eats first,' said Biggest. 'Then we'll be on our way to get your boy for you, my pretty elvin one.

We was going dat direction any hows so it be no problemo for us.'

Sitar nodded her thanks, Istar beckoned to the servants and ordered them to prepare a morning fast breaking collation of monumental proportions and, in deference to Cabbie, he asked for extra helpings of double deep fried everything and a side order of breaded lard.

Whilst the other members of the quest were partaking of the massive pile of elven-supplied victuals, Plob, his mind obviously on other things, approached Istar who sat at the head of the table alongside Master Smegly. 'I wonder, good elf, if I may ask of you a favour?' The assistant enquired of the golden one.

Istar nodded. 'Speak your request, my child and, if it be in my power, it shall be granted.'

'I wish permission to view the scrying pool. To look at an incident some twelve years past at the time of the last of the winter Hobgoblin wars.'

'Ah. I see. Your grandfather.' Istar's face grew sorrowful and, as he looked at Plob, his intelligent elvin eyes radiated both grief and concern. 'You ask the one thing that I cannot give. Slight though the request might seem I am bound by both custom and promise not to reveal to you that very thing that you so desperately want to see.'

Plob, who in his own mind had obviously built up hope that this would help to finally clear his beloved grandfather's name, was devastated and, unbidden, tears of disappointment glistened in his eyes. As he turned his face away in embarrassment at his overt show of emotion Sitar rose from her chair, walked over to him and clasped him in her arms, her luscious hair enveloping him like a silken cloak of deepest dark.

'Grieve not, dear Plob,' she whispered to him. 'Your grandfather was a great and heroic mage. His sacrifice to the people of Maudlin was of a magnitude far in excess of what they know. Although we are bound by custom not to help you we may tell you this – continue to strenuously increase your knowledge of the arts and, in time, the answer to what you seek will come and then, and only then, might you be of sufficient maturity to deal with what you find. I perceive the apparent harshness of this answer but I assure you that it is for the best of all concerned.' She gave Plob, who was now feeling much calmed by her physical presence, one last squeeze and then stood back. 'Well, good questarians,' she addressed all. 'The day marches on and so should you. So without further ado we must bid you *adieu.*' (Be doo be doo be doo).

As the questarians dwindled into the distance, flanked by two fleet-footed elvin guides who were leading them back to the door, Istar turned to his dark and glorious wife, his face betraying an expression of world-weariness. 'Should we not have told him the full story, my light?' he questioned.

Sitar shook her head. 'He is not yet ready for it. There is still a great deal that he must, indeed has to, learn and he is much driven by this pursuit for the truth regarding his grandfather. If he learns too much too soon it may take the edge off his desire for knowledge and, right now, the quest needs all the advantages that it can acquire.'

'But still…' interjected Istar.

'What would you tell him, husband mine? That his grandfather is alive?'

Istar shrugged. 'We know that to be a sham,' he answered.

'Then what?' continued Sitar. 'That his grandfather is dead and gone?'

Istar shook his head. 'We know that also to be an utterance of falsehood.' Sitar stared at her golden-headed husband for a long while, eyes slightly downcast, head to one side. Eventually Istar let out a rueful sigh. 'As always, dear heart, thou art correct. Any attempt to elucidate would only cause the waters to muddy even more. But at times the understanding that we have to bear brings down the grey dawn of sadness on my immortal elven soul.'

Sitar smiled knowingly and held out her hand. 'Come, my liege, let us to the central dell for to gather the other elves together and make song and merriment, for that always lifts the pall of melancholy from thy soul.'

Istar's face lit up immediately. 'Oh great. A sing-song. Can we do that one about the big fat ogre who becomes a stripper?'

'If you like,' agreed his wife, laughing.

'Oh goody.'

They had been riding for some hours now since they had left the inner sanctum of the elves and Cabbie was holding his chest and grimacing from a severe attack of post oily fry up heartburn. As they had not slept the night before. Master Smegly had suggested that they stop at the first good site that they came across so they could set up camp in a leisurely fashion and get some badly needed shut eye.

As usual Biggest had been running on ahead, scouting out the land and using the opportunity to cull the odd head of game that he ventured upon. Cabbie slowed the cab down as he saw Biggest come jogging around the corner, a brace of small antelope hanging from a rope on his belt.

'There's a good spot up ahead,' Biggest told them. 'Nice shady glade with running water and all. A real den from home. Follow me.'

True to his word Biggest had found a perfect overnight spot. They built a goodly sized fire, knocked up a rotisserie and spitted the dressed deer over the flames.

Plob and Smegly hauled out the travelling oven and proceeded to forge a fresh batch of spells. After some discussion regarding energy content and vectors of force, Plob added a few twists to the forgings that they both agreed should get an added degree of impact on the 'earth, attack' spells without effecting their controllability too badly.

Smegly could see that Plob's skills were jumping ahead in leaps and bounds and it wouldn't be long, months as opposed to years, when Plob would be entitled to forever remove the codicil of Assistant from his name and title. After quenching the spells they transferred them to Plob's magic miniaturising carry pouch and packed away the equipment.

Cabbie and Biggest were seated next to the campfire discussing the merits of ale verses Blutop.

'I see where you're coming from,' said Cabbie as he pulled on one of the many bottles of ale that they had been gifted upon leaving the land of the elves. 'It's definitely more transportable than ale and, as you've already shown, it's great for starting fires, cleaning wounds and polishing the riding tackle. But it's not ale is it?'

'Also good for preserving fruit and getting blood stains out of battle gear,' added Biggest.

'Yeah, but it's just not ale is it?' argued Cabbie.

'Can't refute dat,' agreed Biggest. 'Cause it's definitely not of the malt liquor flavoured with hops variety of alcoholic beverage. I reckon if it was ale it would be called ale, or sumptin similar. But as it's most decidedly named Blutop I suspect it's an intoxicating potion of the cane spirit variety called Blutop.' Biggest took a swig from his never ending magical flask of cane spirit.

'But it's still not ale,' insisted Cabbie.

'It's not ale, applejack, armagnac, arrack, beer, bitters, brandy, cognac, gin, kirshwasser, lager, metheglin, pilsner, pombe, porter, pulque, rum, schnapps, sloe gin, stout, vodka or whisky either.'

'Or absinthe or anisette,' added Plob.

'Benedictine, cassis, chartreuse or crème de mocha,' contributed Horgy.

'Curacao, kummel and maraschino,' supplemented Dreenee.

'Or Pernod,' finished Smegly.

Cabbie looked dubious. 'Or ale.'

Biggest playfully chucked a burning log at him forcing Cabbie to duck smartly out of the way. 'Shut it regarding dis alcoholic argument you unbeliever. Dere ain't no way youse is gonna convince me dat ale is better than Blutop. As far as I is concerned Blutop is like water – cause without it all life would cease to exist. So dat would make the adoration of dat particular cane spirit pretty much a religion to me and if there's one thing dat I'm not gonna take from you, Cabbie, is religious persecution. Cease your discriminatory harassment of me or suffer the consequences as I get seriously pious on your ass.'

'Well – if you put it like that,' Cabbie shrugged and held out his now empty ale bottle. 'Give us a top up of your fine faith inducing fire water my sanctimonious friend and let us drink together in celebration of your new found self-righteousness.'

Biggest laughed loudly and dispensed generous quantities of the good liquor freely to both Cabbie and the rest of team.

Chapter 19

Captain Bravad had painfully crawled away into the forest adjacent to the castle, found himself a safe dry spot and passed out into an exhausted dreamless slumber which lasted until midmorning of the next day. He awoke feeling surprisingly revived and healthy considering that he had pretty much opened death's door the day before and taken a good long look inside the grim reaper's inner sanctum. Curiouser and curiouser, he thought as he sat quietly and planned his next move.

Meanwhile, Bil was having the time of his life.

King. King, King. Kingkingkingkingking. King Bil. The man. The head cheese. The honcho. Potentate. Caesar, Kaiser, tsar and pharaoh. The fuehrer of all he surveyed. Man he felt good. Oh well, he thought, time to get amongst my subjects and spread a bit of patricianly largess.

Bil walked into the keep, bedspread billowing in the breeze, wrench swinging by his side. Regal, aloof, functionally disintegrated and crazier than a bedbug. There was a roar of welcome from his large group of cohorts as he entered the central courtyard and waved his wrench aloft in greeting.

On the right hand side of the courtyard, tied to a sticking post was ex-king Mange (and his alleged twin brother Mucous). By order of King Bil he had already suffered numerous abuses including whipping, stoning and general bashing and, although he didn't know it, his suffering was about to be brought to an abrupt end.

Bil strode (yes - strode) across to the bound ex-king and quoth (quothing as well, two higher mortal words in as many sentences. Definitely growing in power and stature this Bil de Plummer lad).

'Behold - the pretender to the throne. The thief of King Bil's birthright. The defiler of the rightful regent's throne. The despoiler. The violator. Begone, foul burglar of de Plummer's pukka place.'

And with that the wrench rose high yet again and, with one dementedly driven blow, the mangy one was dispatched. And now Bil could proudly add regicide (mangycide?) to his growing list of reprehensible acts.

And Evil stood up out of his armchair and cheered hugely, for he was greatly impressed as not a lot had been going right lately, what with that goody-goody group of questarians poncing about doing beneficial deeds the day long. Well – can't win them all, still the regicide scene was damn good and deserved some solid applause, so Evil got to clapping big time.

'We're in luck,' said Terry as he covered the mouthpiece of the telephone (or 'dog-and-bone' as he would have said). 'They only started manufacturing this particular style of wrench in red four months ago.'

Hugo gave him a thumbs up. 'Splendid, old chap. So how many have they sold?'

Terry relayed the question down the line and then looked up, his face a newly turned greyish and pasty look. 'Three thousand two hundred and ninety-seven. As of yesterday.'

'That many?'

'Yes – that many.'

'Oh. Shit.'

Captain Bravad had got lost once or twice as he searched through the maze of streets in the less fashionable areas of the city of Maudlin but had, eventually, found the address he was wanting.

Number twenty-seven Thundermug street, the Shuddery, Maudlin. The address of the erstwhile Mr Tipstaff, Sergeant-at-arms.

The self-same Mr Tipstaff who had just recovered from two badly banged-up knees, courtesy of our Dreenee during the abortive arrest attempt at 'The complete and utter…,' and had thus been bedridden during the last few weeks' events, totally and blissfully unaware of the living hell that his captain and the doomed detachment had been through.

After the captain had filled him in Mr Tipstaff was, to say the least, outraged, enraged and just plain raged. Something, he said, had to be done about this 'orrible little Bil person.

So Bravad r Us, Captain-of-the-guard and Mr Tipstaff, Sergeant-at-arms, poured themselves some ale, sat down in front the fire and put together a plan to exact a little well-needed retribution from the newly declared malevolent simpleton of a Regent and his scummy band of cohorts.

Chapter 20

The last two days of travel had been less than pleasant. The cab had cracked a wheel on a small round boulder that had lain in the track concealed by a tuft of grass and it had taken five hours of back wrenching work to splint it and rebind the metal rim back on.

Then Kashfloh had thrown a shoe and damaged his hoof so, after Cabbie had re-shod him, he was declared unfit to pull the cab for awhile and, since then, their one-horsepower progress had been slow to very slow.

The constant light but bleak rainfall hadn't helped and, to make matters worse, the surrounding terrain had gone progressively from relatively uninviting to downright forbidding and hostile.

Blasted trees and burnt-out areas of stumpy blackened bushes. Cracked and broken rocks were strewn with haphazard hand across the harsh landscape. And the water, what they could find of it, was brackish, rank and bitter.

(All in all the sort of environment one arrives at after parting with your non-refundable, up-front payment for a four-day mid-week budget break in the new tourist Mecca of some torn-to-shreds middle African country that has been specialising in a post apocalyptic form of slash and burn agriculture and has now decided that tourism is the new strip-mining and have mocked up a bunch of re-tinted Hollywood style holiday brochures and dumped them on the unsuspecting UK package tour market).

But this wasn't the worst part of the day. No, the worst of it was that they had now been set upon by a group of dwarvish bandits.

The would-be miniature Dick Turpins were, however, making a considerable meal of things. Right from the outset the ambush and supposedly resultant cab-jacking had gone wretchedly awry, starting from the traditional kick off line of 'stand-and-deliver- your-money-or-your-life' which was conveyed by the gang leader and resident crossbow owner, an impressively bearded dwarf who answered to the name of Budget.

Budget (Budgie to his friends) had delivered the line with all of the usual aplomb and savoir faire demanded of such a classic verbal offering but, unfortunately, instead of the usual 'please don't shoot, grovel, grovel' reaction that was expected he found himself upside down, disarmed and having his small bony head being bashed against a tree by a large Trogre who had reacted with a speed and violence of such instantaneous that, even in his present compromising position, Budget was hugely impressed.

Cabbie had urged his horse forward and deliberately ridden down the small group of four vertically challenged backup archers that were arrayed behind their glorious leader, standing slightly out of his seat and applying his horse whip generously to any exposed necks and faces that came into view.

Plob whipped out his pouch, extracted an 'earth, attack' spell and launched an ice storm at two other mini-miscreants that were hiding in the boughs of a large twisted tree that leaned partly over the track. They fell to the ground squealing in pain at the mass of hail-induced bruises that now covered their bodies.

Master Smegly tidied the whole shambles up by weaving a collection of 'air, restraint' spells and using them to drag the company of dwarves, including Biggest's new bashy toy, into a ragged tightly bound cluster consisting of shovel-shaped beards, funny pointed hats and spectacularly bushy eyebrows.

'Well, my bantam-sized band of bandits,' said Master Smegly. 'Things didn't pan out quite as expected, did they?'

Budgie shook his luxuriously be-whiskered head. 'Not quite, good sir. Not quite.'

Smegly lit up another of his supply of richly fragrant cigars. 'If I release you now I expect you to refrain from doing a runner and, I warn you, if any one of you tries to leg it I guarantee that the first attempted leggee will have all of his appendages forcibly removed by Biggest here who is not only faster off the mark than all of you but also happens to have made an enjoyable hobby out of said limb removals.'

Biggest bowed in acknowledgment and did a little limb removal miming just to push the point home. The clump of dwarves made sounds of general agreement and Master Smegly removed the spellbound bonds.

Budget stood up first, faced the group and bowed deeply. 'If I may introduce myself and my team of merry dwarves, I am Budget and these other fellows are,' he pointed as he talked, 'Bag, Barrel, Basin, Basket, Bin and Box.' As he mentioned each dwarf they stepped forward, doffed their hats and bowed to the team. 'And we are the bandit group known as - "The seven dwarves".'

'Who and the seven dwarves?' questioned Horgy.

'I'm sorry?' said Budget, raising an eyebrow.

'You have to be "Someone - and the seven dwarves".'

'Why?' enquired the hirsute one.

'Dunno,' admitted Horgy. 'It just seems that "The seven dwarves" is missing something. It's too short.'

Budget went snow-white with rage. 'Are you calling us short?' he roared. 'You speciest bastard. I'll have you know…'

'Gentlemen,' interrupted Smegly. 'Enough. No harm meant and I'm sure none taken. Horgy, apologise and, Budget, calm down. Hang it, I've never come across someone with such a short fuse.' The collective of dwarves turned as one to glare at Smegly. 'Sorry,' he corrected himself smartly. 'I meant not long - someone with such a "not long" fuse.'

Horgy mumbled an apology along the lines of 'Frrimph…flub…didn't mean rmmph…whatever,' and Budget, under strict instructions to do so, calmed down.

After the conflict, Master Smegly introduced the quest members to the dwarves and explained the importance and direction of the quest.

Suitably impressed 'The seven dwarves' had led the team to their hideout, a nice dry cave set far back from the trail and supplied by its own spring of fresh running water, an absolute luxury in this area. They pooled their supplies, started a fire and began cooking up a decent sized meal of boiled ham, onion and potatoes. Meanwhile Biggest was distributing industrial quantities of Blutop to the happy-go-lucky dwarves who were blithely quaffing brimful mugs of it in the fashion that only dwarves can do and still stay standing.

After their meal everyone sat around the fire and Smegly gave the dwarves the, much interrupted by other team members, full tale of the quest thus far. There was much oohing and aahing and other sundry vocalisations of an impressed and surprised manner. That is until they got to the part where Istar and Sitar had expressed their theory of their wayward son's alleged abduction and extraction to the ruined city of Sloth by a viscous gang of dwarven thugs and ne'er do wells.

'Hah,' interjected Budget.

'Hah, what?' asked Smegly.

'Hah what no ways,' said Budget and there was much nodding, hah hahring and miscellaneous snorts of disbelief amongst the other homogenisation of dwarves.

'Hah what no ways what?' persisted Smegly.

'Hah what no ways what who would dare,' replied Budget. 'To attempt to take Legles prisoner whilst he's under arms would be liken unto throwing down the gauntlet to a standing militia of a battalion of dyed-in-the-wool, death-before-dishonour, fight to the last man standing, bowmen of the gods. In short - the boy is a one-elf orgy of destruction. A warmonger of note. Mars, Ares, Odin and Bellona all rolled into one longbow-toting-keen-shooting-holier-than-thou-and-deadlier-than-the-plague son of a bitch. Frankly we're all terrified of him. Everyone is, well anyone who isn't brain dead.' Budget shuddered and took a long, long pull of Blutop. The rest of the dwarves huddled a little closer together.

'Are you's saying dat this boy is bad?' asked Biggest.

There was a collective shaking of Lilliputian craniums. 'Not bad,' said Budget. 'Good. Excruciatingly, brain numbingly good. The most moral, straight talking, upright and honest being one could ever hope not to meet. A veritable saint.'

Smegly afforded Budget a puzzled glance. 'There seems to be some sort of essential dichotomy here. Bad - problem. Good - no problem. Why's everyone scared of this chap?'

A nervous dwarvish scuffling ensued. 'What if you're not good?' Asked Budget.

'Well, what?' voiced Cabbie.

'If you're not good - then he becomes bad,' whispered Budget as he looked shiftily around the cave.

Cabbie shook his head. 'Sorry?'

Budget nodded. 'Yes.'

'Yes?'

'Sorry' repeated Budget. 'You will be.'

'Will be what.'

'Sorry,' repeated Budget vehemently. 'If you're bad you will be sorry.' He wrung his hands. 'Let me explain - Legles considers himself to be the elfsonification of virtue, rectitude, purity and chastity. He oozes prudence, undebauchedness and nobility. He sees himself as the font from which all honour springs. Unfortunately what he doesn't have is patience, tolerance or sympathy. In fact he is an impatient, intolerant, unsympathetic, deaf-minded pain in the proverbial. In short,' he glanced quickly at the other dwarves, 'if you'll pardon the expression, good colleagues, he is an immature spoilt brat with trumped-up ideas of his own nobility and the skill of Mars to back it up, although…' Budget shrugged, 'he can be as charming as all hell if he's getting his own way. Or so I've heard.'

'So what do you think has happened to him then?' asked Smegly.

The dwarves held a short (sorry - 'not long') confab amidst much nodding of heads, gesticulating of arms and voicing of opinions. After they had seemed to reach some sort of agreement in principal as to what had happened Budget turned back to Smegly.

'There's only one other gang of any substance this side of Sloth, a group of dwarves that call themselves 'the band of twenty,' and we're all in agreement that, if they inadvertently attempted to rob Legles, the ones left alive will have gladly handed over the burdens of leadership to him. By now they're probably all back at their hideout in Sloth.'

'No problem,' said Smegly. 'You can show us the way there, we'll pick him up and be on our way.'

The dwarves laughed as if Master Smegly was making a joke. 'You can't just pick up Legles if he doesn't want to go. He'll say that you've been not good, and then he'll get bad and that will be the end of it.'

Smegly chuckled. 'Gentledwarves, a word of advice. Remember - no matter how bad someone is there is always, always someone worse - and usually that someone is me.'

The quest members, remembering the casual way that the master had ordered Biggest to break Munge the farmer's fingers, nodded briskly in agreement. 'Right, folks,' continued Smegly. 'Let's all get some shut-eye; we've got a long day ahead of us tomorrow.'

Chapter 21

It wasn't much of a plan. Captain Bravad would have been the first one to admit to that, but given the limited recourses they had available to them, it was the best that they could come up with.

He and Mr. Tipstaff had decided to round up every retired soldier, hopefully still alive, although this was not essential, that had ever served in the king's army. The old, the lame, the sick and the crippled. If they could bear arms then by gods they would be volunteering, once again, for active duty. And then the captain would cry havoc and let slip…the venerable, grey-crowned, hoary old dogs of war.

And soon Captain Bravad, Mr Tipstaff and the Methuselaen mongrels of menace would be marching to meet Bil's malcontent minions of madness and massacre most of them. (Maybe?)

Biggest and the seven dwarves jogged on ahead of the cab. At first Budget had deliberately tried to lead them in a contrary direction to the ruined city of Sloth, his nervous disposition regarding Legles still apparently outweighing his fear of Smegly. The master had remedied this by taking Budget aside and looking deeply into his eyes. After only a sho…'not-long' pause, he was on his knees begging Smegly to stop looking at him. Subsequently he had informed the dwarven collection that, although Legles was definitely one scary elf, Master Smegly was worse. Far, far, far worse. The rest of the day's travel was at pace, in the correct direction and devoid of incident.

That night they stopped to pitch camp in a relatively rock-free area next to the twisting track that they had been following. There was no fresh water, little usable firewood and they had come across no edible game during the day's journeying. They dined on cheese and hard bread, drank a goodly share of Blutop and curled up into their respective sleeping rugs after Plob had erected an 'earth, protect, shield wall' around the camp just in case.

The next morning they awoke with the sun, finished off the last of the rations and hit the road. Around midday they came across a small herd of scrawny unpleasant looking rock-goats. The dwarves insisted that they were good eating so Biggest threw a handful of boulders at the herd, stunning three of them which allowed the dwarves to swarm over and use their battleaxes to administer the necessary coup de grace. They skinned and dressed the animals where they had fallen, threw them onto the back of the cab and continued on their trek on the track to the tumbledown town of Sloth.

That night they were all in higher spirits as they sat around the campfire drinking Blutop and watching the rock-goats sizzle and splutter over the flames. Dreenee and two of the dwarves, Bin and Box, had conducted a successful search for wild potatoes and these sat in a pot of boiling salted water that had been placed on three rocks at the side of the fire.

Smegly re-lit his cigar and stared into the flames, lost in contemplation. 'The quest begins to gain weight,' he said thoughtfully.

Dreenee immediately twisted around in an attempt to look at her perfect posterior. 'What do you mean? Do my buttocks look large in this?' she asked with a look of consternation as she adjusted her skirt.

'Yeah,' grinned Cabbie, 'you'd better take it off.' There was a chorus of hur hur hurs from the dwarven collective followed quickly by a refrain of sorrys when Dreenee turned and impaled them all to the floor with one of her sharpest glares.

'I don't mean weight as in mass,' explained Smegly. 'I mean weight as in momentum. Things are beginning to gain inertia and we must take care lest we lose control. We started as two, are now thirteen and I am without doubt that our numbers will soon begin to swell beyond all of our imaginings. All the signs begin to portend in that direction.'

'I see,' said Horgy. 'What signs?'

'Oh, you know,' answered Master Smegly. 'Signs. All signs in general. A bit of this, a little of that. There's just a feeling of overall portentousness in the air. You get my meaning?'

Horgy looked doubtful. 'I don't know. It's a bit like saying "they say".'

'Who says?' asked Cabbie.

'They,' repeated Horgy. 'They say that drinking too much is bad for you. You know? Them.'

'Oh,' acknowledged Cabbie. 'My Aunty Flem and Uncle Norgam. I didn't know that you knew them.'

Horgy shook his head. 'I don't.'

Well how come you know what they say about drink?'

'It's just an expression. You must have heard it before. Here's another example - They say that sex rots your brain, or they say that…'

'Yes, yes,' interrupted Cabbie. 'I've known them for years and years. I know all those things. Personally I think that Aunty Flem and Uncle Norgam are a brace of fruitcakes, I don't care what they say. I've never cared what they say, and I don't care how famous they are. Up theirs anyway.' Cabbie got up and walked off in a huff mumbling they say, they say, under his breath.

'What did I say?' asked Horgy in a baffled voice.

'Don't worry about Cabbie,' Smegly reassured him. 'He'll get over it.'

After a prolonged group effort at emptying Biggest's magic flask they all crawled into their sleeping rugs at a later than usual hour and, after a short while, a choir of snores and snorts sounded as the newly enlarged team let fall the shadow of their eyes.

The next morning there were more than a few Blutop-induced groans and head-clutchings as they struck camp and started the day's tramp towards the ruined city of Sloth. After a couple of hours both Biggest and the dwarves had run off the effects of the cane spirit and they decided to stop for a break to brew some tea and take a much-needed rest.

After the brief respite they were back on their feet again and continued their Slothward trot. In the late afternoon of that day they came across the first of the vestiges of the age-old ruined city. The sprawling collection of ancient broken-down buildings had existed in its wrecked state for as long as any remembered history. Stumps of once-proud structures and vast megaliths of rubble containing peculiar twisted dowels of steel and what appeared to be blocks of grey stone still showed evidence of some terrible orgy of destruction that had once been visited on the past thriving metropolis.

Plob, who had never been to Sloth before, was utterly overawed by the size of the area of devastation. 'How big is this place?' he asked the party in general.

'It carries on for days,' answered Budget. 'When you get closer to the centre, some of the buildings are still partially erect.'

There was a smattering of hur hur hurs from the other dwarves that was quickly silenced by a shut up from Dreenee.

'Some say it was some bizarre form of natural structure, like a mountain, volcano, something like that,' added Cabbie. 'Some of the erec…still standing buildings at the centre are simply too large to have been man-made. One can tell by the rubble that some were well over two hundred feet in height.'

'They're man-made,' assured Smegly. 'People lived in them, thousands upon thousands of families. Then there was a great war, a terrible conflict that grew and fed on itself until finally it claimed the lives of almost every living being in the land. Mankind almost destroyed itself - almost.' He shivered and pulled his cloak a little closer around him. 'Come, good people, let us start our search for a likely camp site. Tomorrow we will begin our investigation for Legles and his merry band of alleged captors.'

Captain Bravad was by nature both a patient and a stoical man but even his rock-solid endurance was starting to fray around the edges. The plan, although not perfect, definitely seemed workable. What the captain and Mr Tipstaff hadn't figured on was the fact that when a soldier retired he usually moved away from the big city, took his pension and purchased a small place on the coast, or in the mountains, or somewhere else. Anywhere else it seemed but where they were now needed.

They had visited over forty houses and had thus far managed to come up with a mere four volunteers. A selection of ex-soldiers ranging in age from merely ancient to positively gerontic. A collection of rusty, moth-eaten, mossbacked, fossilized old warriors.

And a dog. One of them had insisted on bringing his frosty furred, antiquated bloodhound who went by the name of Pups. Still - it could be worse, thought Bravad, but then, after a brief moment of contemplation, he decided that it couldn't. But, if you only have one plan, even if it's not a very good one and isn't working all that well, it's the only one you have so all you can do is stick to it. So stick to it the captain and the sergeant did.

By the evening of the third day they had no more addresses left to visit. Ninety-eight calls and a sum total of seven extremely venerable old dogfaces and one crusty old dog (with a face).

Berm 'brick wall' Odger, swordsman. Originally nicknamed after his massive masonry like build and prodigious strength.

Pactrus 'pace man' Petracis. Once a young man possessed of great speed and agility.

Dill 'the demon' Bacchus, renown as a berserker of note and a veteran of many a great battle.

Grunchy Fromson, Spectal Petreson, Wogler Manger, Partlee Nobee and Pups. All being in possession of various monikers such as Masher, Killer, Barbarian, Slasher, Dog (in the case of Mr Nobee) and Slobberer (in the case of Pups the dog).

There was no denying it. This was an old, old bunch of guys but, as the captain talked to them and explained fully what their mission would be, he began to see something. Although they were rusty they weren't worn out. Moth-eaten but not threadbare. Mossbacked perhaps, but then so are boulders. Fossilized, definitely, but aren't fossils merely old flesh become rocks? And that is what Captain Bravad had managed to collect – a bunch of stripped-down, no nonsense, hard as stone, old warriors.

He nodded to himself. They had set themselves a goal that was so impossible, so unfeasible and so obviously unattainable that maybe, just maybe, they had every chance of achieving it.

Chapter 22

Plob didn't like Sloth. It was sinister and eerie and seemed to begrudge the very presence of the living. As they searched through the broken remnants of a society long gone, looking for a trace of Legles and the band of twenty, he felt like a tomb raider or grave robber of some sort, disturbing the spirits of the dead.

'Over here,' called Box (or was it Bag, Barrel, Basin, Basket or Bin - whatever). 'A large group camped here not more than two nights ago.' He pointed at the blackened evidence of three fires and various small depressions in the earth where people had lain for the night.

'He's right,' confirmed Cabbie. 'Fifteen, maybe twenty bodies. Probably the band that we're looking for.'

'Right, troops,' said Smegly. 'Let's keep our wits about us. Eyes and ears open, there could be an element of danger about so stay vigilant.'

Biggest took up the trail and the rest, attentive and alert, followed him. Although the band that they were tracking weren't specifically trying to avoid detection it was difficult to keep on their route as it meandered through the ruins and the rubble.

Later that day they came across a second campsite. Some of the coals in the remains of the central fire were still warm and Biggest concluded that the band had slept there the night before and left that morning after what was probably a fairly late breakfast. Smegly told the group to continue the search with weapons drawn, or at least close at hand, just in case.

Throughout the day they slowly gained on the band and the tracks grew fresher. Moist torn blades of grass, small branches broken in passing and still weeping sap and overturned rocks that had revealed damp spots not yet dried by the sun all told their tale.

The team slowed to a wary walk checking and rechecking their surroundings as they moved forward. By the time that the evening started to encroach upon them they had still not caught up with the band but knew that they were getting very close.

They ate a cold meal as Smegly did not allow fires lest they attract attention and Plob cast an 'air, alarm' spell around the camp. They fell asleep easily, tired from the long tense day that had just passed.

King Bil was ensconced in his favourite room in the castle - the throne room. It was everything that he had ever imagined, rich red drapes covering the wall behind the large gold and black throne. Tapestries and carpets, paintings and vases, cushions and ornaments. And a marvellous silver tasselled rope that you could pull and ring a bell somewhere in the depths of the castle, and a servant would appear. And you could order them to do anything you wanted, or just shout at them and watch them grovel, or not. Because you were the king and the king does what the king wants - yes, sire.

Bil leant over, pulled the silver rope and waited, squirming in anticipation, pausing every now and then to gibber. And then howl like a loon.

It was good to see that Bil was still living up to all of our expectations.

To be fair it wasn't Plob's fault. As they woke the next morning he had stood up, yawned, stretched and released the 'air, alarm' spell as he did. It seemed that within the blink of an eye there was a crossbow toting, unknown dwarf standing next to, or above, every member of the team.

As they all attempted to take stock of their surprised situation a tall, green-garbed man with long curled locks of golden-red hair walked into their midst and bowed.

'Top of the morning, good gentlemen and exquisite lady,' he said in a voice that throbbed with such integrity and sincerity that his mere morning greeting made them all feel that they were worthy (worthy of what you ask – just worthy, generally inspiring a feeling of great worth). 'I must apologise for the less than welcoming sight that I have caused you to awaken upon but these are dangerous times and, as you have been following us for the last few days, I felt that a little caution would definitely become us all.' As he talked he walked over to Dreenee who was still seated on her blanket and offered his hand to her, helping her to rise. He gazed into her eyes and smiled. 'Ah, such perfection, my lady. Never before have I had the pleasure of coming face to face with a visage of such elegant loveliness. Your sublimity makes all around seem inelegant and homely. Surely what I see before me is God's handwriting.' Dreenee blushed as he leant forward and kissed her hand. He stood back and faced them all. 'Good people, pray let me introduce myself. I am the elf known as Legles, formally of the inner lands and now the leader, if you would, of this small group of dwarves that were previously the renowned "band of twenty" and are now, after a small misunderstanding with my own self, acknowledged as "the band of eighteen." Now, mayhap you could explain your presence in this sad city of Sloth.'

Master Smegly stepped forward and slightly inclined his head to Legles in greeting. 'First, my good elf, please kindly ask your men to safety-catch their weapons and put them aside. There is no need for such a show of force as we mean you and your companions no harm.'

As Smegly spoke Plob glanced around and noticed that Cabbie was nowhere to be seen. Biggest was still seated on the ground as was Horgy, Budget and the rest of the dwarves but no Cabbie.

'I apologise profusely, my excellent friend,' replied Legles with exquisite manners. 'However, I am sure you can see my problem. Until I know exactly who you are and what you are all doing here I dare not drop my guard even for a moment.'

'I'm afraid that I must insist,' insisted Smegly (insistently). 'You have my word that we will do you or your companions no injury.'

'Ah, herein lies the rub,' said Legles. 'For, in as long as I maintain our guard, I too can guarantee that no hurt comes to us.' The elf shrugged and smiled enchantingly. 'I am certain that you can appreciate my dilemma. So, perhaps, you shall do as you are told and tell me why you are here,' Legles finished off in a slightly harder tone than before.

Master Smegly addressed Legles in an irritated fashion. 'Luckily I can help your quandary,' he said sternly as he folded his arms across his chest. 'Cabbie,' he commanded and, as he did so, Legles' pointed green hat was plucked off his head and impaled to a stumpy twisted tree behind him. The split-second incident being accompanied by the fluted fluttering sound of the yard-long steel tipped arrow that had travelled through the air to accomplish the task. Cabbie stepped out from behind the large bush that had been concealing him, another arrow already notched in his yew bow.

Legles smiled at Cabbie. 'Good shot, sir,' he applauded.

'Maybe,' grunted Cabbie. 'But then maybe not - perhaps I meant to shoot you in the eye and I missed. Maybe it was a crap shot and the next one will be better.' Cabbie drew back on the bow. 'You think - huh?'

Legles' perfect poise shivered for a second and then the wagon loads of self-confidence came rushing back. 'Bravo, sir. Your point is well taken, never assume, yes very good. I'm afraid what we have now is a standoff. If you harm me you shall all come to grief and, conversely, if we hurt any of you I will meet with an unfortunate end. What do you suggest we do?'

Smegly drew a deep breath and asked Cabbie to put the bow down. Cabbie raised an eyebrow, shrugged in an it's-your-funeral-as-well kind of way, un-notched his arrow and lowered the longbow. Legles, looking slightly, ever so slightly, abashed ordered his band to stand down. A collective loud sigh of relief sounded from all concerned excepting Smegly who was lighting up a cigar, Legles who was far too cool to do something as crass as exhale noisily, and Cabbie who had already gone over to check the horses.

That night they all stayed at the main camp of the band of eighteen and were served up a large simple meal that, although not a feast, was wholesome and plentiful. As per usual Blutop was dispensed via Biggest's never emptying flask and soon the atmosphere became rowdier and more convivial. Master Smegly explained the quest to all and, afterward, told Legles why they had had to track him down. The quest was right up Legles' avenue.

'This is a noble venture,' he exclaimed. 'To do good deeds and show people the true meaning of honour and nobility. To be a part of a group entrusted with the fate of the world, truly good folk this is the endeavour for which my life has always been destined for.' He grasped Smegly by the shoulder. 'Thank you, kind master, you and yours have given me a meaning and dedication for which to strive. I shall not disappoint you.' And with that Legles retired to bed so as to better conserve his energy for the deed-filled days ahead.

'Intense sort of bugger, isn't he?' commented Cabbie as Legles left.

'And touchy too no doubt,' added Smegly. 'This sort often are. Try not to antagonise him too much, Cabbie, we need him on our side. That goes for all of you, watch the way you talk to Legles, he'll take offence at the drop of a hat and that'll just provide us with more hassles than we all need right now.'

The team grunted in acceptance except for Cabbie who shook his head. 'He's trying to be so noble he makes my teeth itch,' he muttered under his breath. 'But I'll try to moderate my inveterate humour and razor-sharp wit for a while. Only for a while though,' he finished.

The next morning Smegly took Cabbie, Budget, Legles, Biggest and Plob aside for what he ominously referred to as a council of war. 'As our team has grown larger I feel that we need to formalise some sort of structure or things may start to unravel on us,' he told them. 'We need a chain of command, nothing rigid or militaristic but definitely an agreed set of responsibilities for each of us here.'

This was greeted with a general nodding of agreement from the five questers gathered round him. 'Right,' Smegly continued. 'Firstly, Legles, I'd like you in charge of the dwarves with Budget here as your second in command, both of you must feel free to call on Biggest whenever you need help. Plob here will from now on carry the bulk of the responsibility for all magiks that we need performed, I will be in overall charge and Cabbie, as usual, will take care of any transportation that we need except, and this is important, gentlemen, when any military strategy or decision is needed Cabbie will have the full and final say on it. Any questions?'

'Yes,' said Cabbie. 'How do I resign?'

'You can't,' answered Smegly. 'It's a lifetime position. Live with it.'

'Perhaps we should reconsider,' interjected Legles. 'It does seem passing strange to me to appoint a cab driver as absolute military strategist. Perhaps I could offer my services.'

'No,' barked Master Smegly. 'I mean no offence but we need a professional.'

Legles was gobsmacked. 'You would put the worth of a coachman, a mere carter and gharry-wallah above mine. I find that I must strenuously object to this course of action and, perhaps, even reconsider my gracious involvement in this enterprise.' Legles folded his arms and glared haughtily at Smegly.

'Give it a rest, elf-man,' rumbled Biggest. 'Get off your elevated-equine and come to live down here with us normal earth grubbin' folks. Use your eyeballs, boy, the master don't mean you no abuse, don't you see who Cabbie actually is or is you too involved with your own exaltedness to notice anything but your sorry-assed self?'

Legles, who was now literally spluttering with rage, looked intently at Cabbie. Cabbie stared back at him mockingly with a slight grin on his unshaven face. Legles contemplated Cabbie puzzledly and then abruptly, as if Cabbie had taken a mask off to reveal his actual face, the farthing dropped.

'Tarlek,' he whispered his face glowing like a child who has just had irrefutable proof that, not only does Father Christmas exist, good old Pere Noel is actually his uncle who has just promised him an unlimited supply of pressies for the rest of his life. 'You're my hero,' Legles gushed in a very un-elf like fashion. 'I've studied all of your escapades - you're the reason that I left the inner lands. I wanted to be just like you.'

'What?' responded Cabbie 'A mere carter and a gharry-wallah?'

Legles hung his head in overt shame. 'I apologise, it was an unworthy comment. I had no idea that it was you.'

'It would have been unworthy even if it wasn't me,' responded Cabbie. 'But, in a way, you're right. That is what I am - a driver, a reinsman, a hackman if you would. I am no longer a knight and I except this duty ordered me with the disinclination and reluctance that I feel it deserves.'

'That's fine by me,' said Smegly. 'I didn't tell you to like it, I just told you to do it. Let's go, gentlemen - once again upward and onward.' Smegly rose and the rest of the group followed.

The questers packed up camp and started the first steps of their long route to Bil de Plummer and the capital city of Maudlin. Budget took point followed closely by the other twenty four pack carrying dwarves running three abreast and backed up with the cab containing Smegly, Dreenee, Plob, Cabbie and Legles. Biggest loped behind in the position of rearguard.

As they ran the dwarves started to sing.

'With a lop diddle diddle
and a lum tiddle too
we will run to the middle
of the...'

'Stop that!' shouted Cabbie. 'We'll have none of that. I'm serious, I can't stand it. I've never had singing on a quest before and I bloody well won't start now.'

'But it's traditional,' argued Legles. 'Elves and dwarves always sing when questing. It's a long-established time-honoured custom and, personally, I think that it should be allowed.'

'Listen,' said Cabbie. 'I get full and final say on all matters tactical and military – right?' Legles nodded in agreement. 'So,' continued Cabbie, 'I say that they can't sing. There, argument closed.'

Legles shook his head in disagreement. 'It's not a tactical issue this, it's a morale issue and, as the leader of the troops, I feel that it falls under my auspices and I say they can sing.'

Cabbie pointed his finger at Legles. 'Full and final say, Legles, full and bloody final. That's what I get and I deem that this singing issue is of tactical im-bloody-portance and it irritates the bezonkers out of me and we won't hear it anymore and that is that.'

'Yes but…' continued Legles.

'Do you want to walk?' interrupted Cabbie. ''Cause I'm also in charge of transport and I can feel a transportation crises looming so just shut it. There's a good fellow.' Cabbie turned to face the front and Legles, who could have run all day if it was required but really didn't feel like it, kept it shut.

They kept up a good pace throughout that day, stopping only briefly for lunch and setting up camp as the light was beginning to fade that evening. Their course was going to take them through the small town of Blange the next day, probably around the late afternoon sometime, so Master Smegly had called everyone together and was explaining the necessity for adhering a thin layer of civilization veneer to the dwarves who, due to their banditeering, had not been in urbane company for a while.

'So please remember,' repeated Smegly. 'Just because there are over thirty of us, and we are armed, we can't merely do anything that we feel like doing. Simply because we can do it doesn't automatically give us the right to do it so remember, don't do it.'

There was a general puzzlement amongst the dwarven ones who obviously thought that this was exactly the time to do whatever one felt like - when you were armed and dangerous and you could. It stood to reason that if you couldn't then you wouldn't and now they could but they weren't because Smegly said they couldn't and they thought that they should. They were all becoming very confused.

'Huh?' asked Budget.

'Just behave,' snapped Smegly.

A general nodding of heads and why-didn't-you-say-so-in-the-first-place type comments followed.

They entered the town late that afternoon and immediately looked for some sort of suitable accommodation for the new enlarged team. With access to funds obviously not posing any problem to Master Smegly, he sorted their dilemma out by the simple expediency of hiring the whole of the first decent, large enough inn that they came across. A three-storey, sprawling affair that went by the name of 'The Kneeling Nun.' Smegly settled the bill for all thirty-one of them up front, to the landlord's patent relief, and told everyone to see themselves to their rooms and meet in one hour's time in the central common room. Before they went up to their chambers Plob enquired whether the innkeeper could organise a bath to be brought up to his room.

'Sorry, good sir,' answered the keep. 'But we are not of the custom of bathing in our rooms in this part of the country. We do, however, have a central bathing establishment right next door and, as a paying guest in this inn, you have full access to all the facilities.'

Plob thanked him and, after he had taken his luggage to his room he went next door, accompanied by Cabbie and Legles to treat himself to a good hot soak. They entered the room through an inter-leading door between the inn and the baths and, after being issued with a large rough towel each, were shown to the changing rooms.

They stripped their travel-stained clothes off and went through the curtain into the bathing area carrying their towels over their shoulders whilst Cabbie endeavoured to start a serious debate as to whether one should drink one's best wine first in order to savour fully all of its nuances or whether one should quench one's thirst with cheaper ale or wine before to prevent one quaffing down the good stuff with little or no thought or, if one did quench one's thirst with cheap wine then would one become so drunk as to not notice that the good wine was good and, this is the important part he insisted, if this was the case why bother with good wine in the first place as it cost three times more, gets you no drunker than the cheap stuff and, contrary to what anyone says, gives you the same grade of hangover if you overindulge.

This theory of Cabbie's, which probably bears more thinking about, was completely lost on both Plob and Legles who were gaping dumbstruck at the contents of the baths (actually the contents of the baths was water – as it is oft wont to be) but it is what was in the water that was disturbing our teenager and our decent and dignified noble elf.

The steaming water contained people, naked people, naked people of the very obviously female persuasion. The only reason that Plob knew that he had not inadvertently wandered into the wrong baths was that the water contained people of the male gender as well.

Cabbie carried on his postulation regarding the merits of alcoholic quantity over quality, dropped his towel next to the pool and climbed in. Plob, whose reflexes had been momentarily slowed down by the fact that he was surrounded by almost half a hundred wet naked soapy girls, abruptly realised that he was inadvertently, and quite outstandingly, showing his appreciation of the various female forms arrayed around him and so he hurriedly dropped his towel and followed Cabbie into the dubious cover of the steaming water.

Legles, however, had gone an odd purple colour and seemed to be staring at the mixed sex bathers in something akin to complete and utter outrage.

'This is an affront to decent behaviour,' he spluttered as he suddenly remembered his nakedness and whipped his towel off his shoulder to cover himself. 'It is wicked to be expected to bathe in a place where women shamelessly parade themselves around in font of you like brazen hussies. The whole enterprise smacks of ethical turpitude.'

'There he goes again,' laughed Cabbie. 'Off on his elevated steed once more. Charging recklessly to the aid of the morally corrupt and mentally indecent. Come off it, Legles, it's the custom here, you know, like that stupid singing that you and the dwarves like. Sorry, I should have warned you but I was totally caught up in my cheap booze hypothesis. Now give it a break and jump in.'

Legles was unrepentant in his moral indignation and stormed out of the baths, his face almost matching the colour of his gilded flaming-red locks. Plob and Cabbie sat soaking in the hot water while Cabbie rambled on about the merit of cigars versus pipes and whether smoking tobacco and drinking excessively was good for you or bad for you because his grandfather on his mother's side had drunkenly chain smoked cigars since he was about twenty years of age continuing for every day of his ninety-seven-year-old life. Whereas the grandfather on his father's side didn't smoke or drink and had died at the sadly youthful age of thirty-two. Admittedly, Cabbie continued, he died in a fire that had been caused by Cabbie's other grandfather leaving a lighted cigar on the table after he had drunkenly made his way home after being invited over for supper one evening – so – maybe that didn't count. Still, it was worth thinking about, said Cabbie as he mused to himself whether he should take up smoking to ensure a long and healthy life.

Unfortunately Plob heard none, or at least very little, of this as he was having a hard time (as it were) concentrating on anything and was desperately trying to think how he would get out of the pool and to the cover of his towel which he had dropped a couple of yards from the poolside whilst hiding his testosterone-driven body's massively (well, medium to large at least) embarrassing betrayal.

He'd tried closing his eyes to block out the view but had discovered that the only thing more erotic than seeing two score and ten nude damsels lounging about in the hot water was not seeing them. The fact that they were there, all around you, floating by whilst you had your eyes closed, instantly conjured up such vivid sybaritic images of wanton carnality that Plob was now unable even to blink lest he, quite literally, went off the deep end. And then, to make matters just a little bit worse and a lot more embarrassing, Dreenee entered the baths. Fortunately she was fully clothed or Plob's, by now fast becoming, tenuous grip on reality may have slipped completely when faced with the body that had helped to launch a thousand ardent imaginings.

'Master Smegly says to hurry up,' she told them as she walked up to the edge of the steaming pool of water.

Plob nodded. 'OK, we'll be along soon.'

Dreenee shook her head. 'Now. He said I must wait and make sure that you get out.'

Cabbie climbed nonchalantly out of the water, strolled across, picked up his towel and started drying himself vigorously.

Dreenee picked up Plob's towel and stood, grinning, a few yards away from the pool. 'Come on. Let's go.'

Basically Plob had three options. One, slip under the water, fill his lungs with the warm slightly soapy liquid and slip mercifully into unconsciousness – workable but rather drastic. Two, clamber out of the pool and immediately assume the crawling hunchback mode of perambulation in order to get to the towel – might work but in all likelihood Dreenee would just keep walking backwards until he was forced to stand upright (in all senses of the word). Plob decided on a third option. He screwed his courage to the sticking post, climbed out of the pool and walked with head, and other certain tumescent extremities, proudly held high for all to see. This unexpected act of bravado totally threw Dreenee who squeaked, blushed, dropped the towel and ran from the room all in one continuous movement.

Cabbie doubled over with laughter and slapped Plob on the back. 'Good one, boy – good one,' he chortled wickedly as they strolled forth from the baths.

Plob rose late the next morning with his ears still ringing slightly from the noise and joviality of the night before. As he splashed his face with cold water from the stone bowl in his room, snatches of the eve's revelry played through his mind like a half-remembered dream.

The evening had started fairly quietly as they all sat down to a meal of roasted ox, potatoes and whole cinnamon baked butternut squashes chased down with a large amount of locally brewed mead, a drink that Plob had never had before and, after an exploratory sip, decided it was very tasty but too sweet to be that alcoholic. How wrong he was, how very, very wrong. Incorrect, mistaken, erroneous, fallacious and monstrously wide off the mark.

Over the meal, Master Smegly had informed them all of the slightly adjusted route that they would be taking to the capital city, a journey that would now take them directly through the uncharted bad-lands of the desolate eastern marshes of Grumble, home to goblins, cacodemons, ghouls, flibbertigibbets and perhaps even worse. They were to do this for two reasons he told them, firstly to hone their team to an edge before the probable big showdown with Bil and his minions and, secondly, there was no better place for them to come across opportunities to do good. In fact, he argued, in a place of such all-consuming evil, pretty much anything that they did, within reason, would probably be construed as good.

This revelation was greeted with trepidation by all except Legles who was so pleased with this forthcoming opportunity to display his overabundance of nobleness and gallantry that he wanted to skip the meal and set off straight away in order to 'do good on the minions of evil in all their guises.' Cabbie told him to stow it and the elf had replied that 'evil never stops to eat or sleep so neither should we,' Cabbie then told him to bollocks off so Legles sulked quietly for the rest of the evening, or perhaps he went up to his room, Plob couldn't remember.

The master then advised all to enjoy themselves to the full that night as they would have little chance, or reason, for frivolity over the next few days. The meal came and went and the mead came and stayed, and brought some friends along for good measure.

Cabbie had temporarily lifted his ban on singing and, after the meal, the dwarves started singing in earnest as if to make up for the time on the road that had remained song-free. At first the songs were mainly variations on Cabbie's 'drink, drink, drink' song but, as the candle burnt lower, the lyrics turned more to the 'I am so lonely and many miles from home and I hope that I don't die in a foreign land' type song that makes local bystanders grit their teeth and mutter things like 'why don't you just bloody well go home then, really, if you like coal mining so much and the beer is always so good and the girls are so pretty then go back why don't you' under their breath. (I don't know if you've noticed but why is it that whenever you find people singing about going home or the old country, the ones that seem the most heartbroken about living away from home were normally the first buggers to leave the place or, in some cases, weren't even actually born there. In fact it seems that the crappier the country that they have left then the more vocal the singer and the more rose-tinted the spectacles that their old toilet of a nation is viewed through. Although this is not completely true - I've never actually heard anyone singing about going back to Mauritania but then maybe that's just because nobody's had the sense to leave there in the first place, or maybe nobody really lives there.)

After the gloomy songs had finally drawn to a close, Biggest went around the table topping up everyone's glasses of mead with Blutop and thereby turning a surprisingly potent drink into a sweet pleasant tasting potion with a ferociously high alcoholic content that had an effect something akin to general anaesthetic. After a glass or two of this demon drink, Biggest announced that he was going for a short walk outside to clear his head and Plob had called out for him to wait as he wanted to come as well. Plob had a moment of overwhelming drunken panic as he had tried to stand and realised that, although he was sober from the waist up, all of his lower extremities were gloriously and catatonically intoxicated. Eventually he levered himself out of his chair and staggered zombie-like through the door and outside.

The cold night air hadn't sobered Plob up but it did seem to evenly distribute the numbness throughout his whole system which meant that he could now walk, after a fashion. He then stepped into a knee-deep hole with both legs and simply stood there as he desperately tried to figure out what to do next. At this point Cabbie arrived, took one look at Plob and burst into tears of maudlin sorrow. Biggest hadwent gone over to consol Cabbie and enquire as to what was wrong. 'His legs' Cabbie told him, 'look,' he had said, pointing at Plob's knees. 'He's lost the lower half of his legs. That's so sad. It's a tragedy. And he was my friend and now he's got no legs. Boo Hoo.'

Plob, momentarily forgetting that he was standing in a hole, had felt his eyes well up with tears at the sheer injustice of it all. A young lad like him, struck down, or at least foreshortened, in his prime. Being forced to wander the streets, begging for alms whilst being pushed about in a wheelbarrow. He was completely legless (in more ways than one).

Unable to take it any more, Biggest had leant over and dragged Plob from the small pothole, dropped him unceremoniously on the turf and declared him cured. 'Praise be to the Gods!' Cabbie yelled as he witnessed Plob's miraculous recovery and, overcome with emotion, promptly passed out and crashed to the ground.

Things got really weird after that. More mead. More Blutop. Someone's beard catching alight. Falling off a chair whilst singing. Mead. Undying love. Best of friends. Blutop. I love the whole world. Mead and Blutop and…

Strangely though, the next day Plob didn't have a hangover. But then that's how it goes, he reckoned. No good basing any sort of Blutop-and-mead-doesn't-give-you-a-hangover theory on his lack of any sort of alcohol-induced malady because, ten to one, the next cup of mead that he drank would probably give him a rip snorting headache of the homicidal death-before-sobriety category. He threw his clothes into his small trunk and carried it downstairs to the cab, after which he went to the common room where everyone was seated for breakfast.

'Morning, big-boy,' greeted Dreenee. Cabbie raised an eyebrow at her and she blushed and gazed at her plate. Plob grunted a non-committal morn greeting to all, sat down and spooned some sausages and grated fried potato off one of the laden platters that were scattered around the large central table. The conversation around the trestle was desultory at best as they all applied themselves to their breakfast fare.

Eventually Budget piped up. 'You know the dwarf that was dancing on the table last night? The one that had taken his breeches off and wrapped them around his head. The one that set fire to Basin's beard and then got sick all over the table and then cried and cried inconsolably for the rest of the evening even though everyone kept telling him to shut up. You know that dwarf?' There was a general smattering of agreements. 'That was me, wasn't it?' asked Budget embarrassedly. Another general vocalisation of agreements ensued followed by a chorus of dwarven hur hur hurs. Budget buried his face in his hands and sat very, very still in the hope that it would make his hangover disappear.

After breakfast Master Smegly went into town with Cabbie, his cab and ten or so of the dwarves to purchase sufficient supplies to carry them through the bleak time that they had ahead of them. Legles took his longbow and arrows to a field out back of the inn to put in a little target practice, Dreenee repaired to her room and Plob and Horgy sat with Biggest who had taken a small fold-up wooden board game from his trunk and brought it downstairs to show the two of them.

When unfolded, the board consisted of twelve hollowed-out depressions which contained twenty or so different coloured stones. The way that Biggest explained the game it, seemed to consist of basically moving the stones around until Biggest lost his temper and threw the board across the room. Plob figured that there was probably more to it but, try as he might, he couldn't figure it out. They played a couple of rounds to pass the time but, after Biggest had thrown the board against the wall a few times they lost two of the stones and Biggest claimed that the game couldn't be played properly without the correct quantity of stones so he packed it up and went off to his room.

Plob and Horgy, with nothing else to do, walked outside to the back field to see Legles practice his archery. After watching the elven toxophilite for a short while Plob was suitably impressed. Legles was shooting at a coin-sized knot in an oak tree perhaps some one hundred and twenty paces distant and the arrows that he had already unleashed were grouped so tightly that they had split each other as they drove into the target area. But it was not the accuracy that amazed Plob, although he had never seen its like, it was the speed at which the elf loosed his quarrels that truly inspired awe. He could fire his shafts , one after the other, so swiftly as to create the illusion that he was connected to the tree by one long continuous shank of wood. Plob shuddered as he envisioned the effect that that onslaught of sharpened steel and hardened wood might achieve on a closely packed mass of troops. The dwarves were right - Legles was definitely a one-elf army.

Smegly arrived back a little later that day and, after they had repacked the supplies and distributed them, by weight, evenly about the team, the dwarves shouldered their packs and the team set off towards the malevolent swamps of Grumble.

Chapter 23

'It's no bloody use,' Hugo slammed the phone down onto its cradle and sprawled back in his chair. 'We will never be able to track down where every one of those stupid tooly-wrenchy things went. Plumbers, DIY enthusiasts, merchants. We've got to try something else – anything else.'

Terry, who had already decided that they were wasting their time with their current wrench line of enquiry but wasn't about to admit it, stared at Hugo with a scornful and disbelieving look. 'Oh typical. Mister upper-class wants to give up. No bloody staying power, that's the problem with you public school nanny-boys. A few phone calls and…'

'Nancy.'

Terry stopped in mid blether. 'What?'

'It's Nancy-boy. Nancy-boy, not nanny-boy, you imitation working-class, middle-class pillock. Nancy-bloody-bleeding-boy. And if you don't shut up with the class-orientated taunts I shall come over there and give you a damn good thrashing, you horrid, beastly…beastly…state school wallah.'

'Oh you'll give me a thrashing, will you?'

'Yes.'

'Oh yes?'

'Oh yes.'

The two detectives stared belligerently at each other for a while each waiting for the other to carry the situation to the next step. Eventually Terry, realising that he was actually being a bit of a prat, gave a sigh. 'Should we go get a cup a tea and a sticky bun then? My treat.'

Hugo gave the offer a little thought and then agreed. 'OK.'

'Sorry,' added Terry.

'Me too,' admitted Hugo as they left the building together.

The next to useless guards at the castle gate didn't even bother to check the contents of the donkey drawn cart that was driven rumbling across the moat bridge by two old men. But, even if they had had the wherewithal to do their guardly duties they would not have stopped the cart as it carried nothing that they wouldn't have welcomed into the castle, in fact, quite to the contrary.

The tough looking old men directed the hugely laden cart to the centre of the courtyard, clambered stiffly off the wagon, and pulled back the tarp to reveal…every gourmand's dream, enough for a gathering of gourmands, a group, a pack. A veritable herd. The cart was fully, and more than fully loaded, with hams, cheeses, breads, pickles, sweetmeats and, most importantly of all, gallons and gallons of Wegren Bumbles special medicinal cherry brandy. A drink so potent, so heady and intoxicating as to make Biggest's Blutop and mead blend as milk of a mother to her child. In short - brain fryingly, eyeball boilingly, synapse short circuitly, mind blowingly strong.

Berm 'Brick-wall' Odger and Pactrus 'Pace man' Petracis calmly walked out of the castle, pointed out the overflowing wagon to the guards, and left. On their way back to their prescribed meeting point they met up with Spectal Petreson, Wogler Manger, Partlee Nobee and Pups, all of whom had been spreading the news to the two hundred and fifty or so of Bil's minions camped outside the castle walls that the king had supplied free grub and booze to his worthy followers and they were to report immediately to the keep in order to partake in the revelry. Before the group of iron-hard ancients had got more than fifty yards the initial shouts of rowdy appreciation could already be heard stridently ringing out from the castle.

The old warriors walked into the makeshift camp in the woods that they had constructed but a few days previously and made their way straight to the captain's bivouac.

'First stage successfully completed, sir,' bawled out Brick-wall as he came to a halt in front of Bravad.

'Excellent, men,' complimented the captain. 'Well done. Now all take a well-deserved rest for a couple of hours and then, when those foul denizens are all thoroughly hiccius-doccius and all sheets to the wind, we will proceed with the plan part two.'

The men all retired to their respective bivouacs and within moments, in the manner that only the experienced soldier can, they were asleep.

Chapter 24

The rotten-egg smell of the swamps drifted around indolently in the sluggish bog breeze that seemed to be there merely to transport the putrid miasma from one olfactory organ to the next. Initially Dreenee had bound a perfumed handkerchief about her nose but, after endless masked-bandit type jokes from Cabbie, had decided that the smell was preferable to the driver's eternal maddening attempts at humour.

They had entered the swamps the day before and had yet to see any living thing besides the dense clouds of water midges and the nocturnal swarms of mosquitoes that seemed to be as big as wine bottles. The dwarves who had been in swamps before, although not in the badlands, had built big fires at night and then had stacked piles of the leafy green branches of the horsepiss bush, aptly named after the smell it emitted whilst being burnt, on top of the flames. The smoke and the odour were atrocious but at least it did keep the man-eating vampyre mozzies at bay. Plob was convinced that if any of them did get bitten they would wake up in the morning looking like a bloodless human-shaped prune.

They stopped in the early afternoon and snatched a quick lunch of cheese and ham which Plob had to force down as the constant stench of the marsh gas seemed to permeate the taste of all of the foodstuffs and leave one with a slightly bitter taste in the back of the throat.

Later that afternoon they saw a few smudges of smoke off in the distance and so, that night when they pitched camp, not only did Smegly request an 'air, alarm' spell from Plob but also insisted that they draw up a roster to keep a physical watch with at least three bodies on each shift.

Fortunately the night passed without incident and the next morning, as they struck camp, Plob began to postulate that there were no inhabitants of Grumble at all apart from the palpable constant stench and the teeming quantities of predatory insects. He didn't know it but, that very evening, he was to be proved conclusively and terrifyingly wrong.

Raven-black, sombrous and besmirched. The fuliginous avatar of Evil perched on his throne of birch and leather and stared into the fresh new blood that filled his bone-wrought scrying vessel. He had seen all and was impressed. As far as being evil goes he was definitely the number one diabolist, but then he was none other than 'Typhon the Dark' servant of 'the Father of all lies' and he had been perfecting and honing his odiousness over many centuries and even had the evil cackle down pat. Not that simple to get right the old evil cackle, it can so easily come across like a bit-part actor in a second-rate play, hackneyed and overdone. Not so with Typhon. When the dark one did the cackle you could feel it, fear coursed through your body and overrode all your senses, stomachs cramped, sweat glands overproduced and saliva glands shut down completely.

When it came to bad then Typhon the dark was the real deal. But this Bil de Plummer wasn't all bad (or good) either. He showed real promise, mused Typhon. A new kid on the block, but look at the death and destruction he had already caused. Definitely one to keep an eye on. In fact, thought Typhon, one might even go as far as to lend old Bil a bit of a hand, perhaps get rid of these tiresome bloody questarians who were undeniably putting a spoke in the wagon wheel of evil and who had conveniently placed themselves smack bang in the middle of Typhon's very own realm, the swamps of Grumble.

Decision made, the dark one picked up the bone vessel, drank the gory contents therein in one long gooey protein-imbibing gulp and howled for his werewolf at arms.

The captain and his grizzly detachment jogged creakily through the night towards the castle of King Bil, their various paraphernalia of war bouncing and jangling on their backs and belts. Apart from the usual axes, swords, longbows and daggers of their chosen profession, each of the men carried also a length of pitch-soaked hempen rope and two extra quivers of arrows. As they approached the castle it was apparent that hardly any of Bil's twisted followers were still in their encampment outside of the keep and, as they jogged through the all but empty campground Mr Tipstaff took Spectal Petreson and Wogler Manger and broke away from the group to do a quick search of the area in order to flush out any bad hats that might still be malingering.

As it happens they found only a couple of camp followers, one with a child in tow, whom they told to vacate the area as there would be no chance of any future business due to the fact that their clientele was about to drop off rather seriously, owing to a sudden outbreak of being dead.

After the area had been thoroughly scoured, the detachment deposited the bulk of the weapons into a vacated tent and, carrying only their pitch-soaked ropes and a selection of daggers for just in case, made their way stealthily down to the moat and slid into the water.

They swam slowly through the midnight wet until they were under the bridge and then , carefully, extracted the ropes from their canvas waterproof bags and each man selected a pylon around which he tightly wound his rope. The captain, who had a longer one (hur hur hur) than the others, linked his hemp from one pitch-roped wooden pile to the other, effectively joining them all together. Satisfied with their work, they swam from under the wooden bridge, clambered out of the dark water and made their dripping way back to the tent, being guarded by Pups that held their weapons.

After they had suited up again, Mr Tipstaff took a small tinderbox out of the waxed pouch on his belt and, on the second attempt, put light to a yard-long fire arrow that the captain was holding. As the arrow burst into flame the captain notched it, drew back, took careful aim and loosed it at the bridge.

The arrow flew true to form and thudded into one of the pitch-wrapped wooden pylons. Nothing seemed to happen for what seemed like hours but in realty was seconds and then, the pile broke into a smoky orange flame.

The fire spread quickly, via the connecting rope that the captain had strung up, from one pylon to the next and, within minutes, the entire bridge had become a fiery midnight conflagration. The drunken revellers in the castle were by now so far in their cups that they didn't, not a one of them, notice a thing.

After perhaps ten more minutes the bridge collapsed, unhurriedly and with great aplomb, into the moat. Bil and his minions were now rather effectively sealed up in the king's own castle. The detachment quickly split up, bows at the ready and extra quivers at hand, to cover the sally ports and any other possible points of exit for, as the captain had told them, none of the followers of the insane one must leave the castle alive.

Wraiths. Doppelgangers. Co-walkers. Call them what you may (no - actually don't call them 'what-you-may' because that sounds really stupid. Call them wraiths, doppelgangers or co-walkers then, if you have to, and you do because that's what they're actually called). A person's double usually only seen just prior to or just after their death. Creepy as all hell. And there were hundreds of them. Dead counterfeits of every member of the team. Crowds of cadaverous Cabbies. Droves of dead Dreenees. Lashings of lifeless Legles' and species of Stygian Smeglys. Misty, ethereal and, above all, dead, and in various stages of advanced decay.

Typhon the dark had instructed Lycan, his werewolfian sergeant at arms to gather all but the most pathetic of spectres to him and, with more than a little help from his pandemonic master, the King of Evil, he had made them flesh and then transformed all into the ranks of rotting wraiths that stood arrayed before him. With the promise of everlasting life if they succeeded in their ghoulish endeavour he cried havoc and let slip the demonic doubles of war.

Bil was well pleased. It's not every king that gets cartloads of epicurean goodies from secret admirers. Oh yes, he was a good king. Strict but fair. And obviously well loved by the general populous judging from the size of the gift. He was a little worried though as, although gifts were good, they could perhaps be hinting at the fact that he was perhaps being a smidgeon to not strict enough. Spare the rod and spoil the child. No, Bil would not want to be thought of as a pushover, a dupe, a mooch, a gull, a sap, an easy mark. No, this simply wouldn't do. How dare they. Him, King Bil, a pigeon. A sitting duck. He would show them. Never again would the populous of this execrable little town take him for a patsy or a Simple Simon.

The king started gnawing on his already bleeding and pre-gnawed knuckles, eyes flicking around the room in a little paranoid ocular jig. They were all out to get him. But he knew. And they didn't know that he knew. And he wouldn't let on to them that he knew that they didn't know that he knew. And what made it really funny, what made Bil cackle out loud (unfortunately it did come across like a bit-part actor in a second-rate play, hackneyed and overdone, but then

Bil had only been at this evil thing lark for an infinitesimally small amount of time when compared to Typhon the Dark so he could probably be indulged the odd bit of hammy overacting). Anyway - what made it really hilarious was the fact that they didn't know that…they knew that he…they hadn't…They were out to get him. All of them. Out - To - Get - Him. Blood from the gnawed knuckle leaked out of the side of King Bil's mouth and dripped unheeded onto the knee of his blue boiler suit forming a dark star-shaped stain, and Bil continued his insane musings and started to plan his revenge on them. All of them.

They came at them from out of the dark, slobbering and suppurating and screeching out their deep hatred of the dead for the living. And Plob was terrified. Proper short of breath, whimpering quietly and coldly sweating and horrified fear.

There is something hugely unmanning about fighting against a rotting dead replica of yourself and, to make matters infinitely worse, the doppelgangers were almost impossible to kill. If you hacked off a leg they continued crawling after you. Lop off a head and the decaying body would carry on stumbling around groping for a victim. Luckily they appeared to be incapable of coherent thought and it had not occurred to them to all attack at once. If they did it would be a bloodbath of titanic proportions.

At first Plob had surrounded the team with an 'earth, protect, shield wall' spell but, as they all sat and waited behind the protective magical veil, more and more of the obscenely rotting wraiths had arrived so, eventually, Master Smegly had told them all to prepare for battle, asked Plob to drop the wall, and they launched themselves at them. Plob was unable to use any of his attack spells as the combatants were too intermingled and he was afraid of damaging his quest companions.

Legles had given up using his bow and reverted to his broadsword after he had shot one wraith, a doppelganger of Cabbie's, so full of arrows that it looked like a quiver and still it had continued lurching towards him.

The dwarves, with their widebladed battleaxes were achieving the most success. Although they couldn't kill the already dead they were reducing them to small enough pieces to ignore or at least easily kick away if they got too close. Cabbie was also achieving a modicum of triumph as he hacked and slashed away at a group of his own doppelgangers. Slashing off arms and legs and shouting things like 'so that's what I'd look like if I lost weight' and 'oh look. I'm completely legless.'

But, try as they might, they were losing. Even Cabbie's irritating witticisms had dried up and they were being forced closer and closer together as they continued fighting, now almost back to back.

Master Smegly stood unarmed in the centre of the circle of questarians attempting various different air spells to repel the packs of lunging ghouls and, as Plob stepped forward to decapitate yet another putrescent parody of himself, the master cast an 'air, freeze' spell at the stumbling doppelganger. The wraith froze instantly and Plob's massive overhand strike landed milliseconds after, smashing into the decaying co-walker's head and shattering the deep frozen denizen of darkness into a thousand harmless little crystals.

'Yes!' Smegly pumped his fist into the air and did a little victory dance. 'Come on, Plob,' he shouted. 'Quickly, to me. Let's "air, freeze" these bygone bastards into oblivion.'

Plob and Smegly stood back to back casting 'air, freeze' spells for all their worth and the dwarves leapt forward, ancient battle cries on their lips, to deliver blow upon savage blow to the iced-up evils.

It wasn't long before the area looked like an explosion in a meat packing plant. Tiny pieces of frozen and defrosting decomposing flesh covered the ground all about them but still the wraiths came.

The initial burst of passion with which Plob and Smegly had whipped their 'air, freeze' spells around was fast fading as their reserves of energy began to wane and some of the spells merely caused wafts of frigid ventilation as opposed to blasts of immobilising iciness.

Smegly suddenly started patting himself down as he frantically searched through his voluminous robes causing himself to look like an escapee from lice and flea farm as he dug and pulled at his clothing.

'Aha!' he shouted as he withdrew the small glittering cube-shaped spell enhancer that the masters master's bloody hell etc. had given him during the brief sojourn at his strange ever changing abode. Once again he cast another 'air, freeze' spell but this time, as the enchantment was released, he tossed the enhancement cube high into the air above the team…

…and once, in a time long ago when beasts ruled the earth and man was still but an aspiration to a small, thin-skinned, clawless beast that ran on two legs but did have opposable thumbs, there came a cold. Aloof and unfeelingly did it march across the land destroying all that did suffer its arctic embrace. And the wheel of time turned with aching slowness and the small upright mammal that had since become man did survive. And, yea, he had invented fire and all and he was well chuffed with himself for he did not know that it was all pretty much downhill from there…

…and the cold had come again.

Chapter 25

'And just who the hell is this?' enquired Terry in his usual touchy and obnoxious manner.

'It's the next obvious step in our ongoing, and thus far totally ineffectual, murder investigation,' Hugo enlightened his partner. 'May I introduce Madame Zelga – The psychic.'

'No you may bloody well not,' said Terry. 'We're police detectives, Hugo. Detectives. Not a couple of bleeding ghost-busters. Tell her to get on her bike. We've got work to do.' He picked up a sheaf of loose papers and frantically banged them on the desk in a futile attempt to look suitably harassed and busy.

'Come on, old chap. What have we got to lose? We've drawn a complete blank with the wrenchy thingy. All of the other leads have dried up. Frankly, as far as the case is concerned, we're on the proverbial bones of our bums.'

Terry desperately tried to think of a reason to say no but, as Hugo had said, they were at the end of the road, investigation wise. 'OK. Sit down, Mrs Zelga. Now what can we do to help you to help us?'

The first stages of the captain's plan had worked exceedingly well. He had his small team of warriors, the minions of Bil were well trapped inside the castle and his detachment was of sufficient size to keep them there but, and this was a big but, he was now at a stalemate.

He estimated that the enemy had water and provisions enough for eight to ten weeks, he doubted whether he could keep his detachment tied to sentry duty for that long as they were basically on duty twenty-four-seven due to their small number. The next part of his plan had involved him and Mr

Tipstaff getting together a civilian guard of some sort to help starve the minions out and, if sufficient could be convinced to join, perhaps even precipitate a full scale attack on the castle and drive Bil and his followers from this fair land.

However…a few hours later - Nil, naught, zero, cipher, not a one. The captain stood in the centre of the town square and shook his head sadly at the number of townsfolk that had volunteered for duty. He counted again just to make sure but no, he had definitely been given the old bum's rush. He turned on his heel and went back to his small but loyal band of hardened old veterans.

Chapter 26

The hard dull bitterness of the cold squeezed in on Plob like a large gelid playground bully, compressing his cranium and constricting his airways with its harsh brutal icy hands. It was worse for the dwarves who were, by their obvious physical nature, a lot closer to the ground and therefore had to constantly force their way through the thick snow and ice that covered the swamp for leagues in all directions.

The enhanced 'air, freeze' spell had unquestionably sorted the wraiths. One moment a squadron of putrid shrieking doppelgangers, the next a foot-thick carpet of decayed flesh icicles. (frozen at source for your pleasure and convenience).

The spell had ignited above them with a savage eruption of thaumatic energy, throwing them all to the ground as it screamed away from them in an ever-widening circle of furious glacial frigidity, both freezing and smashing the wraiths as it rampaged through them in an orgy of polar destruction.

It continued outward in its spherical path of frosty devastation, trees shattered as they froze in its path and feathered birds on the wing rapidly became frozen bird-shaped popsicles and plummeted frost-riven to the ground. Mercifully the smell and the swarms of biting insects were also frozen into oblivion so at least the team didn't have to worry about them. This was fortunate as they were busy using all of their available worry on keeping from becoming a new and amusing line in frozen novelty lawn ornaments.

They couldn't even start a fire as the cold had destroyed everything leaving them nothing to burn. Smegly advised that they proceed in the direction that they had last seen the smudges of smoke in the hope that there might be some form of civilization and perhaps a little shelter from the benumbing cold.

Before they had set out all of them had raided their luggage and put on every item of clothing that they possessed. Cabbie, for some reason known only to him, had put his overclothes on first and his underwear on last, making him look like some sort of woollen stuffed baby doll in nappies.

They trudged slowly through the icy wasteland, Biggest and Plob in front, in an attempt to flatten down the snow to make the going a little easier for the dwarves and Cabbie bringing up the rear with Dreenee, Legles and Smegly in the cab.

And they did not know where they were going so they continued their westward plodding, closer and closer to the centre of the domain of darkness, the deep dingy den of demons that was the dominion of Typhon.

To say that Typhon was having a wobbly would be an understatement of monumental proportions. (Turkeys have a mild dislike for Christmas. The Kennedys are a smidgeon gun-shy. The Pope has Catholic leanings. I'm sure that you get the picture).

Flecks of spittle flew zealously around the room. Breasts were beaten, hair was rent, spleen was vent, umbrage was taken and haemorrhages were had. In short, Typhon the Dark was considerably and enormously pissed off. His lycanthropic sergeant at arms cowered whimpering in the corner, bushy tail forced firmly between his legs and ears flat against his vulpine head.

'Hundreds,' screamed Typhon. 'All of them.' He raged back and forth across the stone floor of the dark dank cave of his lair and did a bit more rending and beating for good measure.

'Look,' he bawled at Lycan as he pointed at a sorry group of assorted beings that were gathered before them. 'The rubbish. That's all we've got left. Imps, pixies, sprites, gremlins and bad fairies. I've been reduced to being the leader of a band of children's bloody fairytales.

I am Typhon the Dark. Typhon the bloody Dark. Capital T, capital D. The living embodiment of evil. Beelzebub made flesh. Look at me, seven foot of solid muscle, skin thicker than a crocodile and huge, black leathery wings. It's pretty gods damn obvious that I'm not the bad bloody witch of the west. Give me demons, incubus, wraiths and banshees not Puck the naughty elf boy. This is all your fault you know, you stupid dog.' He kicked Lycan in the ribs.

'Yes, boss. Sorry, boss. It's just that…boss…when you told me to get all but the most pathetic…boss…I took you literally. Sorry, boss. Sorry.' Lycan tried, unsuccessfully, to squeeze into the corner even tighter and curled himself up bracing for the next kick. He wasn't disappointed. Typhon rained a series of blows down on the quivering werewolf.

'So now it's my fault, you moronic trembling mongrel. You dull brainless dim-witted son of a she-dog…'

'Bitch, boss,' whimpered Lycan.

Typhon's rave was stopped dead in its tracks. 'What?'

'A she-dog or wolf, boss. It's called a bitch. My mother was a bitch.'

'Well, she was,' shrieked Typhon.

'Yes, boss' replied Lycan nodding his head in agreement, tongue lolling out and ears flapping up and down as he did so.

'Bitch, bitch, bitch, bitch,' screamed Typhon as he strode outside into the cold spitefully batting a bad fairy out of the air as it flew past. Lycan padded along on silent paws behind him.

The Dark Lord stood outside in the frigid atmosphere for a while breathing deeply as he tried to settle his thoughts. He was in deep poo and that was a fact. Up the old faeces river sans an oar. The team of questarians were headed this way. They were a lot more powerful than he had expected and all that lay between himself and them was a gaggle of mischievous spirits that wouldn't know real evil if it walked up and pissed on their stupid little green pointy boots. It was obvious what had to be done, after all he was Typhon the Dark and did have some sort of reputation to uphold. The decision made he beckoned to Lycan who was hovering around at the entrance to the cave.

'Hey, pooch boy,' Typhon yelled.

'Yes, boss.'

'I've decided to promote you. You are now to be known as General Lycan, leader of the band of subnormals.'

'Ooh. Thanks, boss,' Lycan ran around in a tight circle chasing his tail in excitement and barking.

Typhon held his head in his hands and despaired for a while. 'Right. Now, General Lycan.'

'Yes, boss.' Pant, pant.

'Take your troops and form a defensive perimeter about the camp and, if that group of questers come close, defend this place with your lives.'

'Yes, sir boss.' Lycan loped enthusiastically back into the cavern and started rounding up his fairy-tale team.

Typhon the Dark strode away from the cave towards the paddocks, stopping momentarily at the grain house to pick up a flagon of one by triple distilled grain spirits for the use of, and then proceeding onwards to the small enclosed corral that contained the sable black demon steed Incitatus.

As he approached the darksome stallion it reared dramatically on its hind legs and lashed at the Arctic air, red-rimmed nostrils aflair, clouds of superheated carbon dioxide pluming into the bitter environment, its very stance shouting out to the watching world – I am cruel, callous, uncaring and unquenchable. I am the dark steed and I don't take no crap from anyone so just back off. Typhon strode up, cuffed Incitatus around its equine lug hole and vaulted onto its back.

'Move it, you scrawny rackabones,' he shouted as he dug his spurred heels in. 'Let's get going before those sanctimonious pecksniffing questarians get here. Upward and onwards, my steed of night. To Bil we go for it feels right.'

And with that the Prince of Darkness galloped cravenly (and a little Shakespeareanly) off into the sunset.

It is impossible for the truly insane, the genuinely rabidly monomaniacaly demented, to harbour feelings of doubt. This is why people like Mister Hitler (Remember him? Short guy, bad hair, really stupid moustache, thought that it would be a good idea to systematically kill every free thinking person, including his own guys, in the known world).

Thought that he could justly go about saying that the globe should be peopled only by blond-haired, six foot two inch, lantern-jawed, highly intelligent Aryan gods, whilst looking in the mirror every day and not once harbouring sufficient self-doubt to consider the fact that he was the antithesis of all that he found good and proper.

This sort of attitude takes vast amounts of world-class insanity. People like this would win the Insanity World Championships without even breaking a sweat. And I mean the proper world championship, not some American version where they only play amongst themselves. Where do those people get off, really? Baseball World Series. Guys, no-one else plays. Remember the rest of the world, including Asia, Africa, the Soviet Union and Europe? No? Well trust me you can't be the world champion if you don't play the rest of the world and just because we don't know how to play is no excuse. Anyway – I digress.

The point is that Bil was holed up in a castle with over three hundred rabid followers with limited food and water and he was convinced that things were all going his way. He was a little worried by the fact that his nice wooden bridge had been burned down but the shattered wheels of thought that powered his cognitive process were busy grinding out a reason for this that would dispel any fragment or feelings of doubt.

He was king. King indeed. He sighed happily to himself and leaned over to pull the silver tasselled bell cord in order to summon another servant to abuse in his own inimitable royal fashion.

'I'm not sure,' said Legles who was staring into the distance at the ragged line of defenders ranged around the ex-camp of Typhon the Dark. 'It looks like a mixture of sprites and fairies and some sort of dog or wolf perhaps. It's hard to tell at this distance.'

'What's the dog doing?' asked Dreenee.

Legles shielded his eyes from the glare and squinted once again. 'Seems to be running around in a circle chasing its own tail.'

Dreenee laughed. 'Oh how sweet. Come on, chaps. Lets all go and say hello.'

The team made their way down the hill towards the camp; Biggest, Legles and Plob taking point, Cabbie bringing up the rear and the score of dwarves walking four abreast in the middle, broad-bladed battleaxes on their shoulders.

All in all it seemed like a group well worth steering clear of, in fact, a good group to lie down and avoid completely. Lycan, with his innate sense of animal survival, sensed this whilst they were still over a hundred or so paces away and, as a result, his planned command of ‘attack and fight to the death’ quickly metamorphosised into ‘welcome, masters, we have been expecting you’ followed by a bit of happy barking and the inevitable tail chasing.

Lycan’s band of subnormals were as happy as him with the sudden change of heart because, what mustn’t be overlooked, although they were admittedly on the side of evil they were so peripheral, so far removed from the chain of command, that they were almost on the side of good. Which made them more good baddies than evil baddies. Or maybe even bad baddies, as in they were no good at being bad. They weren’t very good at being good either due to the fact that they were, when all’s said and done, still a bit bad. But not that bad. Anyway, the upshot of the whole issue is, bad or good, they didn’t feel strongly enough about anything to take on a bunch of axe-wielding dwarves and a couple of obviously powerful mages. So when Lycan greeted them as masters – well then masters they were. The subnormals excitedly gathered together to greet their new superiors.

Chapter 27

Typhon the Dark had ridden hard all day and was starting to feel more than a little weary. One would think that the Prince of Darkness wouldn't be subject to common and garden everyday varieties of human weakness such as hunger, pain and tiredness but, as he was fundamentally Evil made flesh he was subject to all of the foibles and weaknesses of the flesh.

So, Typhon was looking for an inn to rest his evil bones, partake of some much-needed victuals and get his demon steed watered. The problem was that, when all's said and done, he was a seven-foot demon with a wingspan of over twelve foot and, whenever he did enter an inn, the reactions were always so bloody tiresome. Cacophonies of screaming, oodles of wailing and lashings of get-thee-hence-thou-devil's-spawn, then he would be attacked by any and all comers and it would end with Typhon wading in blood when all that he really wanted was a good meal and a bed for the night because even he got a bit tired every now and then.

Mustn't grumble, he thought as he saw a dimly lit sign up ahead. 'The Maidens Crotch' – Typhon shook his head, it takes all sorts, he mused as he pulled back savagely on Incitatus' reins and yanked him into the forecourt of the inn.

He tied the horse's reins to the hitching post outside the dreary looking inn, walked up the rickety stairs into the reception area and rang the small tarnished brass bell.

'Greetings, good traveller,' called out a man from the room behind the counter. 'Now, how can I be of service?' the man asked as he bustled up to the reception desk busily polishing a pair of spectacles with a scrap of yellow cloth.

'I would like a room for the night and a stable for my steed,' said Typhon.

'Of course, sir,' affirmed the Inn keeper as he gave his eye glasses a final rub and perched them on the end of his red-veined nose. He squinted short sightedly at Typhon, removed his spectacles, gave them a quick once over with the wisp of cloth, reattached them to his ruddy snout, squinted again and gave tongue to a stream of terrified invective that ended with the good old, tried and tested 'get-thee-hence-thou-devil's-spawn.'

Typhon wearily scrubbed at his face with his hands and shook his head sadly. 'Oh well,' he said resignedly. 'I suppose it's time for the old wading in pools of blood to start. I don't know why I bother trying to be civil, I really don't.'

He drew his saw-bladed black sword out of the scabbard strapped between his wings and nonchalantly beheaded the keep with an indifferent backhanded flick of his wrist.

The headless body slumped forward onto the reception desk and merrily pumped a gallon or so a bright red blood onto the floor. There was a scream from the door and the clatter of a dropped tray as a serving girl unsuspectingly walked in on the grisly scene. Typhon spun around to face her.

'Quickly,' he growled. 'Go and fetch everyone from the common room and let's get this travesty over with.'

The girl screamed once again for good measure and flew off to the common room for reinforcements whilst Typhon leaned on the pommel of his sword and waited. It wasn't long before he heard the sounds of many booted feet thundering down the corridor towards him and he saw a group of perhaps seven or eight tough looking customers run into the reception area carrying an assortment of vicious looking bladed weapons.

'Get thee hence, thou devil's spawn,' shouted a tall bearded man at the front of the group.

‘We’ve been through that,’ responded Typhon as he gestured towards the headless innkeep. ‘Your cranium-free companion here has already dispensed with the preliminaries so if we could just get straight down to the wading through pools of blood bit and I can get myself a decent night’s sleep then I would really appreciate it. Thank you.’

And with that he commenced the battle with a massive overhand blow that caught the bearded man at the juncture between his neck and his shoulder and clove him almost in twain.

Typhon’s attackers were hard and tough and dangerous and dead. They never really had a chance, what with Typhon the Dark being the Evil one made flesh and all. The odd lucky blow that did slip through his windmill-type attack just went to prove that, not only was his skin reptilian in aspect, it was also crocodilian in respect of its armour-like abilities. In short, it was one-way traffic.

Afterwards, the Dark One stabled and watered his steed and then found the kitchens, helped himself to a mammoth haunch of spit-roast beef the approximate size and weight of a nine-year-old male child and a hogshead of ale. He carried them up to the master suite of the now empty inn and, after stripping off his blood-soaked leather singlet, fell upon them with a rapacious gusto born of a combination of exertion and natural avariciousness. After, his appetite sated, he threw himself across the down-filled mattress and fell into the deep conscienceless slumber of the truly wicked.

Legles walked along the untidy row of sylvan fairy-folk, glowering like thunder. ‘You lot are disgraceful, dishonourable, discreditable and downright disgusting,’ he told them as he nudged them into a less ragged formation. ‘You,’ he shouted, pointing at a small elvin figure dressed in a tattered brown tunic and carrying a small bow constructed from what looked like laminated pieces of bone and willow. 'What's your name?'

'Puck, sir,' responded the pointy-eared pixie.

Legles rubbed his jaw and thought for a while. 'Puck you say?' he asked.

'Yes, sir,' the Pucked one answered.

'I think I knew your father.'

'Puck, sir,' acknowledged the pixie.

'Yes, yes. I know. Now, let me think. What was his name?' mused Legles to himself.

'Puck, sir. Puck.'

'Shut up,' shouted Legles. 'I heard you before. I'm not grotesquely stupid. Anyways, it wasn't your father. It was your grandfather. Yes, I remember now.'

'Puck, sir. Puck, Puck and Puck.'

Legles grabbed the hapless pixie by the throat and lifted him to his face. 'Puck yourself, you little cretin. Puck you and Puck off.' Legles threw the unfortunate pixie to the ground.

'They're all called Puck,' interjected Cabbie. 'Surely you've heard of the ancient line of Pucks?'

'No I haven't,' retorted Legles. 'I'm an elf not some sort of sylvanian historian. And stop calling me Surely; it's not funny.' The green-garbed elf stalked off in a strop.

Cabbie faced the worried looking band of subnormals. 'Good people,' he started and then, realising the inaccuracy of that statement corrected himself. 'Dear medium bad, or perhaps slightly good, beings of the sylvan variety. What our esteemed elven friend was eventually going to say, after giving you a good, and justifiable, bollocking regarding your recent apparent flirtation with the dark side, is that you are either for us or against us.

Those who are for us please take one step forward and those who are against us, please proceed directly to the wooden chopping block that our Mister Budget and his fellow dwarves have so efficiently erected.'

After a quick sideways glance at the group of axe-wielding dwarves, standing around a knee-high stump of wood and sharpening their blades with grey whetstones, the subnormals got the hint and fell over themselves to take the necessary single step forward. (Or short flight forward in the case of some of the fairies).

Cabbie grinned hugely. 'Welcome to the quest.'

Later on, in the early evening after the basis of the quest had been explained to all newcomers, the newly enlarged force of questarians settled down around a couple of huge fires and partook of some victuals that had been prepared largely by their newest members.

Biggest and Cabbie were eating with Lycan as, unlike the pixies and sprites and fairies who ate mainly fruit and raw vegetables, Lycan ate red meat, bleeding rare, well salted, with all the fat on and in large quantities. This menu suited Cabbie and Biggest down to the freezing cold ground on which they were encamped.

Biggest had distributed his Blutop to all and sundry with great largess and the talk was flowing freely. Dreenee, already full of ripe apples and strawberries, sat next to Lycan and absent mindedly scratched him behind his ears as he ate his venison. Every now and then he would growl, as is a wolf's wont when he is consuming his evening repast, and Biggest or Cabbie would lean over and casually strike him with a backhanded blow to his canine-like cranium. After this he would wag his bushy tail, whimper respectfully and carry on chewing at the animal protein in front of him. Lycan was, for the first time in his werewolfy life, truly happy. No-one expected him to think, they asked him very few questions and, when he got hungry, all he had to do was whine and look pathetic and Dreenee ensured that he was fed. It had been less than one whole day and already Lycan was regressing to such a canine-like state that he had, by now, almost forgotten how to express himself in human vocal terms.

The fairy-folk, who were not averse to using a little magic themselves (although it was of the wild type, largely unplanned and totally unpredictable), were busy discussing shop with Master Smegly and Plob.

'No, I disagree,' said Plob as he shook his head vigorously in confirmation of his discord. 'One can't go around unleashing magic will-he-nil-he on the unsuspecting public like some sort of enchanted jack-in-the-box.'

'Of course one can,' retorted Puck. 'In fact this one,' he said pointing at himself. 'Does it all the time.'

'But what's the point?' asked Plob. 'With such uncontrolled magiks all you can create is…is…'

'Mischiefs,' laughed Puck.

'Exactly,' confirmed Plob. 'And what is the point of that?'

'That is the point,' answered a small winged fairy as she buzzed around Plob's head. 'That is what we are. Sprites, fairies and such-what. We delight in tomfoolery and misbehaviour. Trickery and artifice, illusions and sleight-of-hand. That is our power.'

'It is also your curse,' added Master Smegly. 'This penchant of yours for misconduct has oft had you spilling over into the realms of evil and this behaviour will, thus, no longer be tolerated. For the remainder of the quest you will use all of your powers for good and only for good. Any transgression from this rule will be met with much sternness and harsh measures of retribution.' The master stood up, his expression imperious. 'Let that rule be known and understood by all, lest its misinterpretation bring pain and heartache to any who lapse inadvertently in this, their newly-appointed mission.'

He then turned and walked over to Legles and, after putting a comforting hand on the elf's shoulder, drew him to one side. 'You have a great talent, my boy,' the master told him. 'You have all of the traits of a first-class leader. You are noble, principled, incorruptible and fearsomely accomplished with that bow of yours.' Legles graciously nodded his head in appreciation.

'Unfortunately,' continued Smegly. 'You also have a huge talent for being a complete pain in the bum and a stand-offish, sulky spoiled brat.' Legles bridled in shock at Smegly's straightforward accusation and muttered a half-hearted denial under his breath.

'It's no use denying it,' said Smegly sternly. 'And it has got to stop. Right here and right now. From this moment forth you will carry yourself with decorum and restraint. No more outbursts of temper. No more sulky huffs and a lot more understanding and acceptance of your peers and your submissives. The time draws ever closer to what I fear will be the final and telling battle with the forces of iniquity and we will need you and your troops more than ever at that final confrontation.'

'My troops?' asked Legles.

'Yes,' affirmed Master Smegly. 'I am putting you directly in charge of the band of subnormals. I suspect that they are more important than any of us know and you, with your sylvan background, are the only one who can truly get the best out of them. Now follow me.'

Smegly walked back to the fires with Legles in tow and, after he had warmed himself up a little next to the roaring orange and blue flames, he clapped his hands and called for everyone's attention. 'Fellow questarians,' he said. 'I have had a brief chat with Legles, son of Istar the first of the inner lands, and he has graciously agreed to assume the sole leadership of our new friends, the band of subnormals. Friends, I give you – Legles. Bowman-of-the-gods.'

A small smattering of applause greeted this followed by a tiny whine of relief from Lycan who by now had reverted to a completely animal stage and was relieved that his final human duty had been disposed of.

'My good companions,' started Legles. 'My friends. I accept this responsibility with great pride and also humility. I will strive to do my duty to the best of my ability and the first thing that I would like to do is to insist that from this moment on the so-called band of subnormals are referred to as the Excellents. Thank you.'

And there they all stood. A master magician, his assistant, an ex-accountant and an ex-almost-knight and apparently a thief in potential, a semi-psychotic tavern waitress, a Cabbie who was once a knight, a huge trogre, an elf of supernatural toxophilitic ability, more than a score of axe-toting dwarves, a werewolf who was fast going animal and a gaggle of semi-magical ex-evilish sylvan creatures of the wood nymph variety. All in all, a collection of over fifty souls who were now committed, to more or lesser degrees, to the quest that Plob had embarked upon in a time that now seemed so very long ago.

The Evil ones still outnumbered them by a ratio of some five to one.

But it was a start.

A good one.

The first concerted attempt to break out had happened at about six o'clock that morning, just before sunrise, and the captain's small detachment were struggling to hold their ground.

King Bil, in a rare moment of lucidity, had decided that being trapped in a castle with nigh on three hundred other souls was not good. Leastwise because the tiny remnants of plumber that still resided in the back of his mind had become vastly offended by the unsanitary stench that was beginning to assault his nasal cavities due to the fact that a couple of gaurderobes are no substitute for water-borne sewage when it comes to evacuating human excreta.

So the new king had called his second, third forth and fifth in command to him. He had also insisted on the presence of a man called Tolley because he had large Dumbo-esque ears and a generously proportioned, bright red nose which the king thought to look hilarious. And anyway, Bil liked to share his rapier-like wit with his subjects by making comments like 'you've got a big red nose, ha-ha-ha' or 'hey, big ears, give us a flap, ha-ha-ha,' which normally proved to be right up their depressively low IQ'ed street and went down a treat.

Tolley thought the king's humour to be a trifle heavy handed but then at least it did make him feel important and, when you looked like Tolley, even this sort of acceptance to the group was better than no acceptance at all. And let's face it, he was being insulted by the king and how many people could say that? The best that most people would ever do would to be insulted by a teacher or government official or, at the very best, perhaps some minor royal so far removed from the actual throne that you would need an extremely powerful pair of far-lookers to even see the castle. Oh yes, Tolley smiled, now that he thought about things he realised that he had made it. This would be a thing to tell the grandchildren. If he ever had any.

The group of commanders, and Tolley, trooped into the royal throne room, arrayed themselves in front of the king and waited for their royal leader to notice them.

Finally Bil acknowledged them. 'What?' he asked.

'You called, King Bil ,' responded his second.

'Yes,' agreed Bil. 'Me called King Bil. What you called?'

There was a moments puzzled silence as the second tried to work this one out. Tolley, in a display of relative cerebral brilliance, arrived at the answer first. 'Him called Blog, sire' he said.

Blog nodded and voiced his agreement.

Bil looked perplexed, and then worried, and then pissed off. 'How dare you call yourself Sire?' he screamed. 'I'm the king around here. Not you. Only the king can call himself sire. Where do you get off calling yourself Blog Sire? You're fired, Blog Sire, finished, kaput, nada. Now bugger off and take that stupid looking floppy eared, red-nosed moron with you.'

'But, sire…' started Tolley.

'What?' shrieked Bil. 'Are you two brothers? How dare you call yourself But Sire. I sire. Me, me and only me. You two, Blog Sire and But Sire, get out of my throne room. Now, is anyone else related to these two treasonous brothers?'

'No, sire,' replied the number three in command as the two other ex-favourites ran from the room.

'All right, No Sire. You can bugger off as well.' Bil paused and waited for the guilty party to scuttle from the room. When nobody moved the King went apoplectic with rage. 'Which one of you is No Sire? Come on. Own up. Own up. Ownup. Ownupownup.'

The number four in command, sensing an opportunity for fast track advancement, pointed at the number three. 'It's him, sire,' he accused.

Bil went purple. 'Him Sire. Well who the bloody hell is No Sire?'

The number five, realising number four's game, pointed at him and shouted 'That one.'

'Get thee hence,' screeched Bil. 'You and the whole Sire family are in deep, deep crud. Now get out.'

The number five in command stood proudly to attention in front of the king, the sole survivor of what could possibly be called a battle of wits, although a very low-level one using little wit, but still, an achievement to be proud of.

'What's your name?' the king asked of his new second in command.

'Patruk, sire' blurted out the hapless survivor, his mouth working just that little bit faster than his brain.

Bil went completely insane.

Patruk, whose surname actually happened to be King, didn't even bother to wait for Bil's command as he turned tail and fled from the royal throne room.

It took King Bil de Plummer the rest of that day to regain a slightly even keel, find and promote a new team of commanders and explain his plan to them. It was, against all expectations, quite a good plan. Simple, doable and effective. Basically all that had to be done was to collect all of the scaling ladders from about the castle, lash them together to form a lightweight but strong portable structure, lay it across the blackened stumps of what remained of the burnt-out bridge and, under the cover of darkness, storm across and kill all and any who dared get in the way.

And so it was that the next morning the captain and his men found themselves fighting valiantly for their lives.

Captain Bravad had split his detachment into three small teams. Number one team consisting of Berm 'brick wall' Odger, Dill 'the demon' Bacchus, Partlee 'dog' Nobee and Mr Tipstaff. Team two being Grunchy 'Masher' Fromson, Spectal 'Killer' Petreson, Wogler 'Barbarian' Manger and the captain himself in control. The third team, Pactrus 'pace man' Petracis and Pups Slobberer the dog were being held in reserve as well as being used as runners to fetch additional weaponry, water, bandages and arrows.

Team number one would rake the charging enemy with an arrow storm (although, due to their lack of numbers it was more like an arrow drizzle. Still, even ten or twelve accurately discharged arrows landing amongst a tightly packed group of men attempting to charge across a rickety construction of wooden ladders balanced over a moat tends to be quite seriously off-putting).

Team two would then form a shield-wall (again, perhaps wall is a little ambitious. More like a shield-picket-fence). And run forward at top speed, ancient limbs creaking, old sinews groaning, and go crashing into the enemy that had made it through the arrow drizzle and, whilst swinging massive overhead strikes with their battleaxes, drive them back into the moat. They would then quickly disengage and then team two would rake the survivors with arrows once again.

They had done this perhaps four or five times already this morning and, although the detachment was still relatively unscathed, they were tired. Tired as only extremely old men can be tired. Bone weary, stiff, sore and completely dehydrated. The captain knew that the next skirmish would be their last. Bil's cohorts gathered together at the gate and, after downing a quick shot of cherry bandy each for a bit of the Old Dutch courage, they attacked once more.

Team number one gritted their teeth and drew back on their long bows, team number two tensed their protesting muscles and shouldered their axes once more and, with a loud splintering crash, the makeshift bridge collapsed into the moat taking perhaps ten men with it to a watery grave.

'Yes,' the captain punched the air in jubilation.

The detachment lived on to fight another day.

Chapter 28

Typhon the Dark awoke from his slumber, arose from the feather bed, put on his blood-encrusted leather singlet and strode downstairs as he sheathed his black blade that he had kept at the ready next to him through the night.

He noticed the three men, standing in the shadows under the eaves, as he exited the building. He noticed that they were armed. He noticed that they were big and he noticed that they were extremely bad looking.

He also noticed that the tallest one, the one standing slightly in front of the other two, had a subservient, ingratiating grin on his battle-scarred face. The other two, stood back, eyes cast down and feet a-shuffle as the leader greeted Typhon.

'Good morning to you, your magnificence,' he smarmed obsequiously as he touched his greasy forelock.

'What?' questioned Typhon as he strode towards the stables.

'Pardon us, sir, for our presumption,' the apparent leader continued as the trio jogged after Typhon. 'But we heard the rumour, sir, and we came to look and, sir, we couldn't help but to notice that the rumour appears to be correct.'

'Sir,' barked Typhon. 'You forgot to say sir again, you obsequious toad.'

'Sir, sorry, sir.'

'That's better,' acquiesced The Dark One. 'Now do tell. What rumour might this be?'

'That you're a demon,' blabbered the leader.

'Sir,' snapped Typhon. 'I'm a demon - SIR,' he finished with a bellow.

The trio went into such a paroxysm of bowing, fawning, scraping and forelock tugging so as to actually cause two of them, the leader and the one with the scraggy ginger beard (yes I know that I hadn't mentioned the beard before but it wasn't necessary), to cramp over as their overworked thigh and abdominal muscles went into repetitive stress spasms and caused them both to prostrate themselves on the sod in front of the Dark One. The third rogue, (no beard, the shortest of the three, mulberry birthmark on the right side of his face - there, happy now?) sensed that he was looking a little prominent in his upright position and so threw himself to the horizontal alongside his partners.

Typhon the Dark, mightily impressed at such an outstanding show of first-class grovelling, stopped in mid stride, placed his fore-claws upon his hips and contemplated the prone trio of ne'er-do-wells.

'Doest thou posses transport?' he asked, to be met with a triplet of blank stares. 'Steeds?' he continued to a repeat of the uncomprehending gapes in triplicate. Typhon sighed. 'Have you got horses, you sub-moronic triad of imbeciles?'

'Yes, sir,' replied the moron in chief. 'Good ones. Fresh stolen only yesterday.'

'Good' affirmed the Dark One. 'Come with me.'

They rode hard through the whole of that day, Typhon and his demon steed out in front and the moronic trio strung out behind him like a trailing tail of stupidity. Tough, well-armed and violent but stupid nonetheless. Not that evil has the sole agency for idiocy, far from it, but still, it was nice to know that our heroes were a cut above Typhon's triplicate trio of twits.

They stopped at another wayside inn that night and, as was to be expected, the chain of events that ensued were almost a carbon copy of the night before. Except that this time Typhon had a lot less work to do as his triad of hard-hitting nit-wits showed their mettle by dispatching all but the most resilient of dissenters.

The next morning five more unctuous creatures wished to join the ranks of the foul individual that was represented by Typhon the Dark. And the next day, many more. And the next. And the next.

For Evil does beget Evil - and don't you forget it.

Kleebles' mother, dressed all in black and her head still swaddled in bandages from the effects of Bil's violence, sat at the front of the temple and sobbed. (Ha - bet that you'd all forgotten about poor little Kleebles, hadn't you? Shame on you. A pitiable innocent child, so brutally and unnecessarily battered to death in the third chapter, merely to provide a small twist in the plot and already all but forgotten. My heart haemorrhages at your callous and insensitive attitudes).

'Is there not a man amongst you?' she wailed. 'Evil walks the Earth unmolested and no-one, bar that brave captain and his dilapidated old men, seek to do aught about it.'

She slid off the bench onto her knees in front of the congregation. 'Oh woe and despair, sadness and anguish, misery and wretchedness. A gnashing of teeth and a rending of hair. Breasts to be beaten and hopes to be dashed. Oh, if I were other than a middle-aged woman with a partly bashed-in head and a pathological fear of physical violence, I would stride forth and do vengeance upon the vile Bil and his minions for the savage and untimely death that he brought down upon my poor little Kleebles. If but for the cruel twist of fate that has…'

'All right. All right,' shouted the priest from behind the pulpit at the front of the temple. 'We get the picture. Unlike some amongst us,' he continued, glancing directly at Kleebles' mother's husband…no - not Kleebles' father. It's a little complicated but let us put it this way. Kleebles' mother's husband was a pale, tall, rangy red-headed man with watery blue eyes and size fourteen feet. Kleebles favoured him in absolutely none of his predominant physical properties but did, oddly enough, appear to be the splitting image of the king's tax collector, small swarthy man, bad teeth, black hair and small of foot. The whole town knew this apart from Kleebles' mother's husband - no, I'm not going to tell you his name as it isn't necessary to the plot and we really don't have the time to be drawn into vague and unnecessary asides such as that - because Kleebles' mother's hus...all right. Kopy. His name was Kopy.

Anyway, to shorten this whole explanation, Kopy was not a man possessed of any overt sense of cleverness. In fact it was rumoured that when he was born his parents had come across a two-for-one special offer on Stupidity and, being the types that could never refuse a bargain, they had loaded up on an entire barrow load of Stupid for poor old Kopy.

'Unlike some amongst us,' the priest repeated. 'We don't have to have everything repeated twenty or thirty…thousand…times.' The priest cleared his throat wetly, noisily and unpleasantly, in the manner of all teachers, minor government officials and men-of-the-cloth. 'We feel for you in this, your time of need. Your pain is our pain but, in all fairness, what do you expect us to do? We are not soldiers. We have no military training. We are helpless.'

Kopy stood up and, as he did so, a shaft of light blazed through the stained glass window and backlit him with a bright blue glow. He turned to face the congregation, his simple slow features set in a look of calm resolve, his watery blue eyes showing a small hint of flint.

'It seems to me,' he said, in his dim halting way. 'It seems to me that none of us have been trained to be cowards either but we've been making a damn good job of it. I'm going to avenge my son.'

Kopy strode from the temple, head high, shoulders back and oversized feet slapping loudly on the hard packed earth.

They arrived in ones and twos throughout the rest of the day, and that night, and the next day. Men, women and children. And not only to fight but also to cook food, draw water, roll bandages and fletch arrows.

And with them all came a huge assortment of weapons, longbows, horse bows, crossbows, broadswords, rapiers, daggers, axes, morning stars, cudgels, pitchforks, spades and sticks, and the desire to use them. The reason being that, for as long as they all lived, from that day forward, they would all have to live with the fact that they were shamed and humbled, in the temple, by a simple man. And they were all determined to do what they could in order to be able to stand proud once more.

The captain was pleased. And Mr Tipstaff set about organising the newcomers into teams of bowmen, swordsmen, armourers and carriers.

Fate galloped on and the forces of good and the forces of evil were once again neck and neck. And the elves breathed a sigh of relief – for Captain Bravad r Us was no longer living on their borrowed time.

Chapter 29

There had definitely been a change. Plob wouldn't go as far as to say that things were idyllic, because they weren't but, all things considered, the world seemed to be on a much more even keel than it had been before, at the beginning of the quest.

The days passed, if not without incident, then unquestionably without any serious upsets. The villages that they passed through seemed happy and untroubled by all but the most usual of rural complaints. No plagues of locusts, rains of frogs or even unusually dry, or wet, weather. Normal, normal, normal.

However, if they had been travelling back via the same route as Typhon the Dark, things may have appeared a little differently. But they weren't, so they didn't, so there.

When Plob brought up this sudden un-normal spate of normality with Smegly, the master simply smiled in a self-satisfied way, nodded and said something obtuse in reply, such as 'it's almost time' or 'the moment draws near' or once, 'who the hell rolled these buggers? They fall apart after the first decent puff.'

And so they continued their way back to the castle of King Bil the pretender, making good time, stopping at inns or barns along the way and, all in all, feeling relaxed and ready for the fast approaching final showdown.

The next day they came to the outskirts of New Grumply, the first large town on the route since they had left the frozen ex-swamps of the realm of Typhon. Smegly, unsure of the sort of reaction that they would receive if the entire detachment marched, fifty strong, into the town centre, ordered Cabbie, Plob and Horgy to go in for a quick recce of the local populous.

They rode into town in the cab, parked outside a local pub, the Meal and Bucket, and strolled in. Cabbie went straight to the counter of the almost empty but pleasant place and ordered a brace of ales for himself and one each for Plob and Horgy.

'So,' said Cabbie as he paid the keep for the refreshments. 'We've been on the back roads for a good few days. Pray tell us, my good man, of all and any news that has reached your ears in this fine establishment of your'n and, so that your throat does not suffer from drought whilst you talk, please draw yourself an ale, on us, to carry on with.'

The barman acknowledged Cabbie with a smile and nod of the head, drew himself a brimful mug of the fine dark brew, blew the froth off the top and sank it in two long swallows, stopping halfway to snort lustily in appreciation. 'Thank you muchly, governor,' he said as he banged the empty mug back onto the counter top. 'We don't see much of that sort of generosity here in New Grumply. Now, how can I be of service?'

'Firstly,' started Cabbie. 'Draw yourself another and a second brace for me, and tell us of the doings and going ons.'

'Well now. Old Mister Numson on the other side of the stream, the farm near the watermill, with the ducks and that strange black pig - his wife left him to run off with a travelling snake oil salesman that comes around here every year about this time. And her not a day under seventy-five. Scandalous if you ask me, and you are so I'll tell you, scandalous. If it weren't for Mrs Scrompy who lives on Badgers Bum farm on the old side of town who's keeping Mr Numsom company, if you know what I mean, and, being men of the world I'm sure that you do, well he would be distraught with shock and sadness. Mind, some say that if Mrs. Scrompy hadn't been so friendly in the first place then Edwinda Numson wouldn't have left old man Numson and run off with that homing pigeon salesman.'

'Snake oil,' corrected Plob. 'You said snake oil salesman.'

The keep shook his head. 'No, young sir. That was this time. I'm talking about last fall when she ran off with the pigeon salesman.'

'A busy lass our Mrs Numson,' interjected Cabbie.

'Oh yes, every year for the past decade she runs off with some itinerant salesperson. Always comes back within a fortnight or two. She could never leave old Numson for good. Would break her heart it would. Now if we're talking about heart breaking there's the widow Mrs Clam, lives on Fuzz Street next to the peach cannery, beautiful woman. Can break your heart at twenty paces, fifty on a clear day if the wind is blowing in your direction. Why only last week…'

The barkeep rambled on and on pausing only to refill their mugs or deliver the odd ale to one of the other drinkers in the tavern from time to time. Plob lounged back in his chair savouring the relaxed comfort and hovering in that Zen-like state brought on by alcohol, warmth and the background drone of the keep's monotone and he could see that Cabbie and Horgy were in a similar stress-free state. After almost half an hour of background hum, something scratched the surface of Plob's relaxed ruminatory state bringing him out of his semi-trance and pricking his ears up.

'Wait,' he said. 'What was that? Sorry, repeat. I missed what you were saying there.'

'Why, I was only talking about the frightening rumours flying around the country about this terrible man, Bil the something-or-other…'

'Plummer,' said Plob. 'Bil de Plummer.'

'Yes,' the keep nodded. 'That's the one. Apparently he's deposed the king and set himself and his followers up in the castle at Maudlin. Not only that but he also has allegedly hired the services of the evil Typhon the Dark who is, as we speak, travelling around the country side collecting up an army of mounted men of such wickedness and depravity that no one will be able to stand in his way.'

'How big is this army?' asked Cabbie as he lent forward, a worried look on his face.

The keep shook his head. 'I can't be sure of that, good sir. Why, after all, this only rumour not substantive fact that I base my ramblings on.'

'Guess,' urged Cabbie. 'Approximate, estimate. Apply a little conjecture to the subject.'

'Really. I couldn't…'

Cabbie lent over the counter, grabbed the keep by the collar and twisted it until the man's face started to go an unpleasant shade of puce. 'Approximate or asphyxiate, my good man. Your choice. Do you understand?'

The keep nodded almost imperceptibly. Cabbie let go and, as the keep drew breath once again and his face returned slowly back to its normal colour, he started to talk once more. 'I've heard tell that he rides already with over two hundred men and, by the time he gets to the castle, he may have as many as four or five hundred with him now could you please go you are not welcome here anymore.' And with that the keep shrank to the back of the bar as far away from the counter as possible and chewed nervously on his greasy dust-laden cleaning cloth.

Cabbie threw a handful of coins on the counter. 'For your trouble,' he said to the keep as the three of them left the tavern at a fast walk, got into the cab and hastened back to Master Smegly and the rest of the questarians.

Typhon the Dark rode at the head of the host, seated on Incitatus who pranced and snorted mightily in true demonic style and, it must be said, the Dark One and his allies made for some seriously troublesome viewing. The innkeeper of the tavern at New Grumply had been pretty much spot on with his estimations.

Spread out behind Typhon was well over two hundred assorted miscellaneous motley members of the race that we loosely consider to be human. Short ones, skinny ones, fat ones and tall ones. A malicious myriad of foul individuals with nought but one thing in common. The will, nay - the need, to do evil upon their fellow man. And they were drawing closer, ever closer to Bil and his minions in the castle of Maudlin.

'Well I'd say that pretty much screws things up big time,' said Cabbie in a depressed sounding voice as he got to the end of the telling of the current Typhon situation to Smegly.

'No. Not necessarily,' disagreed the master.

'So you think that there's hope?' asked Plob.

'No. Not necessarily,' answered Smegly. 'However, one thing's for sure. We have to get to the castle before Typhon or things will be screwed up big time.'

'No. Not necessarily,' rejoined Plob.

Smegly stared at him. 'Yes. Necessarily. Necessarily and definitely. A host of mounted men will ride roughshod over whatever small resistance that the captain has managed to raise in next to no time at all and then Typhon's troops and Bil's minions will gather together to form the biggest baddest army that this poor peaceful world of ours has ever had the misfortune of witnessing. Necessarily and definitely. So, gentlemen and others, time is of the utmost importance to us now. From this moment on we shall all have to endure forced marches and thin rations. Get all of the rest that you can tonight, for tomorrow, and the days after, we rise early, begin our march at first light and keep going until dark. We will eat twice a day, before dawn and after twilight, no other stops will be allowed and, the gods willing, we will arrive at the castle of Maudlin long before the Dark One.'

The next few days were the hardest that Plob could recall in all of his relatively short life. The first day of forced march was not too bad. True to Smegly's orders they arose and ate before sunup and, when they finally ate for the second time, it was well into the night.

Before they slept they readied what they could in preparation for the morning and then fell into an exhausted, dreamless slumber.

The next day was far worse and, by the third day, every step was another yard more into each person's own internal valley of pain and fatigue.

Strangely enough, by the fourth day things seemed to get a little better and, by the sixth day, as they crested Maudlin's western hills and got their first look at the city spread out below them, they had run off all excess fat and toxins that had formerly taken up residence in their bodies and they looked exactly like what they were. A well-honed team of lean, mean fighting machines. Legles spotted the smoke from the camp fires around the castle and, proudly, with their heads held high, they marched, in tight formation, into the captain's camp.

Chapter 30

Captain Bravad r Us had just finished the detailed telling of his story on what had thus far transpired in his battles with King Bil de Plummer and, to put it mildly, the questarians were hugely impressed. It was not often that one came across such leadership, bravery, fortitude and general common-or-garden good sense wrapped up in a single package.

Smegly harrumphed, not out of any disrespect for the captain but merely because the situation in which they found themselves looked to be, if not impossible, then at least damned difficult to get out of.

'The way that I see it,' started Master Smegly. 'Is that our first priority is getting rid of Bil and his minions before Typhon gets here with his host and we become even more totally outnumbered. Any suggestions, anyone?'

'The trouble is that we're in a bit of a stalemate situation,' said the captain. 'We have no siege equipment capable of battering down the walls and, according to my reckoning, the bad ones have unlimited water and enough rations to last them another ten days or so, as long as they live a little frugally.'

'That's no good,' said Cabbie. 'We can expect Typhon to be here within the next three to four days, five at the outside. We've got to find a way of either all of us getting into the castle or, somehow, getting all of them out here onto the plains.'

'I've got an idea,' contributed Horgy. 'And it's a bloody good one too,' he added with uncharacteristic intensity.

King Bil stood on the battlements of the highest tower and contemplated the scene below. His new number two, three and four stood in a row behind him. No one with big ears or funny nose was there as Bil had not yet found a replacement for Tolley (or But Sire as the king thought him to be called) in fact, if the truth be known, Bil missed all of the Sire brothers that he had dismissed in a fit of pique during his last meeting. These new advisors were simply not up to it. And to top it all, with no one to use as a foil for his razor-sharp wit, he was starting to become downright unfunny and more than a little depressed. 'What do you think it is?' he asked as he turned to his second in command.

'I can't be sure, Lord King (nobody called Bil sire anymore after the news of the last debacle had reached the ears of his followers - and anyway, Bil preferred Lord King as it smacked more than a little of godliness). 'It looks a bit like some sort of mobile bridge.'

'My thoughts exactly,' agreed Bil who had actually thought that it may have been some sort of Trojan Horse but, on reflection and taking his second's opinion on the matter, it probably was some sort of bridge. 'Right. Put double guards on the gate. Lots of archers, people with javelins, rocks, fire - that sort of thing. Let them put the bridge in place and, as soon as they attempt to cross it, let loose a rain of death on their blasphemous heads. Then, when we've routed them, we charge across the bridge and massacre them all.'

Yep. He would show them. King Bil. Lord King Bil. Lord. God. Bil the Lord King God. He pulled his bedspread a little tighter around his shoulders, straightened the seams on his blue boiler suit, shouldered his bright red drop-forged wrench and strode, insanely, from the battlements.

Budget hammered the last nail into the wheeled bridge-like structure that he and the rest of the dwarves had been building through the night by the light of fires and torches and stood back to admire his work. 'That'll do,' he commented as he turned to Box. 'Go and call the master. Tell him that we've finished.'

Box jogged off to inform Smegly who returned with Horgy, Legles, Cabbie, Biggest and Plob who all inspected the structure. 'Excellent job,' admired Legles. 'Well done.'

Budget and the rest of the dwarves beamed in pleasure.

'OK,' said Horgy. 'I suppose it's time for the next phase of the plan. Where's the captain?'

'He's with Dreenee,' answered Cabbie with a grin. 'The two of them seem to have spent every waking moment together since we got here. She even goes on his rounds with him. It's like they're joined at the hip or something.'

'Box, Basin,' Smegly called. 'Go and find him and tell him to report back here sharpish.' The two dwarves ran off to do the master's bidding. 'So – you reckon that you're up to this, Horgy. It's a big risk and, I won't beat about the bush, there's a good chance that you won't make it back out alive.'

Horgy shrugged. 'It has to be tried,' he said. 'It's no good just running the bridge up to the gates and hoping that they'll all come pouring out. They'll be too suspicious that we didn't try to storm across and, if we did try, they would kill too many of us. I can't let that happen. We've got to give them a reason to cross that bridge onto the open ground and the only one that I could think of was Bil's sceptre. If I can steal that and bring it out onto the plain there's no way that he'll stay bottled up inside the castle. From what we've heard they all hold that sceptre in very high regard. It seems to have some sort of religious significance or something. If we get the sceptre then they'll attack.'

'Let me try,' begged Legles. 'I have more experience at moving silently. My battle skills are far superior to yours so I'll have a much better chance at staying alive than you.'

Horgy shook his head. 'It has to be me. Don't ask why because I don't know. Maybe it's something the master's masters master whatever master alleged – he said that I was the thief so, if thief I am, then thief I be.'

As Horgy finished talking, Dreenee and Bravad ran up, hand in hand. Cabbie raised an eyebrow but said nothing. 'Well, it looks like it's time,' said the captain. 'OK, you all know what to do. Let's get to it.'

Upon his command the dwarves gathered around the wheeled bridge and started to push it slowly towards the moat and the castle gate. 'Faster,' urged the captain. 'If we don't get up enough speed then there's no way Dreenee and Biggest will be able to keep it going until it falls into place.'

Dreenee and Biggest ran behind the dwarf-driven bridge and, as they ran, Dreenee activated her protective bracelet which spun a shimmering blue shield of light around her and Biggest. This was the one part of the plan that both Smegly and Plob were less than happy about but, as it was impossible to maintain an 'earth, protect', shield wall around any moving object they were forced to rely solely on Dreenee's magical bracelet and, as it was specifically gifted to her, it would only work if she was wearing it. They had teamed her up with Biggest in the hope that his enormous strength coupled with Dreenee's aggression would be sufficient to keep propelling the bridge towards the gate after it got within bow and arrow range and the unprotected dwarves were forced to drop out.

As the bridge started rolling forward, Horgy slipped his colour-shifting cloak on and began his run around to the other side of the castle, relying on the fact that all eyes would be on the advancing bridge and, should anyone glance in his direction, his cloak would provide sufficient concealment. He ran swiftly around the edge of the moat until he reached the partly hidden sally port that the captain had made his escape from so many days before. He slid into the water and swam slowly, so as not to cause any ripples, across to the port.

When he got there he clambered quickly into the opening and lay there for a while catching his breath. Then, he crawled into the castle.

Meanwhile the bridge rattled towards the gate joggling and bouncing frantically as it picked up speed. Shouting came from the walls and turrets of the castle and arrows started flying out in the direction of the trundling structure but most fell well short. As they pushed closer and closer the arrows started to home in on them until, when they got too close for comfort, the captain ordered the dwarves to fall out and, as they did, he followed them.

Dreenee and Biggest threw themselves at the bridge as they put their full weight into keeping it going. Sheets of arrows bounced off Dreenee's magical shield and lay scattered on the ground around them and slowly, ever so slowly, the bridge ground to a halt, a scant two or three feet from the moat. Dreenee screamed in frustration and Biggest threw his head back and bellowed. Together they leant against the wood, counted to three, and threw all they had into it. But it was just too massive, more than strength it now needed weight to shift it, and weight they did not have. Knowing that it would do no good they tensed themselves up for another attempt and, as they did, they heard a whooping and hollering from behind them and turned to see the captain and his detachment of geriatrics screaming and yelling and running at full tilt towards them, shields held above their heads to ward off the arrows.

But the arrow storm was thick and strong and one of them went down before they even got to the bridge, as they threw themselves against it they had to drop their shields and another quickly followed his comrade to Valhalla. Dreenee heard the captain grunt in pain as an arrow slammed through his left shoulder and all but pinned him to the bridge. Another old man, Dreenee thought that it might have been

Pace Man, went down cursing and shouting insults at the foe, a four-foot javelin appearing, seemingly magically, between his shoulder blades. And then, finally, the bridge was there, falling into place with a loud quivering crash. Dreenee, Biggest, the captain and his valiant group of veterans turned and ran. One more octogenarian fell under a hail of arrows on the return trip and Biggest leant down, picking him up on the run and throwing him over his shoulder and then, mercifully, they were out of range.

Plob and Smegly ran up to the injured captain and his surviving men. 'You idiot,' Smegly shouted. 'Why didn't you tell me what you were going to do? We could have given you some covering fire, thunderbolts or something, anything.'

To Plob's surprise the captain and his men, far from looking upset at the falling of their comrades, were hugging each other and laughing out loudly as Pups and Lycan ran around them barking boisterously. Bravad extricated himself from his comrades and faced Smegly. 'Sorry,' he said. 'It wasn't exactly planned. We saw that they needed help and we just couldn't stop ourselves.'

'But three of your men are dead' exclaimed Plob.

The captain shrugged. 'They're soldiers. Soldiers die. It's an integral part of the job description.' Plob was about to interject with a retort but held back at the last moment as he looked at Bravad's face and saw the look of intense anguish and grief that completely belied the gruff words that he had spoken.

Dreenee and Biggest walked over and, wordlessly, Dreenee laid a lingering kiss on Bravad's lips and then led him away to the medical tent to have his shaft-pierced shoulder seen to.

Biggest called Berm 'Brick Wall' , Partlee Nobee, Spectal and Wogler over, and when they got there he opened his flask of Blutop and offered it around. After each of them had taken a good long pull of the cane spirit, Biggest shook each of them by the hand. ‘Thanks, ole folks. You guys is welcome to fight on my team anytime. I’m sorry about your brothers. They was good men. Old – but good.’

Brick Wall chuckled. ‘You’re right there. They don’t come any better – or older – than them, and us. All of us. But save your congratulations for later. There’s to be a lot more hunting and grunting before there’s to be a picking and a grinning.’

Biggest nodded sagely in agreement. Plob, who had no idea what Brick Wall was saying decided to look blank instead, then he changed his mind and decided to nod his head in a knowing way. The two conflicting expressions and the vague head nodding cased Brick Wall to stare at him concernedly. ‘What’s wrong, boy?’ he asked. ‘You in pain? Your stomach acting up or summat?’ Plob shook his head.

‘Nothing to be ashamed of, boy,’ offered Wogler, ‘it happens to the best of us. When I was your age I couldn’t keep anything inside me before a battle. Sluices used to open up at both ends. Probably still would, come to think, but I’m not as regular as I used to be. Takes more than pre-battle nerves to get this old gut going, I tell you.’ He pulled an antiquated battered silver goblet out from under his moth-eaten cloak and held it out towards Biggest. ‘Top that up for me, Big my man,’ he said and Biggest leant over and poured a brimful helping of Blutop into the bent and buckled goblet. Wogler took a good swig of the fiery spirit, winced slightly and sat down next to his pack, a look of contentment on his wrinkled face.

Plob didn’t bother arguing over the misunderstanding, he took a sip from the magic flask as it was handed around once more and then lay back on the grass and wondered how Horgy was getting on.

The stench inside the keep was horrendous. Over two hundred and fifty unsavoury lowlifes crammed together in a not-so-large castle, with no running water or provision for waste removal other than pushing it out of the way as you walked through it, meant that the atmosphere had become a little less than wholesome. The reek was the least of Horgy's problems though as he sneaked through the piles of waste and attempted to remain undetected from the gazes of Bil's unholy entourage. He was looking for the main tower, as Bravad had told him that the king's private chambers were on the third floor, just below the level of the walls.

As Horgy scuttled along he was undecided whether to adopt the furtive sneaky approach or the brazen I-belong-here approach to his cross-castle wanderings. As a result he vacillated rapidly between the two and so appeared, to the casual onlooker, to be a man, attired in a strange colour shifting cloak, attempting to take a morning stroll whilst having a world-class attack of St. Vitus' dance. Strolling, crouching, striding, crawling and leaping Horgy made his inefficient undecided way across the keep.

As it happened Bil's followers were so used to strange and off- beat behaviour amongst themselves that this random pattern of movement was, by chance, the best form of disguise that Horgy could possibly have chosen – he blended right in.

Plob and Smegly, who had both been hammering away for a couple of hours, were now hunched over the small portable oven muttering to each other and poking at the spell inside with the tongs and the poker, set looks on both of their faces as they collectively harrumphed, in Smegly's case, and umm-er-ed, in the case of Plob. They were attempting to create a spell that they both knew couldn't be created whilst, at the same time, knowing that it had to be done or, in every probability, the impending battle was all but lost.

'It must be possible,' said Plob wearily. 'You've managed to recreate Blundelberry's eternal intensifier. Surely it's just the same thing – only different.'

'That's precisely what it is,' agreed Smegly. 'It's exactly the same thing as Blundelberry's eternal intensifier – only different. Absolutely, completely and utterly different. So much so that it could, in fact, be referred to as Not Blundelberry's eternal intensifier because of its pure unadulterated unlikeness to the aforementioned spell of Master Blundelberry's. So stop being so slow, Plob and start thinking a little more laterally. OK?' Smegly harrumphed. 'And that goes for me too,' he finished as he gave the super-heated spell another irritable poke with his tongs.

Cabbie, who had been watching the two mages from a distance, wandered over, ale in hand. 'Exactly what are you two toiling enchanters up to?' he enquired.

Master Smegly harrumphed in reply and hunkered down over the oven, glaring at the now totally overheated spell with a look of disgust.

Plob stripped the sweat off his forehead with the palm of his hand and flicked it at the fire where it sizzled momentarily in a small vaporous puff of steam and was gone. 'Thought control. Mind meld. Perhaps using some sort of intensifying spell. A combination of air and earth. Change others perception. Bugger.' He kicked at the oven and missed - on purpose.

Cabbie nodded. 'Right. Fine. OK. Now let's, just for the sake of argument, pretend that I had absolutely no fornicating idea what you were saying and you could re-explain the entire thing using standard English. Who knows, perhaps I may even be able to help.'

Plob put the poker down and then placed himself on the grass next to it, grimacing as the exhausted muscles in his back pulled up tight. 'We're trying to forge a spell that, allegedly, hasn't been done before.'

'Not allegedly, my boy,' interjected Smegly. 'Not allegedly.'

Plob grimaced as he changed position. 'He did it. I'm sure of that. He did it – he just couldn't control it.'

Sadly, his face downcast, Smegly shook his head.

'He did,' insisted Plob. 'Somehow he did.'

'Who did what?' asked Cabbie.

'My grandfather. He created a spell during the final Hobgoblin wars that enabled him to control, or at least affect, the hearts and minds of the enemy. The only problem is that, somehow, he lost control of it and…well…he just disappeared. Poof. Gone, never to be seen again. They say that he ran away, transported himself to another place, but then how come the Hobgoblins suddenly withdrew – and never came back?'

Smegly sighed. 'This is all conjecture, my boy. I, for one, think that you are partly correct. Your Grandfather Slodong probably did lose control of a spell, but it could have been any of a number of the attack spells that were being thrown around the place. One of the Hobgoblin spells could have vaporised him.'

Plob shook his head stubbornly. 'They can't raise enough power. And how do you explain the fact that they unexpectedly quit the battlefield?'

The master shrugged. 'They're Hobgoblins, Plob. Who knows why they do anything? Who knows? Any road – mayhap it can be done. With our combined skill and some luck we might be able to create a confusion spell of some sort. If we can, it could give us some help, perhaps a little edge over the dark ones. Let us continue our experiments.

Come on.' He stood up, set his shoulders and hunched back down over the oven once more.

Horgy stood outside Bil's chambers, sweating in a nervous fear. Somehow he had managed to get this far unchallenged but, now that he was so close, he had no idea what to do next. As he stood, sweating and vacillating outside the hall of the counterfeit king, he heard the tinkling of a bell, far off in the womb of the castle and, not long after, saw a man come jogging down the corridor towards him, hands flapping and face a fluster. He drew up short as he laid eyes on Horgy. 'What are you doing here?' he demanded in the standard super-officious tone of the extremely low-level servant. Horgy stared at him, eyes bulging, ears twitching, skin sweating and face alternately glowing red and then draining to white.

'Ah,' the servant nodded. 'You must be Tolley's replacement. Come with me.' He opened the large steel-bound door and strolled in, beckoning to Horgy to follow suit. And, without any idea as to what was going on, he did.

Hugo adjusted the cords on the blind, twisting them to cut out the weak London sun that dribbled in from the internal light-well. Turning, he walked back to the desk, pulled his chair closer to Madame Zelga and sat down.

'All right, gentlemen,' said the psychic, her low and husky voice a little above a whisper. 'Shall we ready ourselves for the journey?'

'I'm not holding hands,' interjected Terry. 'I'm willing to go along with this but no hand-holding. It's too naff for words.'

Madame Zelga glanced at Hugo who rolled his eyes heavenwards. 'Terry, come on now, old chum. We have to hold hands. Madame has explained all of this already. The room has to be darkened, we have to be seated in a circle, four candles have to be lit, incense to be burnt and hands to be held. We've all agreed. You've agreed.'

'Changed my mind.'

'Why?'

'Just have.'

'Why.'

'Well what if someone walks in? We'll be the laughing stock of the department.'

Hugo sighed and raised an eyebrow. 'Too late, old chum. The way that we've been handling this case so far we're already the laughing stock of the force let alone the department.'

Abruptly Terry leaned forward in his chair and grabbed Madame Zelga's hand in his own. 'Well come on then,' he snapped as he held out his free hand to Hugo. 'What are you waiting for? Let's get psychic.'

Master Smegly and Cabbie looked on as Plob's jaw clenched tight in concentration Mentally he wrestled the three separate spells in to a compact ball of thaumaturgic energy his breath hissing out little by little between gritted teeth as slowly, ever so slowly, he released it in the general direction of an unwitting Biggest and a group of about ten dwarves. A combination of an 'earth, attack, thunderbolt' to provide enough energy to project the spell over distance. An 'earth, protect, shield wall' to stop the energy dissipating as it was released and, finally, a completely adapted form of Blundelberry's eternal intensifier combined with a large dash of Plob's personal advice, suggestions and proposals which, if all went according to plan, would manifest themselves into the targets' psyche causing them to believe what ever it was that Plob had proposed.

The air around Plob shimmered like a heat mirage and suddenly Biggest, who was busy partaking of his magic flask, yelped in the manner of a whip-struck hound and spat a mouthful of cane liquor onto the floor. 'Ouch,' he voiced. 'Dat burnt. I think dat the alcohol content of dis drink is possibly too high. I think dat I'd better switch to drinkin ale from now on, this Blutop drink is no good.'

The group of dwarves, who were also enveloped in Plob's spell, nodded their agreement and, as one, upended their brimful mugs of Blutop onto the grass with sundry expressions of distaste.

Master Smegly, who was standing next to Plob, whooped with delight and flung his portly frame into the air. 'You did it, my boy,' he shouted. 'You did it.'

Plob, however, was too exhausted to celebrate. Sweat rolled down his face and his muscles jumped and twitched with fatigue. Smegly walked over and patted him on the back. 'A job well done, my boy. You were right about using a variation on Blundelberry's eternal intensifier, I apologise wholeheartedly and without reservation.'

Plob shrugged. 'Dat is not a problem, magic man. I tink dat I am in serious need of some Blutop and a bit of shut-eye.'

Cabbie frowned. 'Why's he talking like Biggest? What's going on?'

Without answering, Smegly cocked his arm and delivered a stinging slap to the side of Plob's face raising a red glowing hand-shaped imprint.

'Hey, master mage jus what does you tink you is doing?' shouted Plob. 'You'se had better apologise before I open a whole can of whip arse on you.' He folded his arms and shuffled around in a circle.

The next slap that Smegly landed was, if at all possible, probably even harder than the first one. Plob staggered back and then fell to his knees shaking his head. 'What the…how did…why are you hitting me? Ouch. That was seriously painful,' he continued as he rubbed the side of his jaw vigorously.

Smegly nodded. 'That's better,' and he helped the assistant to his feet.

Biggest came wandering over, magic flask in hand and puzzled look on face. 'I don'ts feel too good,' he growled as he looked suspiciously at his never-ending container of Blutop. 'Here,' he thrust the flask at Cabbie. 'Taste this.'

Cabbie took the container and had a good swig, crinkling his eyes up against the fumes that rushed out of the neck of the flask as he raised it to his lips. 'Yummy. Excellent as always. Why what seems to be the problem?'

'Hey, why were you guys hitting me?' enquired Plob once again, to no avail.

Biggest shook his shaggy head. 'The problem is dat for a short while dere I thought that I didn't no longer like Blutop. Sort of like a waking nightmare. Very strange.'

'It's no use pretending that it didn't happen, I can feel the welt on my jaw where I was struck. Why was I smacked in the face?' continued Plob plaintively.

'We all felt the same way,' exclaimed Box, who had just walked over. 'A sort temporary anti-alcoholic insanity. Extremely disturbing.'

'It's damned sore. Why? Why me?'

Smegly chuckled. 'Gentlemen, what you have just experienced is a dose of "Plob's temporary auto-suggestion intensifier." Through a clever combination of spells, our young magician here has managed to almost perfect the art of mind control over distance. I say almost because for a moment there he overextended himself and, instead of controlling your minds, the feedback was causing his mind to work in sympathy with yours. Or to put it simply – for a time he thought that he was Biggest. Actually I thought that we'd lost him there, it was a close call. If I hadn't slapped some sense of self back into him who knows what would have happened.'

'Oh. I see,' said Plob as he slowly collapsed into an exhausted, unconscious well-slapped mage-shaped heap on the turf.

Chapter 31

'And who the hell are you?' bellowed King Bil the bonkers as he twitched and rubbed and squirmed uncomfortably in his throne due to the dirt-induced stiffness of his as-yet-unwashed royal blue boiler suit.

Horgy stared wildly at the king, his mind working overtime as it tried to churn out some sort of vaguely acceptable reason for his presence in the imperial throne room. 'I…er…I'm…your…your personal…bard. Yes, that's it. I'm your personal bard, come to sing your songs of praise to the entire known world. Hallelujah, great King. Praise and extol your virtues, O grand one. O your magnificence, your radiance, your…your grandiosity, your…' Horgy glanced at Bil, hoping to find a reason to stop his frantic praise chanting before he ran out of synonyms for greatness but there was no chance. Bil had stood up out of his throne and, beaming face held high, wrench aloft, he soaked up the obviously false flattery with huge relish.

'…your imposingness, your splendaciousness…' Horgy chanced another look. '…your luxuriousness, your…your…' Horgy was really reaching now. '…gorgeousness, sportiness…' Now scraping the bottom of the proverbial barrel. '…gaudiness, obtrusiveness…' Through the bottom of the barrel and into the chaff below. '…pomposity, fandangleness…er…er…attitudinatarianismismanali…'

'All right,' commanded Bil. 'That's enough. Now sing some songs about me. Start with your favourite top ten and then we'll see how it goes from there.'

Plob lent over the bucket of cold water that Dreenee had brought to him and splashed his face liberally with cold water, puffing his cheeks out and blowing at the same time in an effort to jolt himself awake.

'Plob's temporary auto-suggestion intensifier.' His spell. His very own spell. He was well chuffed but, as he continued to chuck cold water at his face, he knew that, however hard he concentrated, he would never be able to use it to effect more than six or seven people at once and manage to keep control. Still, it would definitely prove to be useful in the upcoming battle and, moreover, he was now more convinced than ever that he was solidly on track regarding his grandfather's mysterious disappearance.

He stood up, scrubbed himself dry with the rough towel that Dreenee handed him and then followed her to the fires where a bowl of thick venison stew and mug of ale waited for him.

Horgy slid carefully into the water and gasped involuntarily as the coolness of the moat rapidly lowered his sky-high body temperature. He swam with one hand across to the other side, holding the king's red heavy metal sceptre above his head with the other to keep it out of the wet. When he reached the other side and climbed out, it took all of his remaining strength to stop himself pitching forward onto the sod such was the depth of his post-fear-induced exhaustion.

It had been a close-run thing. Very close. Too close. If not for Bil's seemingly insatiable appetite for fawning flattery, however devious, disingenuous and deceitful it may be, he never would have been able to obtain the sceptre without a great deal of bloodshed – probably all of it coming from Horgy.

His break had come when he started singing Bil's top-ten praise songs, a process which basically involved Horgy dredging up faded old schoolboy memories of religious hymns and replacing any mention of the gods with Bil's own regal name, the rendering of which sent Bil into ecstasies of self-important delight. When he got to the part in the second hymn that went - *praise him, praise him, praise him, praise him, for King Bil is his name,* Bil went into such paroxysms of conceited rapture that he literally swooned from the sheer delight of it all and Horgy, taking note of Bil's temporarily incapacitated state of rabid self-acknowledgment, whipped his belt off and wrapped it tightly around both Bil's mouth and through the back of the throne thereby both gagging and imprisoning him in one swift move. He followed this up by cutting a length of the tasselled silver bell-pull and binding Bil's arms and legs and then, wrapping the sceptre in his coat, he frantically legged it back to the sally port and out into the moat.

And now, as he staggered on shaky legs back towards the fires, he felt well and truly pleased with himself for, mayhap he was not the best of knights, but he was, for the moment, both the best, and the happiest, of thieves.

They came howling out of Bil's castle at first light, bent on the retrieval of the wrench, gibbering and screeching like the very personification of the king of dementia that they represented.

Captain Bravad brought his arm down and the first volley of arrows went sheeting through the still, crisp morning air with an appealing fluting sound like a flock of sugary-voiced songbirds in dawn flight. The wet meaty smack of the missiles riving human flesh and the ensuing screams of pain quickly dispelled any such temperate and poetic thoughts and, with the steely whispering rush of the unsheathing of a multitude of swords, the battle for the castle was joined by all present.

The candles wavered and guttered fitfully in a wind that wasn't there. The heavy oaken desk shuddered and bumped and the incense flared briefly in a self-destructive orgy of flame and then went out. Terry tried to remove his hand from Madame Zelga's grip but it was no use, she clasped his sweaty appendage in her own with a grip like a carpenter's clamp. Her eyes rolled back in their sockets and her head swivelled three hundred and sixty degrees on her stout middle-aged neck.

And then, with the all encompassing sound of fury ringing in their ears, their world went black.

And over the hill, surrounded by the billowing dust raised by over a thousand hooves, came Typhon the Dark and his dastardly, devious, deceitful and dishonest minions of evil. And as they broached the rise he did stop and survey the battlefield.

The tears of grief rolled freely down the parchment-like skin of his cheeks as Partlee Nobby held Pup's doggie corpse to his chest, the yard-long arrow still protruding obscenely from the dead dog's ancient torso. Cabbie stood protectively over him, his massive two-handed, ever-sharp broadsword glowing redly as its sticky layer of congealing blood reflected the light of the weak mid-morning sun.

All around him the dead and dying lay, clothes and flesh torn asunder, friend and foe alike, oft draped over each other in death like some perverse necrophillic orgy.

And with a baying battle cry that rent the heavens did Typhon command his cohorts to fall upon the fast dwindling army of good. And Master Smegly looked up and knew that all was lost.

Flickers of light assailed Terry's stinging eyes and, suddenly, like a child bursting free from the womb, he and Hugo and

Madame Zelga and a budget priced Government Issue desk, were in another place, and another time, and another world. And there a vast medieval battle raged around them and Terry for one was hugely confused. So much so that he almost forgot to be terrified. Almost.

Plob gathered himself, tensing his will as he readied his mind to form the spell that he was going to cast. 'Plob's temporary auto-suggestion intensifier,' and he was going to give it all he had and bugger the consequences to himself. Ready - one, two, thr…

And, not for the first time in his career, Terry wished that he carried a gun. And a couple of grenades. And a bloody tank. He crawled under the desk to join Hugo and Madame Zelga and started praying as fervently as a missionary in a cooking pot.

'Stop. Don't do it, my boy.' The voice rang in Plob's head like the sound of fornication in a cathedral - loud, clear and totally unexpected.

'Grandfather?'

Cabbie was no more, for in his place, striding the battlefield like the gods of war, was Tarlek Honourusson son of Glimburble Honourus son of Swain Honour. Tarlek Honourusson 'the Dragon slayer.' Knight at arms and keeper of the sword of the nation and the most deadly wielder of the double-handed blade in the known world. And the enemy were as blades of grass before him as he exacted a furious vengeance upon all in his path.

'Well yes - and no,' said the strangely choral voice in Plob's head.

'Where…where are you?' asked the assistant.

'I am we. And we are here,' chimed the multitudinous tone.

And through the forest came the ululating hordes of the Hobgoblins. And they fell upon the evil ones like a storm of wrath from the heavens.

And Typhon the Dark unfurled his leathern wings and, as was his bent, cravenly flew from the tumult of battle.

And Tarlek leaned upon the pommel of his awesome sword and surveyed the vanquished foe.

And Dreenee, who had fought back to back with the captain, turned to embrace him, and kissed him, and stared into his eyes noting well the look of love that was reflected back at her.

And Biggest took a swig of Blutop, and passed it to Legles who, in turn, passed it along to the six or seven surviving dwarves.

And Horgy sat down next to Master Smegly, a grin on his cut and bleeding face and, wordlessly, the two of them clasped each other on the shoulders and then laughed.

And Bil, who had somehow, impossibly, regained possession of his wrench during the course of the battle, was surprised to find himself wrestled to the ground and handcuffed by a shaven-headed man in a Marks and Spencer suit shouting, 'You're nicked, you psychopathic bum-hole.'

Plob faced the King of the Hobgoblins who communed wordlessly to him via the mental part of him that was still Plob's grandfather. The small part that had come to exist when Slodong the Mage had overextended himself whilst exerting his spell of 'temporary auto-suggestion intensification' and became a small part of every living Hobgoblin.

Plob's grandfather was more alive than one would ever believe possible but he was also dead and gone. The goblin king gravely bowed to Plob and the voice in his head sounded one last time as it bade him goodbye. And with that the Hobgoblins melted back into the forests from whence they came, taking their fallen with them.

And Madame Zelga's head revolved once again and, like a smearing of a picture, the psychic, Terry, Hugo and the insane plumber exited the scene, leaving the desk behind them.

And Plob - Reetworthy Plob - Reetworthy Plob the IIIrd - said, 'Well how about that.'

And the rebuilding began.

THE END

Printed in Great Britain
by Amazon

49745423R00166